Dark Harvest
MAGIC

Dark Harvest MAGIC

Ella Grey Book Two

JAYNE FAITH

Dark harvest magic / a novel by Jayne Faith

Paperback Edition ISBN: 978-0-9970260-8-5

Edited by: Mary Novak
Proofread by: Tia Silverthorne Bach of Indie Books Gone Wild
Cover by: Deranged Doctor Designs
Interior Design and Formatting by

E.M.
TIPPETTS
BOOK DESIGNS

www.emtippettsbookdesigns.com

Published in the United States of America

For Charlie,
whose love is better than magic

The pulse of the reaper's presence tapped against the inside of my forehead as I smashed sauce-smeared paper plates into my nearly overflowing kitchen trash can. I was in the middle of a pizza-and-movie night, a little informal reunion for several of us who'd banded together to free a demon-possessed young man who'd become trapped inside a gargoyle.

Usually I'd have to be bribed with something damned good to host any sort of gathering, but I'd given in when my best friend Deb told me Roxanne missed all of us. She was the young girl whose brother we'd saved. I realized that deep in my crusty, solitude-loving heart I missed Roxanne, too.

I'd done my best to try to make it a nice night for her, but all day I'd been hyper-aware of the shadows swirling around the edges of my vision. It was probably my imagination, but at times I could almost swear I felt a chilly swirl behind my breastbone. Right in the spot where I imagined the reaper soul was curled up all cozy and munching on my own soul like it was a glazed donut with sprinkles.

My Demon Patrol partner Damien, Deb, and Roxanne were the only ones still left out in the living room. Witchy Lynnette Leblanc and supernatural rights activist Rafael St. James had both only made brief appearances before sailing off to Thursday night destinations unknown.

The doorbell chimed. I straightened and shoved the trash can back under the sink, and tucked my hair behind my ears. Blowing out a slow breath on the way to the front door, I relaxed my face into the semblance of an easy smile despite the tightness in my chest.

Johnny Beemer stood on the front porch holding the handle of a black, hard-sided case in one hand, a bunch of white daisies in the other, and a warm spark in his dark brown eyes.

I swung the door open and felt my lips widen at the now-familiar sight of his leather jacket, tousled chestnut hair, and expressive mouth quirked in a half-grin.

"Hey, sugar." He leaned in to kiss the soft spot under my cheekbone, sending a pleasant web of tingles stirring through me.

"Come on in. So, you always bring your scanner when you call on a lady?" I was going for a lighthearted tone, but it came out tighter than I'd hoped. I was glad to see him, but preoccupied by the changes I sensed within.

He grinned anyway, seeming to understand I was trying to be jokey, but a flicker in his eyes said he picked up on the strain in my voice. "Only when I really, really like her."

I managed a little laugh.

Though he had no magic ability, Johnny worked as a supernatural P.I., and he'd developed all sorts of instruments that could detect different types of magical phenomena. The scanner in his little black suitcase would tell me how much more of my soul the reaper had devoured.

"Johnny!" Roxanne jumped up from where she'd been tucked between Deb and my dog on the sofa. She half-skipped, half-ran across the room but stopped short, suddenly a little shy. Johnny passed the flowers and case to me with a wink and then engulfed the girl in a hug.

Loki, a big hellhound-labradoodle that had followed me home the night I'd met Roxanne, hopped to the floor. With his tail waving enthusiastically, he loped over to Johnny and circled him, nudging his thigh. Johnny fished a dog treat out of the pocket of his jeans and, in a habit he and Loki had established over the past few weeks, waited for the dog to sit. Then Johnny lobbed the treat up in the air, and Loki followed the arc of it with his eyes and caught it with a chomp of his jaws.

While Johnny said his hellos to Damien and Deb, I went to the kitchen with the flowers, filled a pint glass with water, sawed a few inches off the stems with a bread knife, and plunked them into the makeshift vase.

". . . been a fluctuation in the Boise Rip," Johnny was saying when I returned to the living room. I felt his eyes following me as I went to place the flowers on the table near the door. "The past day or so, the energy surrounding it has started to swell and recede in a rhythm, like a tide."

I sat down next to Johnny, close enough for my shoulder to press against his arm, and curled my legs up. He shifted back slightly so he could slide his arm behind me. It rested along the back of the sofa, just close enough for me to feel the warmth of his skin across my shoulder blades.

"Energy around the Rip?" Deb asked, tilting her head.

Damien's eyes lit with interest, and he leaned in as if to be sure to catch whatever Johnny said next.

"The interdimensional rips emanate their own power," Johnny said. "That's one of the reasons access to the major rips is restricted."

The local Rip was a permanent tear between dimensions, a doorway that allowed hellspawn to invade our world. My job on Demon Patrol consisted of trapping and killing the minor demons that came through smaller spontaneous interdimensional burps that occurred randomly. Minor demons didn't have enough demonic energy to possess a person, but they were nasty pests that would attack small pets and scratch the hell out of you with the claws that tipped their bat-like wings and talons, if given the chance. Minor demons were mostly just a nuisance. It was the arch-demons that really caused trouble. They were much larger and more powerful hellspawn, capable of possessing humans. If the possession could be reversed in time through exorcism, separating the demon from the human before the creature drove the person to kill, the possessed could usually fully recover. But if a person took another life while possessed, the fusion was permanent.

Damien was almost literally on the edge of his seat. As a life-long student of supernatural phenomena and a high-level magic user, he lived for this stuff. "And this fluctuation is new?"

Johnny nodded slowly. "As far as I can gather."

"I wonder what's causing it." Damien's eyes flicked toward his Demon Patrol backpack, which sat on the floor against the ottoman just out of his reach.

I'd bet anything his fingers were itching to dig out his ever-present notebook so he could scribble down things to look up later. Not that Damien would scribble. His handwriting was so legible and consistent it was practically its own font.

Roxanne looked up from her phone. "Maybe it's 'cause of Halloween. I'm dressing up as Supergirl. Hey, can we start the movie now?"

"Actually, there could be something to that," Damien muttered to himself, giving in to his urge and reaching for his pack.

While Damien bent over his laptop, the glow of the screen revealing his squint-eyed focus, the rest of us settled in to watch the latest superhero flick.

I kept thinking of what Johnny had said about the Rip fluctuation. *Rhythmic*, he'd called it.

I'd asked him to bring his scanner so he could check how much of my human essence was still left. A few months back I'd briefly died after a call on the job went awry, and when I came to on a gurney that was queued for the morgue, things had been, well, *strange* ever since. The soul of a reaper had hitched a ride with me back to the living. Johnny had been doing measurements every two or three days, and over the past several weeks the reaper soul that had tethered itself to me had seemed to slow its consumption of my soul. But when I'd woken this morning, something had felt different. At first I'd thought it was due to a particularly vivid vision of my missing brother Evan, but the unsettled feeling had stayed with me. A new sensation had taken root deep in my gut, too, coming and going in waves like a stomach cramp. Vague hunger was the only way I could think to describe it, but nothing I ate seemed to satisfy it. My eyes felt twitchy and strained, too. I didn't have proof that any of this was related to the reaper, but I felt sure it was, and I was equally certain it wasn't good.

By the time the credits rolled, Roxanne was half-slumped against the back of the sofa and over Loki's rump, asleep. Deb touched her shoulder, gently waking her. When I turned on the lamp next to the sofa, Damien looked up, blinking as if he'd forgotten we were all here.

Deb stood and made a beeline to the bathroom that neither of the men seemed to catch, but I glimpsed the green-around-the-gills look of her face as she passed. I eyed the closed bathroom door, trying to gauge how sick she might be. Sometimes the morning sickness only made her queasy and retchy rather than all-out pukey.

I stood, stretching. "Hey Damien, would you mind doing Deb a favor and dropping Roxanne at home?" I tipped my head toward the bathroom and gave him a pointed look.

"Ah . . . oh, sure," he said, catching on.

He packed up his things and Roxanne bade us all a droopy-lidded goodbye.

I went to tap on the bathroom door with one knuckle. "You still alive in there?" I called softly.

"Yeah," came Deb's hoarse voice. "Just need a few minutes to collect myself."

"No rush, holler if you need anything." I quickly stepped away, relieved to avoid hearing any barf noises. I felt bad for Deb, but in my opinion sympathy puking went beyond the requirements of friendship.

I turned to find that Johnny had his black case open. I eyed the souped-up tablet inside as he pulled it from its bed of molded foam.

He glanced up at me. "Ready?"

"As ready as I'll ever be."

Johnny held the tablet up by one of its handles—a modification he'd added—and used his other hand to swipe through the instrument's controls. He aimed the device's camera at me, tapped the screen, and then gave me a nod.

I sank onto the sofa, watching his face as he examined the readouts on the device. His brows drew low with the concentration that came across his face whenever he used one of his supernatural detection instruments. But when his eyes flicked up to mine, I knew the news wasn't good. He came to sit beside me and propped the edge of the tablet on his jean-clad thighs.

I stared at the image on the left of the screen. It was a multi-colored blob roughly in the shape of a standing person—me—with a rainbow of colors radiating out from the center of its chest, marked by a dark purplish circle the color of a fresh bruise.

"It's eaten more of my soul, hasn't it?" I asked.

Johnny drew a solemn breath in through his nose. "It looks like it."

"How much?"

He scrolled down the columns of numbers on the right.

"Another seven percent."

My stomach dropped like I'd just stepped onto a fast-moving elevator. "I'm barely three-quarters human now?"

Flipping his finger over the edge of the device to darken the screen, he shifted to face me, and his expression tightened to worried sympathy.

"You're still *you*, Ella. You're still walking, breathing, talking, and thinking under your own power. But now would be a good time to get something in place to halt the reaper's progress." He gave me a pointed look. "Or you could just let Lynnette exorcise it."

Deb's friend Jennifer Kane was trying to figure out a magical solution that would preserve what was left of my soul. So far, she'd come up empty. Jennifer and Deb—and Johnny, apparently— wanted me to get the reaper soul exorcised, if that was even possible, but I wasn't willing to do it. Not yet. The reaper gave me visions of my brother, the only clues I'd had that he was alive since he'd disappeared five years ago. I knew I was taking a terrible risk, but I couldn't give up the one link I had to Evan.

"No exorcisms." I felt my forehead furrow. "I'll get in touch with Jennifer tomorrow."

His jaw muscles pulsed a couple of times, as if working to contain something else he wanted to say.

I didn't like the way he was looking at me. All that focused worry made me twitchy.

"Maybe you should call her now," he finally said in a carefully measured voice.

"Nah. If she thought she had a cure, she would have contacted me." I pushed to my feet and shot him a wry smile. "Besides, if the reaper kills me overnight, a call to her now probably wouldn't have made a difference anyway. But maybe you should stay and make sure it's a damn good night, just in case."

I said it partly to cut the tension but also because I really did want him to stay.

He chuckled, and some of the seriousness in his eyes began to dissolve in the heat that stoked in his gaze. He leaned in so his lips brushed my ear as he spoke. "I'll give you a night you won't forget."

A warm shiver spilled down my neck and spine, but just then the bathroom door flew open. Deb lurched out with her phone pressed to her ear and a look of sharp concern in her blue eyes.

"Have you called the police?" she said into the phone.

I broke away from Johnny, honing in on Deb.

"Okay, yeah, I'm coming now," Deb said. Her gaze finally focused on me. "I'm at Ella's. She's coming too."

She lowered her arm slowly.

"What, *what*?" I asked, impatiently waving my hands.

"Jennifer's house was trashed." Deb's voice was tight, and she sounded a little out of breath.

"Is she okay?" I asked.

"Yeah, she wasn't home when it happened. She's upset, though. She doesn't understand how someone could've passed through the wards around her house without her noticing. And the person took something from her altar room. Ella, her scrying mirror is gone." Deb said the last part with emphasis and then paused as if expecting a reaction.

"Oh . . . okay?"

"It's the mirror she used during her session with you. If someone knows what it is and how to use it, they can basically see everything that happened when she helped you identify the reaper soul."

My brows pulled lower as my frown deepened. I shook my head. "Well, that would suck, but mostly just in the sense of invading my privacy. Other than that, I don't really see the danger."

She sighed, and I could tell she was stressed and struggling to be patient with me. "You're a *necromancer*, Ella. Anyone who knows enough to access what the mirror holds will recognize that. There are only a few of you in the world, and there are a lot of people who would love to have that talent at their disposal. Plus, the fact that you can wield magic and you have two souls, one of which is a reaper's, probably makes you completely unique. In the supernatural community, rare talents and configurations like yours are incredibly valuable. There are plenty of people and organizations that make a point to recruit rare talent. Sometimes by force."

My breath stilled as I took in what she was saying.

Yeah, I'd recognized that since my untimely demise and return to life I'd gained the ability to see through the eyes of demons and was just learning to manipulate them with necromancy. Necromancers could drive demons and other death-touched beings, including vampires and zombies, by penetrating their minds and taking command of them. But I couldn't do a whole lot with the skill yet. I'd only barely begun to try it out. I sure as hell didn't think of myself as someone to be categorized along with Phillip Zarella, the notorious psychopath and one of the most powerful necromancers in the world. But Phillip didn't have any magical ability, and I was betting that most other necromancers didn't either. I was unskilled, but Deb was probably right about my unique configuration.

I tried to process what she was implying, clearing my voice to stall for a second. "Okay. Well. I hadn't thought of it that way." I glanced at Johnny. "We can both come. Johnny can do some scans, maybe help her figure out what went wrong with her wards."

He nodded, already moving to pack up his tablet.

"I've got one more piece of equipment I want to grab from my place. It's close by, so it'll only take a second," Johnny said.

Deb jammed her arms into her coat and grabbed her purse. "Thank you, that would be amazing. She really doesn't want to report it, but I think she should."

She hurried toward the door and then turned with her hand on the knob to look back at me. "Okay, I'm going over there in my car. You go with him, and I'll see you both there."

I took a couple of steps and opened my mouth to protest her going by herself, but she was already out the door.

With a grumble I strapped on my service belt, and Johnny and I went out to his Mustang and jumped in. He headed toward his North End bungalow-style house, about two miles from my place and roughly on the way to Jen's.

"Maybe we can help her figure out what happened so she doesn't have to call the authorities," I said.

Johnny shook his head. "Sorry, but I agree with Deb on this. She needs to call it in. Only someone with ill intentions would take a scrying mirror. For all you know, Supernatural Crimes could be trying to track someone who's been stealing these types of items. Letting the authorities do their job is your best chance at catching the person and recovering the mirror. Not to mention the fact that a scrying mirror is on a list of magical items that are *required* to be reported to SC if stolen. Jennifer is breaking the law by not reporting it."

"You'll have to take that argument up with her, I guess," I said mildly. I really wanted to get a look around before SC took over, and I wasn't in a hurry to involve any bureaucracy, despite what Johnny said. The more I thought about it, the more uncomfortable it made me to think that my session with Jennifer could be revealed through the mirror.

"Unfortunately, it's more than just a disagreement," Johnny said. "I'm a licensed P.I., and I'm a registered Supernatural Crimes contractor. Both of those designations mean I'm required to report this, or I could lose my accreditations."

Damn.

My jaw tightened. I'd thought it would be a good idea to bring Johnny along. I wasn't aware of his legal obligation in a situation like this, but it was too late now.

"Can you at least give us a chance to look things over first?" I asked.

He gave a tight nod. We'd reached his place. He parked on the curb, left the motor running, and was in and out in less than a minute. He came back carrying something that looked like a large camera case with a shoulder strap.

"Where are we heading?" he asked.

I hesitated for a split second. "Jennifer lives in Sunshine Valley."

His brows rose. "The vampire community?"

"Yep."

A mix of surprise and interest danced in his dark eyes as he shot me a sly smile. "Never a dull moment with you, Ella."

Johnny took full advantage of his Mustang's MagicBoost engine to get us to Sunshine Valley in fifteen minutes. By the time we turned onto Jennifer's street, the moon was up. I glanced at my phone to check the time. Nearly eleven.

The vampire witch had left her outside lights on, and the front window of her small house was illuminated as well. I didn't see any damage to the house from this angle. Johnny parked at the curb.

"Let's hang back for a sec," I said. "I don't want to screw up anything if they're trying to figure out what went wrong with Jennifer's wards."

We got out of the Mustang, and Johnny went around to the trunk and his instruments while I sent Deb a text to let her know we'd arrived. I adjusted my belt around my waist, the familiar weight settling on my hips. A moment later, the front door opened and Deb and Jennifer emerged.

Johnny stepped forward, nodded at Deb, and offered his hand to Jennifer.

"Johnny Beemer," he said. He'd assumed the focused, business-like air that I recognized from the few occasions when we'd been at the same crime scenes. "Sorry to hear about the break-in."

She grasped his hand. "Jennifer Kane. Yeah, this is as shitty as it is mysterious."

Deb patted Jen's arm sympathetically.

Jen turned to me, pushing her fingers into her bangs and scraping her hair back from her forehead in an agitated gesture. "I'm so sorry about the scrying mirror, Ella. I just never thought anyone could get in so easily and without my knowledge. I probably should have just destroyed the mirror after our—"

She abruptly cut herself off and shot a look at Johnny and then back at me.

"It's okay, he knows," I said. "And no apology is necessary, Jen. You took all the precautions you thought were necessary. Besides, whoever took the mirror might not even know what to do with it."

"I wish I could believe that, but unfortunately, I don't think it's the case," Deb said.

"I'm happy to do whatever I can to help," Johnny said. "But you should know that due to my profession I'm legally obligated to report knowledge of a stolen Class A magical item."

I winced as I watched Jennifer's face pull into a frown.

"I'm sorry," I said to her. "I didn't know about that when I told him. I thought he might be able to help you figure out what happened, and it just didn't occur to me that it would be an issue."

She made a low noise in the back of her throat, clearly unhappy with this development. "This is gonna expose my witch status. I've been so careful to stay under the radar."

A vampire with magical ability was extremely unusual. Deb had told me that the few she knew of generally kept a very low profile, even in the supernatural community. But Jennifer was making a bid for Lynnette's newly formed coven, which in itself would raise Jen's visibility to some extent, and I felt my defenses prickle as I recalled this tidbit.

"Again, I apologize," I said, swallowing back my irritation.

"Well, it's done, so let's try to sort out what we can on our own," she said.

"I think in the long run it will be better to involve the authorities," Deb said, trying to console Jennifer. My best friend shivered visibly, and I could almost see her intuition clicking in. "I don't think this was meant to be just a robbery. Something feels off here."

I took a breath, ready to ask her to elaborate, but the words stuck in my throat as a tremor rippled through my senses. My gaze rose to the rooftop and the nearby trees.

"You feel that?" I asked Jennifer and Deb. "Minor demons nearby."

Deb gave me a squinty look. "I don't sense any demonic energy."

Jennifer shook her head. "Me either."

The shadows edging my vision were twisting and dancing like campfire smoke, and they crowded inward, narrowing my field of sight. The tingle passed through me again, like a finger plucking a string deep in my brain.

"It feels . . . odd," I said. I drifted a few feet down the sidewalk, trying to zero in on where the signal originated. "Jen, can I walk onto your property?"

"Sure, go ahead. We've already examined the wards."

I kept my eyes up, scanning for minor demons. They'd be hard to spot in the dark, but the thumping pulse of the reaper had awoken in the middle of my forehead. I could feel Deb, Johnny, and Jennifer's attention trained on me, but I turned my focus within.

Moving across Jennifer's front lawn, my shoes brushed through papery fallen leaves and stirred up the mild scent of leaf decay and cold, moist soil. The tingling hum grew stronger as I approached the gate leading into her back yard.

Three. There were three minor demons somewhere back there. My job as a Demon Patrol officer had put me in proximity to hundreds of minor demons over the past several years, and I knew the feel of them as well as I knew my own face. But this time there was something different, a thrumming quality I'd never experienced before.

As I unlatched the gate and quietly pushed it open with one hand, I started to reach for my stun gun with the other. But instead of the service weapon, I grabbed my Patrol-issue guided net launcher, realizing I wanted to trap a demon for a closer look.

The back yard was all shadows and dark shapes, with only some weak interior light leaking out from the house. The far end of the fence was vertical metal bars rather than the wood slats that made up the front and sides. Beyond Jennifer's yard there appeared to be a tree-lined walking path. Sensing the demons were out there, I quickly crossed the grass to the back gate. Wincing at the metallic squeak it made when I opened it, I froze for a few seconds, waiting to see if it scared the demons away.

"If you're gonna help me, now would be the time," I whispered, speaking to the presence within me. I suspected it could be a key to further unlocking my powers of necromancy, which included my ability to probe into the minds of hellspawn. I had no idea if the reaper soul understood my actual words, but I hoped it would at least grasp the sentiment.

I started to move my awareness out toward the creatures, intending to connect with one of their minds.

I stiffened as my sight suddenly blanked to black. A bolt of cold panic shot through me. The darkness began to clear almost immediately, resolving into the yellow and blue tones I knew from my visions. My pulse quickened. My necro-vision had kicked in.

Perhaps the reaper had decided to assist.

I swayed in the dizzy sensation of having my visual perspective shift so abruptly. I was no longer looking away from Jennifer's back fence, but down from above. Down at myself. I blinked several times, trying to breathe through the disorientation.

Blindly gripping the net launcher I still held, I started to raise it, but then stopped. How could I aim it accurately when I was looking down at myself from my target?

A sharp pain drilled into my right eye, and I squeezed my lids closed, groaning softly through clenched teeth. When I opened them, I pitched back a couple of steps, nearly crashing into the iron fence. My head swung wildly as I tried to make sense of what I was seeing. My sight seemed to be bouncing between my normal eyesight and the necro-vision that was sighting through the demon's eyes. But then it hit me. I had necro-vision through my right eye and regular sight through my left.

A grin tugged at the corners of my lips as I steadied myself. "*Nice* trick."

I checked the demon's position one last time with the necro-vision and then lowered my right eyelid and raised the net launcher.

Just as I was about to let the magically charmed net fly, my target and his two buddies bolted.

Cursing under my breath, I lowered the net launcher and sprang into a sprint. Quickly accelerating into a swift rhythm of pumping elbows and legs, I sped down the walkway after the creatures. They were following the line of trees along the path, probably trying to use them as cover.

Honing in on the thin tether of awareness between me and them, I could sense their positions as easily as if I saw them. I reached out more strongly, trying to be careful so I didn't lose them. I wasn't entirely sure if these demons were different than the ones I usually encountered or if the growing presence of the reaper was giving me a new sensitivity to them. Whatever it was, they seemed more like feral neighborhood cats than spawn of hell. They'd stopped fleeing and had taken refuge in another tree.

Mentally feeling along the strand of awareness to one of the demons, I realized it was too far away for me to use any of my limited elemental magic on it. Instead, I focused on our connection, forcing it wider until I could sense the creature's mind. A shiver ran over my scalp and down my back.

I'd tried this before on the job. My partner Damien had held demons with his magic while I attempted to use my necromancy to take control of them. It took a few tries, but in the past few weeks

I'd succeeded in penetrating the minds of several minor demons. Once I got better at locking into a connection, I tried things like looking through their eyes and trying to direct their movements. Most of the time I couldn't hold on for more than a minute or so. After, I always felt as if my insides had been coated with dark, cold slime. Unpleasant, but it mostly faded away after a few hours.

Now, all I had to do was get this demon to stay where it was for just a few seconds. I felt the mental click, like a deadbolt sliding into place, that told me I'd touched its mind. I gripped it lightly, not needing to command it but only keep it where it was, and I felt the creature give in to my control. On stealthy feet, I moved closer to the tree where it hid.

One bough suddenly bobbed, sending down a shower of crisp autumn leaves, as the other two demons flapped away. But the third remained.

"Gotcha," I whispered under my breath.

Aiming at the shadow-shrouded spot low in the elm to my left where I knew one of the demons was perched, I pulled the trigger on the net launcher. With a springy recoil of the gun and a soft whir, the net shot upward, a faint glowing blur in the night. Its sensors locked onto the demon, activating the net to yawn wide and wrap around the creature. It all happened in a blink.

Amid high-pitched screeches and thrashing noises through the dry branches and leaves, the glowing white net tumbled to the ground. It writhed around as the pissed-off demon tried to escape. If I'd had more magical juice, I would have trapped all three demons in bubbles of earth magic like I'd seen my partner Damien do. But I was only a weak Level I on the Magical Aptitude Scale, and it was way beyond my ability. One demon would have to do.

I let out a breath and strode forward to retrieve the net. The contraption was made of a very fine mesh that wouldn't allow the creature's talons to pierce through, but I still carried it well away from my body as the demon continued to struggle. The interior of the net was charmed with a sedation spell, which would take effect any second.

When I'd pulled the net launcher instead of my stun gun, I wasn't exactly sure what I'd intended with the trapped creature, but now I knew—I was going to use this demon to try to try to gain some information. If it had been here when the robbery took place and I could access its memory, I might be able to tell Jennifer who'd taken her things.

I jogged back to her place. As I reached for the iron gate, I glanced into Jennifer's yard and froze.

Blurs of magic the dark black-red of blood wound around the side of the house, streaked the patio, and smeared over parts of the back door. It shimmered in my perception, and I realized I was sighting it strongly with my necro-vision and more faintly with my regular sight. I'd become somewhat accustomed to the yellow and blue tones of the necro-vision, and this new color felt oddly foreign. I closed my left eye, and the bloody energy came into focus. In fact, everything through the necro-vision seemed more crisp than ever before.

Maroon-colored magic? I'd never heard of such a thing, let alone seen it. It was a color distinct from the flaming orange-red of fire magic, nothing like the green of earth, blue of water, or yellow of air energies. My eyes traveled upward as I realized I could also see the faintly glowing magenta sphere of the ward Jennifer had cast around her house, made of a brand of magical energy unique to vampire witches. Only the top half of the sphere was visible, as the rest extended underground to complete the bubble. The widest circumference of it was a slightly brighter magenta line that traced the arc of a ring along the ground.

I squinted as I realized there was fainter blood-red magic trailing across the grass, to the back gate, and—

I sucked in a breath as I looked down and realized I was standing in a pool of it. I raised one hand and watched open-mouthed as a maroon aura gently pulsed around my fingers.

I sidestepped and watched with alarm as my movement left a trail of maroon. It wasn't as distinct as the magic clinging to the patio and back door, but it was unmistakably the same type of magical energy.

My mind spun. What did it mean?

"Ella?" Deb's voice floated from the side of the house, and a second later her petite shadowed form came into view. "Is everything okay back here?"

I swallowed, trying to work some moisture back into my dry throat. "Yeah. I found the demons." I started back across the yard, retracing my trail of maroon. "I trapped one of them, but the other two got away."

The creature's struggles had subsided to weak twitches as the sedative took effect.

Jennifer and Johnny came around from the front, too, and the four of us congregated on the patio. In spite of her down jacket, Deb had her arms wrapped tightly around her middle, and her shoulders hunched forward. Jennifer was eyeing my netted trophy, and Johnny carried an instrument the size of a milk carton that was emitting soft beeps. There was a bulky black bag slung across his body.

My eyes kept drifting back to the maroon-smeared door, and I was waiting for Deb or Jen to notice it.

"See anything strange back here?" I asked.

"I see that my damn ward is still in place," Jennifer said with obvious annoyance. "I just don't understand it. I should have sensed something. Not to sound full of myself or anything, but my wards aren't like standard elemental wards. Being a vampire gives me the ability to use our pink magic, and if anything, my ward should have been more difficult to sneak past." She planted her hands on her wide hips and hissed through clenched teeth.

My vision seemed to be resolving, the necro-vision fading away. But I could still see the maroon smears. As my eyes traveled from Jennifer to Deb, it finally dawned on me that neither of them could see the blood-red trails.

"I can see another type of magic, too, but it's not Jennifer's hot-pink vamp magic," I said. I pointed toward the door. "It's all over the patio and smeared up to the doorknob."

The three of them whipped around.

Jennifer walked toward the door and bent over to peer at the knob but then straightened and turned to me. "What does it look like?"

"It's the color of blood," I said. I licked my lips. "And there's something else. It appears I'm leaking the same variety of magical energy."

Their heads swiveled again to stare at me, almost comical as their movements happened in unison.

"But I didn't touch the door, I swear," I continued quickly. "That's not from me. My trail is a good deal more faint than the other, so it's actually fairly easy to tell them apart."

"Show me where," Johnny said. He flipped a switch on the box, and it stopped beeping. He shoved it into his bag and then pulled out the familiar souped-up tablet he'd used to scan me earlier. He powered it on, and his face lit in the cool glow of the screen.

I pointed, tracing the maroon path along the patio, and then to the door. The shadows were going wild in my periphery, and the center of my forehead throbbed as if something inside were fighting to escape the cage of my skull.

"There's also a trail around the side of the house," I said. "Not the side we used, the other side."

He shook his head and looked up at me. "My scanner senses supernatural energy but can't identify it."

"Hey," Jennifer said to me. "Could you move across my ward? I want to check something."

I walked several steps away from them until I was outside the magenta ring.

"What the . . ." Jennifer followed me to the edge of the ward, staying just inside. "Cross it again?"

I did as she asked.

"You're not tripping it, Ella." She looked up at me in confusion.

Wards weren't barriers, but more like magical doorbells that alerted the owner to different things that passed through them. Jen should have felt a magical ping when I walked across her ward. One of her wards was a sort of all-purpose alert system, and any human or supernatural creature should set off the alarm. It was the first and most basic ward that was typically used around a home. She had other wards as well, probably designed to signal with more specificity, such as the level of magical ability of a crafter who crossed it.

"Let me try," Deb said, and she passed through the magical bubble.

"Yeah, I felt *that*," Jennifer said.

Even I saw the flicker of disturbance when Deb crossed the circle. My stomach gave a little twist. How could I not be tripping the ward?

"You've always had this ward set, right?" I asked. I was thinking of the first time I'd been here. I hadn't been able to see the ward then. Actually, I hadn't seen it when Johnny and I arrived tonight, either.

I pressed the heel of my hand to my temple.

"Yeah, I've had wards set since the day I bought the house," she said.

My heart lurched uneasily in my chest. Something was shifting within me, and it was happening quickly. My ability to sense magic seemed to be changing, and I already knew the reaper soul had devoured more of me.

Returning my attention to the maroon smears, I lifted my palms and looked at Johnny, hoping he had some knowledge from a scene he'd worked or buried in the recesses of his considerable expertise that would help explain what we were seeing—or not seeing, as the case was.

"I'm not exactly sure what's going on, but all I can think of is to state the obvious," he said slowly. "If I had to guess, I'd say the thief and Ella have something major in common. Something unique, a rare type of magic."

My pulse seemed to stutter. Was there really someone else out there like me? Someone with a tethered reaper soul? A tiny point of hope sparked in the middle of my chest. If there was someone like me, maybe they'd figured out how to live with it, how to keep the reaper from killing them.

"I hate to be the one to bust up this party, but I can't wait any longer to report the stolen scrying mirror. I need to call this in," Johnny said.

Jennifer cursed softly under her breath.

"Sorry," Johnny and I both said at the same time.

She planted her hands on her hips. "Go ahead, I'll get over it. I'd appreciate it if Deb and Ella could help me take one last look around inside before anyone else arrives."

"If you don't mind using the front door, I'll do some more scans back here. I'd like to collect additional data," Johnny said. He had his phone in his hand.

Jennifer nodded, and Deb and I followed her back around the

side of the house.

"I don't mean to be such a bitch," the vampire witch said with a sigh.

"I'm sure he understands," Deb said. She shot me a sly look that I caught even in the dark. "And Ella can do her part to help soothe any hurt feelings."

"I'll mesmerize him with my endless reserves of feminine charm," I said. Deb snorted a laugh before she could control herself, and I smacked her shoulder with the back of my hand. "Hey, it's not *that* funny."

We moved swiftly to the front, our shoes brushing against the grass and scattering a few fallen leaves. Once inside, I blinked a few times in the light. Jennifer's trashy magazines had been scattered around, her balls of yarn and knitting needles spilled from their basket, sofa cushions were askew, and a potted plant lay on the floor in a mess of dirt and broken pieces of its ceramic container. It looked as if a tornado had whipped through the set of a shabby-chic interior design photoshoot.

The blood-red magic overlaid much of the room, while the distinct smell of sulfur and burned leather hung in the air like a sinister mist. It was similar to what demons smelled like if you got close enough to them, but there was an additional note of spice and rot.

"You see it, don't you? The maroon magic?" Jennifer asked. One of her hands was aglow with yellow air magic, and in the other she held a lavender crystal on the end of a thin chain, which I assumed she would use to try to pick up traces of the intruder.

"Yeah," I said. I glanced down to see a faint tinge of maroon around my boots. "Do you want me to stay outside? I don't want to contaminate things here."

"Nah, that's okay." She was focused on whatever she was trying to detect with the pendulum.

I made my way to the back door, picking up the trail of maroon, intending to try to follow its path through the house. It seemed to have gone first to Jennifer's bedroom, and when I flipped on the light, I found the mattress tipped onto the floor.

Vampires, even dociles like Jennifer, didn't need sleep the way humans did. The bed and nightstand were more of an homage to her human beginnings than any sort of necessity.

"It's just terrible," Deb said quietly behind me. "I would feel so violated if someone did this to my home."

A fist pounded on the front door, and we jumped and whirled around.

"Supernatural Crimes, please open up!" a voice bellowed.

Jennifer went to answer, and Deb and I trailed after her.

A woman with a blond pixie cut, dressed in crisp dark jeans, a white button-down shirt, and a navy blazer held up a green glowing SC badge. I sensed she was a low-range Level III on the Magical Aptitude Scale, which was expected for SC personnel. Impressive, but nowhere near Damien's level.

"Lead Detective Arianna Barnes," she said brusquely, looking around at the mess. Two men and a woman wearing green SCSI jackets—the Supernatural Crime Scene Investigation—crowded behind her. She finally turned to Jen, and flipped a glance at me and Deb. "The three of you should have stayed outside. Now your fresh signatures are all over the crime scene. Come with me."

Detective Barnes wasn't a large woman, but she was clearly used to being in charge, and her demand that we follow her left no room for protest. Outside, two SC officers fell in step behind us as Barnes led the way to an SC van the size of a food truck.

I glimpsed Johnny off to one side, speaking with a man who, judging by his badge and blazer, was also a detective. There weren't any sirens, but the SC cruisers, detectives' cars, and van were enough to draw attention. A couple of neighbors had emerged to get a closer look at the commotion.

At the open door of the van, Barnes stopped. "We need full scans of the three of you so we can cancel out your signatures in the crime scene readings. Has anyone else been in the house?"

"No. And I really don't think all of this commotion is ne—" Jen started.

"A stolen scrying mirror is a serious matter," Barnes cut in. She squinted at Jen, giving her a hard look. "I can see you have some magical ability, so your mirror was no prop. You should be at least as concerned as I am that it's missing."

The detective's piercing look turned suspicious.

"I *am* concerned. I just didn't want to make a fuss." Jen glanced around, and tucked her chin as if she wanted to hide. Her usual confidence had evaporated.

The van's door opened, and a SCSI tech beckoned us up the two steep steps. The inside of the vehicle looked like a surveillance unit from a futuristic movie, with monitors and control panels everywhere. The tech asked for our I.D.s, passed us tablets with waivers to read and sign, and then used a handheld device to scan each of us.

Supposedly, according to the paperwork, the scans recorded only our aura signatures, a sort of energetic fingerprint that all people, supernaturals and normals alike, give off. But I suspected Supernatural Crimes gathered additional information. Regardless, it didn't take any special scan to see that Jennifer was a vampire, and Barnes had already commented on Jen's magical aptitude. The vampire witch looked dazed and unhappy, as I was sure all of this was running through her mind as well. As for myself, I had no idea what I registered on the scan—they were tight-lipped about all their technology. I was getting more and more concerned about what Supernatural Crimes would be able to pick up at the crime scene. Could they detect my strange blood-red magic in their crime scene scans and link it to something that showed up in my signature? There was nothing I could do about it now—I was officially in the Supernatural Crimes database

Barnes and two other detectives were waiting when Deb, Jennifer, and I exited the van. For a moment I scrutinized the people scurrying around and in and out of Jen's house, watching for any telltale reactions that might mean they'd uncovered something about me. I looked around the dark sidewalk and driveway for

Johnny, but he was nowhere to be seen. I realized his car was gone from the curb.

"We need to ask you some questions. The homeowner will go with Detective Davis. You're with Detective Lagatuda." Barnes nodded at Deb. Then the Lead Detective's gaze drilled my eyes. "And you're with me."

I wanted to ask why we were being treated like criminals, especially poor Jen, but it was obvious I wouldn't do myself any favors by getting combative with Barnes.

I followed Barnes's blond head to a sedan, pulling out my phone to see if Johnny had at least sent a message.

They asked me to leave the scene. Text me when they're done and I'll pick you up.

I frowned. Leave the scene? Maybe they were trying to keep his professional neutrality.

Barnes opened the back door and waited for me to get in and then climbed in after me, forcing me to scoot across the seat, as if she thought I might try to escape. She grabbed a tablet from the center console and powered it on.

"I'll be recording our conversation while I take notes," she said crisply.

"That can't be legal," I burst out, unable to contain my irritation any longer. I wasn't completely certain what was within the bounds of the law. We didn't do things like question suspects on Demon Patrol, and I wasn't trained in SC protocol.

"You think I'm breaking the law?" She fixed me with a challenging look, and I felt myself bristle even more.

I was tempted to argue but refrained from responding. I just wanted to get the hell out of here.

"Let's just get this over with as quickly as possible," I said evenly.

"State your name, your date of birth, and your connection to the homeowner."

I did so, figuring they already had that information anyway.

"What time did you arrive here tonight?"

I hesitated. Johnny and I were here for quite a while before he called it in. "I don't know, I didn't look at the time."

"Why did you come?"

"Deb and Jen asked me," I said.

"Why?"

I decided the briefer my answers, the better. "For support. They were alarmed."

"Why didn't they call Supernatural Crimes first?" Barnes asked.

"You'd have to ask them."

"You arrived here with John Beemer?"

"Yes."

"What's your connection to the individual who allegedly broke into this home?"

I pulled back, my pulse tripping at the unveiled accusation. Was she serious or just trying to trip me up?

I narrowed my eyes. "I don't know who it was, so therefore any connection is unknown to me."

She'd been flipping her gaze back and forth between the tablet's screen and my face, but then her gaze settled on me. She just sat there, staring at me. I knew she was trying to make me nervous, to rattle me into saying more. I returned her steady stare, refusing even to blink.

"Seems like we're finished," I said, when I was satisfied she knew she wasn't going to get anything more out of me. I didn't wait for her to answer, but reached for the handle and got out of the car, and quickly slammed the door behind me.

With a slow breath, I mentally shook off the claustrophobic sensation the interview had left me with and looked around for Deb and Jen. They were both standing in the driveway with one of the Unit investigators. When they saw me, they came out to meet me at the sidewalk.

Jen looked as if she'd swallowed something sour.

"What a mess." She shook her head. "These people need some fricking sensitivity training, for one. And they're tracking dirt and shit all over my carpet."

I was glad to see some of her fire had returned.

"How were your interviews?" I asked, flipping a glance around to make sure no one was within earshot.

Deb shrugged. "Just standard stuff. It was fast. Why, what did she ask you?"

"She asked, and I quote, 'What's your connection to the individual who allegedly broke into this house?'"

Deb and Jen both looked at me in dumb silence for a moment.

"Wow," Jen said. "What a bitch. How did she justify *that*?"

"She didn't," I said. Mentally kicking myself, I realized I should have challenged Barnes on that point. "I had nothing interesting to give her, so the interview pretty much ended with that."

Deb's brow furrowed. "That's not good. Do you think she knows something about the—" She paused and lowered her voice to a whisper. "The magic you saw?"

I shrugged. "I don't know what she knows. But I think I need to make my exit before she gets any new bright ideas about me. Will you guys be okay? You're welcome to come stay at my place."

"We'll be fine," Jen said. "As soon as everyone clears out, I'm going home with Deb."

I nodded. "Good. Call if there's anything I can do."

"What happened to your ride?" Deb asked, looking around.

"They made him leave, apparently." I pulled out my phone and sent Johnny a quick text. "I'm going to walk down the street and have him meet me."

"I'll walk with you," Deb said.

Jennifer went back to her house, and Deb and I set off down the sidewalk.

"She's right," I said. "This is a *mess*." I huffed and swore under my breath.

"Don't worry about Jen, she'll be fine. I'm more concerned about what Detective Barnes said to you."

I blew out a breath and pushed stray strands of hair back from my forehead. "Well, I was with you guys all evening before we came here, so I have an alibi."

"How are things going between you two?" she asked.

"We're not, you know, exclusive or anything at this point. But it's been good," I said. "Taking things kind of slowly."

"Turning over a new leaf, eh?" she ribbed.

I shot her a wry look and then my feet scuffed to a halt. "*Damn*, I left the demon." I looked at Jen's house. I couldn't go back to get it. Walking out with a sedated demon in a net would just raise a dozen more questions.

"Johnny grabbed it and put it in his car," Deb said.

My shoulders sagged with relief. "That's the first good thing I've heard all evening."

Headlights rounded the corner ahead, and I recognized the purr of the Mustang's MagicBoost engine.

Deb stepped close and rose to her tiptoes to give me a quick hug.

"Try not to worry about any of this," she said. "Hopefully it'll all just blow over."

Right. There was the scrying mirror that would announce my necromancy talent, reaper soul, and who knew what else to anyone who knew how to use it. The detective who apparently thought I had something to do with the break-in. Someone out there with rare magic like mine, who could sneak past wards undetected . . . And those were only the *major* points of concern.

But I appreciated Deb's intent.

"We'll talk tomorrow," I said and climbed into the passenger seat of Johnny's car.

"How'd it go?" he asked, wheeling around in a U-turn and driving under the arch that marked the main entrance to Sunshine Valley.

The quicker we could get out of here, the better.

I scrubbed one hand down the side of my face and gave a short laugh. "You're gonna love this." I quickly filled him in on everything.

He didn't respond right away, and I watched his jaw muscles flex in the red gloom of the stop light in front of us.

"Well, I can vouch for you, so that's something," he said. "And, I've got your little buddy in the trunk."

"Thank you for grabbing the net," I said. "I'd probably still be there trying to explain *that*."

"Strange night, huh?" he mused after a few seconds.

"Like you said, never a dull moment."

He reached over and squeezed my hand, and my shoulders loosened the tiniest bit. "At least you've still got one more day off, right?"

I nodded. On Demon Patrol, officers were scheduled in shifts of four days on followed by three days off. The ten-hour days on foot felt long at times, but regular three-day weekends helped make up for them.

"That reminds me, I need to make sure Damien's coming over tomorrow." I pulled out my phone and sent a quick message to my partner.

"How are the magic lessons coming along?" Johnny asked.

"Slower than I'd like, but I'm making some progress," I said. I gave a short laugh. "I'm probably the most difficult project he's ever taken on."

My Demon Patrol partner, Damien Stein, was a high Level III

on the Magical Aptitude Scale. In fact, he was the most powerful crafter I knew. For the past couple of months we'd been meeting a few times a week so he could help me develop my skills. As a low Level I, I'd never bothered trying to hone my magical talents because my capabilities were so limited. But Damien had insisted that I could do more than I thought, so I'd challenged him to prove it.

Johnny shot me an appreciative smile. "That charmed whip he gave you is sexy as hell, sugar."

I cracked a grin, remembering how I'd splattered gobs of magic all over my living room and tangled the whip in a curtain. "I've gotten a lot better than the last time you saw me use it."

"Why didn't you have it with you tonight?" he asked.

I touched the spot in front of my left hip where I usually had the whip coiled and then remembered. "He has it, actually. Apparently my skills have improved enough to warrant some upgrades."

"That's hot."

I laughed. "Thanks."

I could tell he was trying to recapture some of the ambiance from before Deb got the call from Jen. I appreciated his attempt to heat up the mood, but with everything I had weighing on my mind, I wasn't feeling it at the moment.

I was already anticipating something else, which had become part of my nightly routine: bonding time with the reaper, as I'd started calling it. Part meditation, part appeal, I turned to the reaper soul and asked for it to help bring more images of my brother. Usually what came were random and sometimes disturbing images of demons, death, and a dark place that didn't seem of this world.

Since the first time I'd done it two months ago, I'd received only one more glimpse of Evan, aside from the vision I'd had in my dream last night. My chest clenched at the memory. As in my dream, it appeared he was still at a secluded compound that served as a vampire feeder den. He'd looked thinner than before, barely moving except for slight shifts of his glassy eyes. One of his arms had hung limply, his inner wrist mangled from vamp fangs. The wound would heal, the vampire who'd created it would make sure of that, but it still made me ache inside to see it.

Tonight I was more eager than usual to try to get something useful. Maybe it was the knowledge that the reaper's soul had consumed more of me and time was running short. The bizarre discovery of the maroon magic at Jennifer's, and Detective Barnes's accusation, had also put me on edge.

Johnny pulled up to the curb in front of my apartment and turned off the engine.

"Let's get your new pet out of the trunk, and I'll walk you to the door," he said.

My stomach took a little dip as I realized he'd definitely picked up on my down-shift in mood, and I wasn't quite sure if my reaction was disappointment or relief. Maybe a little of both.

With only a little visible cringing, Johnny carried the net containing the still-sedated minor demon up to my front porch. My next-door neighbor's familiar, a pissy black cat who seemed to have something against me, appeared at the window. Its gaze roved over me and Johnny with feline dismissiveness. Then it zeroed in on the net and bared its teeth in what was probably a fit of hissing. It went full-Halloween, with arched back and puffed tail, its yellow eyes glued to the demon.

Johnny dropped the net near the door and stuffed one hand in the front pocket of his jeans. His eyes searched my face for a moment, a faint smile playing on his lips.

"Not exactly the date I had in mind," he said.

I pushed a few stray strands of hair back with one hand, tucking them behind my ear. "Yeah, me either."

He took a step forward, closing the distance between us and bringing us eye-to-eye. "Try again soon?"

I took a breath and nodded. "I'd like that."

With a shift of his posture toward me, his lips met mine in a warm, lingering kiss. The masculine scent of his leather jacket and the freshness of his aftershave filled my nose. For a split second, my worries faded and I was tempted to invite him in to try to prolong the escape. A loud yowl from the cat next door and an answering yip from Loki inside my apartment returned me to reality.

Johnny pulled back with a good-natured chuckle.

"Thank you," I said, reaching into my pocket for my house key. "Let's talk tomorrow."

"Sounds good." He walked backward a couple of steps. "'Night, sugar."

I watched him turn and go down the steps to the walkway. As he went around to the driver's side of the Mustang, I spotted the glow of his phone in his hand. Would he look for another place to spend the night? I wouldn't completely blame him. I wasn't dating anyone else, but I had no illusions that he wasn't.

With a small sigh, I grabbed the net, went inside, and flipped on the living room light. Loki hopped around me, growling at the demon and darting in to get a closer look at it.

"Down, boy. This one isn't going to hurt anyone."

Not knowing what else to do with the net, I went into the kitchen and set it in one side of the double stainless steel sink. I shooed Loki outside to keep him from worrying around the demon. While I waited for him, I rummaged in the fridge, realizing that we'd never gotten around to eating. I pulled out a piece of leftover pizza and ate it cold.

Loki and I settled on the sofa with the lights out, and I closed my eyes and focused within. The pressure under my breastbone was still there along with a faint gnawing sensation that the pizza hadn't subdued. I felt the stir of the reaper's soul, like a whisper of cold breath curling around my heart, as it sensed my attention trained on it. In my mind's eye, I brought up the most recent image of Evan and held it.

I felt the shift inside my head, a slipping or turning, before anything else changed. I clicked into the mind of a demon so swiftly I started. My heart jumped with the hope that the demon I'd connected to had seen my brother. I opened my eyes to the yellow and blue tones of my necro-vision. My pulse jogged as I scanned eagerly for a glimpse of Evan. But the scene was a very familiar one—my own dark kitchen.

The sofa shifted as Loki moved, and over his low growl I heard soft scrabbling noises of claws against metal coming from behind me. Apparently the minor demon was awake, and I'd connected to it.

"Show me," I whispered and probed deeper into its brain, trying to get to its memory. I pictured Jennifer's back yard and the trails of blood red magic. If the demon had been perched with the right line of sight, it might have caught a look at the thief.

The image blurred, distorting and then dissolving, and when it clarified it showed a partially obscured view of the back of Jennifer's house. There was a tree bough blocking some of the yard, but I could see the back door.

I sucked in a sharp breath. There were some visible trails of maroon magic. I watched, barely breathing, as a breeze shifted the drying fall leaves of the tree where the demon sat. Through its senses, I could smell the presence of the other minor demons nearby, the ones that had escaped when I'd trapped this one.

Then someone, a man bathed in blood-red magic, came into view. I knew what I was seeing had already happened, that it was only the memory of what the demon had seen, but my heart pounded in anticipation. The demon's night vision was extremely sharp, and if the man would just turn this way, I might get a good enough look at his face.

He moved quickly but carefully, making no noise. Even dressed in a full-length duster, it was obvious he had an athletic build. By his posture and the easy way he moved, I guessed he was probably mid-30s or younger. At the back door, he paused with his hand on the knob and looked out across the yard, giving me a three-quarters profile view of his face. I froze, zeroing in on his features and locking them in my memory.

The man disappeared inside. I hoped the vision would continue so I could watch him emerge and perhaps get a more direct look at him and see whether he'd left with the scrying mirror. But the vision was already dissolving.

I swallowed and blinked hard as my eyes once again showed my current surroundings. Behind me, the demon's movements were sounding feistier, and it was beginning to make annoyed little screeches. I stood, looking toward the dark kitchen. What should I do with the thing? I had a couple of brimstone burners from work, so I could easily kill it. I'd hoped to get more information out of it, but I wasn't going to be able to sleep if it flopped around in the net and screamed all night.

Without turning on any lights, I walked into the kitchen and watched the magic-laced net writhe around in the sink. Its glow had faded as the sedative had worn off, but the magic that kept the demonic energy contained would persist for quite a while. The nets weren't meant for long-term capture, though, only as an intermediary to use when it wasn't practical to zap a minor demon with a stun gun. The idea was to trap the demon in the mesh and then drop the whole thing onto a brimstone burner. I tapped my lip with a fingertip, thinking.

Unable to come up with a decent solution for keeping the demon quiet the entire night, I realized I'd either have to kill it or set it free. If I let it go, there was a good chance it would return to Jennifer's house—minor demons tended to stick near where they came through from their dimension to ours.

It completely went against my Demon Patrol training to let the creature live, but . . . I wasn't on duty, was I?

I lifted the net from the sink, went into the back yard, and under the cover of night I sliced through the magic-laced webbing with my pocket knife. Taking several steps back to keep clear of angry talons, I drew my stun gun just in case the creature decided to try to dish out any payback for being held captive.

The bat-like demon shook free of its prison, hopped a couple of times on the patio, and then took flight. Within seconds it blended with the darkness and disappeared from sight. I could still sense it heading west, though. Toward Sunshine Valley and Jennifer's house?

I went in and locked up, changed into the Demon Patrol Recruit t-shirt I liked to sleep in, and crashed.

The next morning, Damien arrived after my morning run and calisthenics and just as I started on my second cup of coffee.

My Demon Patrol partner was lean and tall, with a patrician noise, medium blond hair, and fine bone structure that suggested he was of high-bred stock. That was actually the case—he came from the most notorious mage family in modern times. Now firmly rooted as an old-money family of the East Coast, the Steins' power went back generations. Mages kept themselves apart from the rest of the supernatural community. They were extremely powerful and equally secretive.

Damien had come west, here to Boise, in part to escape his lineage. Though his abilities couldn't even touch what a mage could do, he was the most powerful crafter I'd ever met—an extreme

Level III on the Magic Aptitude Scale. But as he said, in his family anything less than mage-level talent didn't count.

"Morning," he said as I let him in. He lifted the whip that was coiled in his hand. "I upgraded the charm to use fire magic as well as earth magic. It's time you learn to sling flame along with earth."

I grinned in anticipation, realizing I'd actually missed practicing with the whip and carrying the weight of it on my belt.

"Sweet," I said. "Show me what you got."

Magic was more fun to sling around in the dark, when you could really see the glow of it, but most of our practice sessions took place in daylight hours. Earth magic, which manifested as green in the visible spectrum, was the easiest and most abundant energy to work with, and thus the one I knew the best. Not that I was any sort of expert. Up until recently, I'd only learned enough about using magic to be able to call it up without hurting myself, and I'd never pursued more refined skills such as stirring spells or making charms. I'd always assumed my low-level ability just wasn't worth developing and felt more comfortable relying on my service weapon, my wits, or if all else failed, my sprinter's speed.

Damien believed that magic ability could be not only highly honed, but in some cases bumped up. When he'd first told me he'd discovered how to change a person's aptitude, I'd been incredulous. His claim went against one of the basic laws of the supernatural world: magical aptitude was a fixed quality. The ability emerged at puberty, and you were stuck with whatever level you tested at, end of story.

I was a 1.3 on the Scale. Damien tested at 3.99, which was the highest the Magic Aptitude Scale registered. He hadn't outright said so, but I speculated he'd acted as his own guinea pig in the aptitude-manipulation research he'd mentioned, and his score hadn't always been practically off the charts.

He wanted me to become more skilled at my current level before he attempted to help me bump it up. He'd hinted that the transition to a different level was pretty hairy and potentially quite dangerous. At first I hadn't really cared one way or the other about altering my ability, but the more I practiced, the more interested I became in knowing what it would be like to command more magical juice. It seemed to have awakened my competitive side. Or maybe it was just that for the first time in my life my magic actually seemed interesting.

He passed the whip to me, and I felt a pleasant zing of energy up my arm as the charmed object connected with my magical capacity. I waited while he poured himself a mug of coffee from the pot in the kitchen, and then we went out to the back patio.

Loki came with us, heading straight for a corner of the yard to sniff around the stone figure that stood there. It was actually a gargoyle in statue form, the creature I'd helped free from the clutches of Gregori Industries a couple of months back. *She, not it*, I reminded myself. Johnny had scanned the creature and informed me the gargoyle was female. She often roosted in my yard despite the fact that she and Loki weren't exactly best buddies.

I gripped the handle of the whip and let the tail unfurl. Drawing up some earth magic, I flicked my wrist and sent the whip straight out with a satisfyingly crisp snap.

"Before we move on, I feel as though I should mention something," he said. He set his mug down on the glass-top patio table.

His serious tone piqued my curiosity. "Sure, what's up?"

"My family caught wind of my involvement with Gregori Industries and the gargoyle," he said. One corner of his mouth pulled down a touch. "I knew they would disapprove, and I wasn't wrong."

He'd been tense after we'd rescued Roxanne's brother and the gargoyle from Gregori Industries, but weeks had passed and he hadn't mentioned any fallout, so I'd assumed he'd worried for nothing.

I straightened with alarm. "You're not moving back East, are you?"

"No, no." He shook his head and then shoved his fists into the pockets of his khaki jacket. "But they've forbidden me from taking part in anything else that's . . . high profile."

"I see." I peered at him, trying to gauge how he really felt about the demand. "So, no more big, flashy, press-saturated rescue missions."

"Right. And I'm fighting it, but they want me to come back and swear some kind of oath before the Mage Council."

I tilted my head in confusion.

"They see me as a loose cannon," he said. I fought the urge to snicker. Damien was one of the most rule-conscious people I knew, and he'd spent most of his life within institutions—first the world of his patrician family of mages, and later extensive schooling. "They're afraid I'm going to give away mage secrets. Not that I really know all that much."

"Oh. Well, that doesn't sound *so* bad."

"They're also insisting that I quit Demon Patrol. Because it's too . . . too . . ."

"Low-brow? Blue-collar? Embarrassing to the illustrious Stein family?" I offered. The thought that the Steins were trying to shame him out of his job irked me, but the idea of losing him as a partner made me downright unhappy.

He scratched at the back of his neck, clearly a little uncomfortable. "Something like that."

I regarded him for a moment, thinking about how much he'd done for me in the short time we'd known each other. On the surface, he seemed whole-heartedly devoted to guiding me as I developed my skills as well as helping me get out of jams. I had no doubt his actions were genuine on one level, but I also sensed it all could be part of a larger agenda. Like how he'd joined Demon Patrol as a means to learn about local demon activity, with the implication that once he'd gained what he needed he'd move on. A tiny part of me couldn't help wondering if in some way our relationship might eventually get the same treatment.

I shrugged a shoulder. "Eh, let's not worry about it unless they find a way to press the issue. You're an adult. You have your own life. We'll figure it out, right?"

He gave a weak nod. "Sure. Right," he said with forced brightness.

A beat of silence passed.

"Okay, back to school." Damien crossed his arms, seeming to shake off the previous moments. "Fire magic. Worked with it before?"

"Yeah, but it's been a very long time." I rolled my head a little, trying to relax. The mere mention of fire energy made me edgy.

It had been over a decade since I'd touched fire, actually. My mother, who'd been my mentor when I'd come into my ability, had shown me how to draw fire magic, traditionally the second type of magic a new crafter learned. But my control was poor, which made it dangerous for me to try to use it. Earth magic was my elemental comfort zone, if I had one at all. You couldn't burn your eyebrows off with earth magic.

"So you can call it up at least, that's good," he said.

He bit his lower lip for a moment, maybe thinking about whether I had a fire extinguisher on hand. But on second thought I doubted that was really his worry. Hell, with his command of magic, he could easily douse any of my misfires in an instant. The tension across the back of my shoulders eased a little. He wouldn't let my house burn down.

"Let's put the whip aside for a minute and just practice," he said.

I nodded and laid the length of the weapon over a chair. Instead of reaching downward for earth magic, I aimed my senses inward to a point just above my belly button and focused on the heat generated by my own body. There were other ways to summon fire magic, but this was the method that had usually worked for me. It took almost a full minute before I felt the telltale spark—I was definitely rusty with this element. Heat grew as I mentally fanned it outward from my middle and into my limbs.

My pulse jumped at the unfamiliar feeling. Earth magic was neutral to cool in temperature, and I'd forgotten about the prickly sensation of the hottest magical element.

"Okay, form a flame," he said, prompting me to run through the most basic fire magic exercise.

I raised my right hand and directed the flow of magic to that area. Already sweating with the effort, I watched as a dime-sized red ball illuminated and hovered above my extended index finger.

Waiting until it I was sure I could keep it steady, I arced my arm downward and aimed my index finger at the patio we stood on. A mental push sent the tiny red orb to the ground with a pop like a firecracker. The fire magic hit the concrete in a burst of heat and light and then extinguished, leaving a smudge of black ash. A whiff of smoke drifted to my nose, sweet with a metallic edge.

It was a pretty weak-ass display, but I was just happy I'd managed it without burning my hand or setting anything ablaze.

I looked up at Damien to gauge his reaction.

"We can work with that," he said, nodding slowly. "You played it very safe, though. You have the capacity to pull a lot more fire."

"Yeah, and I have the scars to prove it." I held up my right hand and fluttered my fingers.

I didn't actually have scars, or if I did they were faint, but the memory of fire magic blisters along my index finger was still vivid enough, even so many years later. Fire magic was the second easiest to access after earth, but it was also the most dangerous to the crafter—and to any flammable objects nearby.

For the next hour, he coached me while I attempted to draw

earth and fire simultaneously and send the magic through the whip. I could see why he wanted me to command more than one element. Even a tiny addition of fire magic made the whip tenfold more responsive in my hand. It was like the difference between shooting a gun at sounds with my eyes closed and firing with the lights blazing with the aid of a laser sight.

But it took its toll. Ten minutes in and sweat was dripping down my temples. At the end of the hour, I had to sit down.

"Now that you're using magic so much more, you need to find a healer," Damien said. "Occasional magical exhaustion isn't dangerous, but you don't want to push it too far."

I ran my hand down my arm as the vague chill of magical drain set in. I frowned. "I completely forgot about the brain damage aspect of overuse. It's never been an issue for me."

Crafters who used magic heavily or on a daily basis needed frequent healing sessions to ward off its detrimental effects.

A reaper eating my soul and magical exhaustion rotting my brain. Well, at least there was an easy solution for one of those problems. I'd ask Deb for a referral.

Damien had been lounging in one of the patio chairs with his hands clasped behind his head while I rested for a few minutes. His eyes were closed, his face tilted toward the sun. Just as I felt the crawling tingle of nearby Rip spawn, his eyes popped open and he straightened.

My right hand reflexively moved to my stun gun, and I rose to my feet.

"Single minor demon," he said, also standing.

Scanning the sky, I spotted a bat-like shape flapping toward us. "Yeah, I feel that, too. I think I know this demon."

Damien flicked a quick glance at me, and my skin prickled as he drew magic. The green glow of earth energy surrounded his right hand. I was too tired to summon much elemental energy, but I didn't think I needed it.

"Don't do anything just yet," I said.

We watched the demon alight in the maple that stood near the sidewalk on the other side of my fence. The tree was large enough to send boughs sprawling into the space above my yard. Like some sort of prehistoric raven, the demon perched on a branch and began preening.

Allowing my eyes to unfocus, I reached outward toward the creature.

"I don't think it's going to hurt us," I said. My voice sounded far away as I slipped more fully into a trance-like focus. "But if it tries to take flight, trap it in a bubble of earth magic."

"Trying to make friends?" I heard Damien ask, but my focus was already too deep to respond.

I found the thread of connection stretching between me and the minor demon like an invisible wire and sent my focus through it. Swaying on my feet, I probed for the energetic throbbing swirl at the other end—the creature's mind. My scalp crawled as I pushed inside.

This demon felt familiar, somehow, like the one I'd brought home from Jen's. It wasn't the same one. I'd learned to recognize some of the tiny things that differentiated one creature from another.

The demon began to struggle as I probed deeper, and I sensed its panic just before it took flight. Damien caught it in an orb of glowing green.

"Don't bring it any closer," I said, my voice barely above a whisper. Since I'd come back from the dead, demons were wary of me, and I didn't want it to freak out.

I sank into the trance, allowing my awareness to flow into the creature's mind while another part of my consciousness pictured Jennifer's house and searched the demon's memory for the areas that rang with a similar vibration.

Random images and sensations whirled through my senses—trees, dark sky, the feel of wind over leathery wings. Then a scene settled out of the chaos. It was the path behind Jennifer's house and along it moved a figure bathed in blood-red magic. A man, the same one as before. My breath caught in my throat as I watched from the demon's vantage point in a tree.

Other minor demons were nearby, and as the man walked, they called out to him. Not the usual ear-bleeding screams and screeches, but soft clucks and caws. He looked up in acknowledgment, and I froze as I saw his face full on. His features were angular, the maroon magic making him look almost alien. I locked onto every detail, trying to commit each to memory. There was no scrying mirror in his hand, but that didn't necessarily mean he hadn't taken it.

My curiosity rose as I remembered what Johnny had said and wondered what this man and I could have in common. Since I knew what the man looked like, how he moved, maybe I could probe—

My phone jangled and vibrated on the glass table, jolting me out of my link with the demon.

I blew out a harsh puff of air through clenched teeth, annoyed at the interruption.

Scooping up my phone, I noted Deb's name on the caller I.D. "Hey, what's up?"

"Oh, god," Deb's voice was trembling and airy, as if she couldn't catch her breath. "Amanda is dead. She's *dead*, Ella. Oh my god."

"Where are you?" I demanded, already in motion. I pinned my phone between my ear and shoulder so I could coil up my whip. It tingled with a small current of residual magic.

"Amanda's house. I brought Roxanne to do some training. I think the killer is the same person who was at Jennifer's." Deb ended with a little sob.

The man I'd just seen through the demon's eyes?

Damn, I hoped Roxanne didn't see anything. She was just a kid, only fourteen. I waved urgently at Damien. He released his magic, and the orb holding the demon dissolved. He followed me into the house as the creature flapped away.

"Get back in your car," I said into the phone. "Lock the car doors and send me the address."

"Okay," Deb said, sounding lost and miserable. "I'm going to have to tell the other witches."

I paused for a split second. "Is Amanda part of your group that's trying to get into Lynnette Leblanc's coven?"

"Yeah."

Jennifer was, too. Two witches vying for the same coven attacked by the same person? I didn't believe in coincidences.

"Hold tight, Deb. Damien and I will be right there," I said and disconnected the call.

I hadn't told Damien about Jennifer's house, the blood-red magic, or the person—the *killer*—out there who had something in common with me.

I started filling him in as I called Loki inside, locked up, and grabbed my keys. I strapped my whip onto my belt as we headed down the front walk.

"I'll drive us." He interrupted me, angling toward his late-model Lexus parked on the corner.

I nodded and followed him to his car.

As I slid into the luxurious leather seat, I vaguely noted the odd flu-like feeling in my body. I was chilly from the drain of using magic but also still sweaty from slinging fire energy. My necro-vision was fading in and out of my right eye. All of that, combined with the fact that I probably needed to eat something, gave me a tilted, off-balance sensation. I used my phone to send the address Deb texted me to the car's navigation system.

"I want to know more about this maroon magic," Damien said. He pulled up to a stop at a red light and turned his head to give me a long, piercing stare that roamed the air, surrounding me as if examining my aura.

"You can't see it, can you?" I asked. I held up my arm and saw a weak halo of the magic, like a bloody mist hovering over my skin.

"No, and that bothers me."

At his high level of magical aptitude, Damien could do and sense things that lower-ability crafters couldn't. He was also extremely knowledgeable on the topic of magic, having grown up in a family of mages and possessing two degrees in Magical Studies. I suspected he didn't encounter too many things in the supernatural realm that were new to him. I had to admit it bothered me, too, that he couldn't see the blood-red magic.

I could almost see the gears spinning in his mind as he drove.

"Theories? Hypotheses? Wild speculations?" I prodded.

His jaw muscles flexed a couple of times before he responded. "We're getting close to Samhain."

I looked at him askance, though he didn't see because his eyes were on the road. "Halloween? What's that got to do with anything?"

"It's not the same as Halloween," he said. "In the pagan calendar it's the final harvest, the point in the year that marks the beginning of the dark half of the year. It's a festival of the dead. It's also the time that the veil between the living and the dead is the thinnest."

His words fell heavily between us, and my heart seemed to also drop in my chest.

"You think the killer is carrying out some sort of black ritual connected to Samhain?"

"Not necessarily. But this blood-colored magic—I don't know, maybe it has something to do with the fact that we're already within the lunar cycle that leads up to Samhain. Maybe it's something that emerges this time of year. Lots of strange things can happen when the veil thins."

He glanced over his shoulder into the backseat, where he'd tossed his backpack with his ever-present notebook.

"It's not just the final harvest of the year, which makes it sound relatively benign," he said, shifting into professor mode. "It's also the final slaughter. Originally that was the final slaughter of livestock before winter. Historically, black magic practitioners and dark arts worshippers have taken some latitude with the interpretation. This year Samhain falls on a new moon—a dark moon."

"So this is a special year for the dark arts?"

"Yeah, and not just symbolically," he said. "There are a lot of events converging on that date this year which will undoubtedly boost certain magical energies. I have some experiments planned to quantify it, actually."

Damien turned onto a residential street in the Boise Bench—a low plateau in the south-central area of the city that in some spots overlooked the river and valley. In other places the Bench was a mixed area of refurbished homes interspersed with overgrown ramshackle houses that had fallen into disrepair. This street had more of the latter, though the address Deb had given me turned out to be a cute little yellow cottage with a cobalt blue door and a bed of roses next to the front porch. The door was ajar about half a foot but revealed only a vertical slice of darkness within. A faint trace of a still-intact ward arced around the foundation of the house. Blood-red magic trailed up the front walk.

Deb's Honda was parked next to the mailbox, her face pale and stricken behind the windshield. Roxanne sat next to her in the passenger seat with the hood of her sweatshirt pulled up and her eyes wide.

When we parked, their doors swung open. I stepped out of the Lexus, and Roxanne rushed to me and wordlessly threw her thin arms around my waist. I touched her chin, tipping her face up so I could look in her eyes. She looked alarmed but not shocked. I didn't think she'd seen anything that would give her nightmares.

"You okay?" I asked, squeezing Roxanne's shoulders and wincing against the sensation in my skull. The middle of my forehead was thumping like a cadre of bass drums in a homecoming marching band. Around the edges of my vision, the shadows danced in a blurring frenzy.

She nodded and stepped back, turning to Deb.

"I just called 9-911," Deb said. The emergency number for Supernatural Crimes. That meant she'd seen or sensed something inside that made her believe magic was involved. Her eyes slid toward the front door, and her face pinched in distress. "Better get in there if you want a look before they arrive."

The upper lid of my necro-vision eye was twitching, and my stomach was rolling around like a rock tumbler. I took a slow breath in through my nose, trying to steady myself as I jogged up to the front door. I wasn't particularly nervous about seeing a corpse—no, there was something else going on within me that had me much more on edge. A strange sense of anticipation flooded through me like a shock of adrenaline.

I used my elbow to bump the cobalt door open wider, careful not to leave fingerprints on anything.

In the dimly lit little entry, I could see the trail of maroon magic. My forehead thumped so hard I reeled.

I shook my head hard and managed to stay on my feet, but my eyes rolled back as a deep chill, thick with black dread, welled in my chest.

The cold inside me began to feed the little gnawing sensation in my gut I'd noticed lately, transforming it into what I could only describe as the deepest, most desperate hunger I'd ever felt. Moving beyond hunger, it tipped into an obsessive, yearning ache for something I had to have or else I'd explode from the need.

Blinking to clear my vision, I looked around. Gray mist swirled through the house on airy currents. I exhaled in pleasure as they caressed my skin. The gray was softly pulling at me, coaxing me to follow where it flowed.

As if in a dream, I moved forward, not even feeling my feet touch the ground.

Around a corner. Through a doorway.

There.

This was what I sought: Amanda, the dead witch collapsed on the floor in a dark pool. She was on her side, facing away from me, but there was an ugly, deep slash that ran over her bare upper arm and across her back. Something very strong had lashed out at her with a large blade, and she'd twisted to try to protect herself from the blow.

But it wasn't her mangled mortal shell that I'd come for. It was the ghostly, translucent image of her that hovered above, bobbing on the currents of gray mist as if it were a balloon still tied to the woman's wrist. The soul's face was blank, slack.

And suddenly I knew what was calling me, what deep hunger was driving me.

With a desire so strong it pushed me to the edge of insanity, my reaper yearned to free the still-bound soul.

I couldn't resist. I didn't really *want* to.

The reaper within me was going to use my hands to cut it loose. Even as the tiny piece of Ella that still remained was repelled by the thought, my every cell seemed to reach out in longing.

I was going to reap Amanda's soul.

A sickening, dark wave of fire and ice surged into my veins. I knew this sensation. I remembered it. This was the same pain that had invaded me the night the reaper marched me out of my apartment and through the dark city to the abandoned ghost house filled with unreaped souls.

I wanted to vomit, to fall on the ground and writhe and turn myself inside out. And yet I also craved more, wished the unfamiliar rush would overtake me until I lost myself in its oblivion.

The gray mist swirled in little eddies as I drifted toward the body and its still-attached soul. I watched it as it flickered, like a hologram that one moment looked more or less like the mortal form of a woman and next was a pale cool blob of pulsing light, swaying in the unfelt breeze of the in-between.

That's where I was—the *in-between*. I'd passed into a space where ethereal energies seemed more solid than physical objects. Where souls awaited the ones who released them into the *beyond*. These were the storied places of which every young crafter was told.

My entire being thrummed with anticipation, the expectation of the darkly magnificent thing I was about to do. The sheer power of it.

With the suddenness of a reflex, my right hand shot up to eye level. In my fist, a curved blade had appeared. It was hook-shaped and black, glinting as if reflecting the silver of moonlight. My movements had changed, taking on a sharp, reptilian quality.

As I moved closer, ready to sever the cord, the soul seemed to awaken. It began to flap madly, like a windsock in a hurricane. It's eyes were wide and fixed on my left hand rather than on the knife I held.

Confusion passed through the part of my mind that was still Ella. Didn't souls *want* to pass on? But then I knew. Through the reaper I understood that I had two choices. I could release it to the *beyond*, or I could collect the soul devour it and keep it for myself.

The maddening hunger I felt wasn't the desire to cut the soul free.

I looked down at my left hand, raised palm-up at my side. It cradled a smoke-black orb with bright pinpoint lights throughout it, like a galaxy shrunk down to the size of a tennis ball.

Souls. Those tiny lights were souls that my reaper had claimed instead of liberated.

Revulsion welled up through me at the realization that those souls—dozens of them—would never pass to the *beyond*. They were forever trapped in darkness. But still, I wanted to devour Amanda's soul, I physically yearned for it as if I'd been lost in the desert for a thousand years and her soul was a cool oasis.

My left hand drifted outward, reaching. I just needed to touch the cord with the orb and this soul would be mine. But those little lights, all those trapped souls . . . My heart lurched at the wrongness of it, and that was enough to momentarily lift the haze of soul-hunger. Before the crazed desire could pull me back under, I lunged forward and arced my right hand out. In a blur, the blade sliced the cord and the soul vanished.

"Ella? Supernatural Crimes just pulled up. We need to get out of here." Damien appeared in the doorway just as I turned at the sound of his voice. He beckoned at me with a hurried flap of his hand. "Come on, let's go out the back."

I looked down at my empty hands and then over at Amanda's still form. The mist had vanished. I was back in the world of the living.

"*Move*, Ella," Damien hollered, his voice pitched high with urgency. "Go!"

I finally jolted from my stupor and sprang into motion, noting as I raced to the back of the cottage that maroon magic had marked the bedroom. I knew it wasn't from me because it glowed too strongly. I'd bet my paycheck that Deb was right—this was the work of the same man who'd messed up Jennifer's place. The one whose face I'd seen through the demon's memory.

My insides tightened as something occurred to me. Why had the man, the one with blood-red magic like mine, not taken the soul? Maybe I'd been wrong when I'd guessed he also carried the soul of a reaper. But I didn't want that to be true. I actually hoped he was like me, even if he was a murderer, because it meant I might have hope of surviving my reaper.

I followed Damien numbly through the neat little back yard, past the raised beds where the season's tomato plants still held some heavy red fruits. Grave chill from the *in-between* still seemed to saturate me clear to my bones, and my brain felt fuzzy like the morning after a long night of drinking. I pulled my hands down my face and gave my head a shake, trying to clear the fog. The soul-hunger still stirred around in my stomach, now only an echo of the overwhelming urge I'd felt just moments ago. I shivered, remembering just how close I'd been to stealing the soul instead of freeing it.

He stopped at the gate and rose up on his tiptoes to peer over.

"Shit," he muttered. "There are a bunch of SC cars parked out there. We either go through the gate or back through the house. Either way they'll see us."

I looked around at the little yard, completely fenced in with six-foot-high wooden slats. There was a black plastic composting bin the size of a washing machine in one corner, nearly hidden by more rose bushes.

I pointed at it. "Let's go over."

We ran to the bin, and I carefully stepped up onto it, hoping it wouldn't collapse. Bracing my hands on the top of the fence, I bent my knees, ready to pop over into the neighbor's yard.

"*Hey!*" a female voice called. "Stop right there!"

Swearing under my breath, I turned, already knowing who I'd see behind me.

"Down on the ground, now!" Detective Barnes barked at us, drawing her gun and swinging it up to aim at us in one swift, smooth motion.

I went to step down just as one side of the plastic bin buckled under my weight. My boot slipped, and I scrabbled at the fence with my fingers but lost my hold. I went shoulder-first into a hedge of peach-colored roses.

Thorns scraped my face, neck, and bare arms. They poked through my shirt and into my skin in painful little points. My cargo pants were just heavy enough to keep the woody needles from piercing through to my legs.

Groaning, I struggled to free myself from the thorny entanglement, and the bush gave me dozens more scratches as a parting gift.

By the time I rolled free of the roses, my skin burned from punctures and scratches, and Detective Barnes loomed over me with her gun pointed at my chest.

I held up my hands in surrender. "No need for that, I'm not going anywhere," I said bitterly.

She was staring at my arms, and I glanced down expecting to see some especially gory rose bush wounds. But she wasn't interested in my scratches. The sigils on my arms, the tattoo-like markings that had first appeared the night the reaper had forced me to the ghost house, were glowing cool pearly white.

Shit.

I flicked a glance at Damien, chest-down with his arms out on the brownish fall lawn. He'd raised his head to watch, and he saw the markings, too.

Without a word, Detective Barnes reached under her blazer and produced a set of handcuffs. I knew they were charmed to prevent the wearer from using magic.

"Eat dirt," she said through clenched teeth. "Wrists together."

Groaning, I rolled to my stomach and joined my hands at the small of my back.

She shouted at one of her colleagues—the tall detective I remembered from Jennifer's—to come and cuff Damien. They pulled us to our feet and marched us through the side gate to the front of the house.

Deb's mouth dropped open when she spotted us, and a look of misery came over her face when she took in the cuffs on my wrists.

The detectives took us to a yellow-and-black Supernatural Crimes patrol car and unceremoniously shoved us into the backseat. Damien looked like he either wanted to puke or cry. He'd probably never been in the back of a police car.

"They didn't read us our rights," I said with a hopeful raise of my brows. My eyes flicked to Barnes, who was talking to the tall detective. "We're not officially arrested."

"Yet," he said with a sour turn of his mouth. "Are you okay?"

I glanced down at my arms, twisting a little to try to get a full view, which was awkward with my hands secured behind my back. The scrapes had already healed, and the thorn punctures were only faint red dots.

"Yeah, it looks like I'll be good as new in a sec. Did I happen to mention how fast I heal lately?"

He shifted to turn his full attention to me. "Another reaper effect?"

"Reaper Effect, hitting theaters this Christmas," I said in my best movie announcer voice. "It'll scare the soul right out of your body."

One dark blond brow quirked, and I grinned hopefully. Damien and I had only known each other a few months, but it seemed like I was making a habit of getting him in trouble. Not intentionally, of course. But still, I couldn't help feeling bad about it.

"Yeah, must be," I said in my normal voice. "You saw the sigils on my arms, too?"

He nodded, tilting his head and squinting at my bare upper arm.

I sighed. "More reaper effects. And Barnes noticed them."

"It's not symbology I'm familiar with. I wish I could have taken a couple of pictures so I could study them later. They're starting to fade."

"They've glowed like that only a few times. I don't know what the marks mean, but she looked interested in them, which can't be good," I said.

"When I found you in the bedroom, you seemed like you were in shock. Did you know the woman who was killed?"

I shook my head. "We'd never met."

"First dead body?"

"Yeah, but that part didn't actually bother me too much." I paused, biting my lower lip for a moment, debating about whether to tell him. "I . . . reaped her soul."

His blue eyes widened. "Damn," he said in a low whisper.

"I know. The reaper took over." I squeezed my eyelids closed for a second, remembering the feel of the souls in my left hand, the crazed desire to add another to the collection. "I'm not sure if I can even explain it. Something strange happened—stranger than reaping a soul, I mean. I know this sounds bizarre, but if there are good guys and bad guys among reapers, I think mine might be a bad guy."

He peered at me and looked like he was about to ask something, but the car door next to him opened. Tall Detective stood there in his navy suit, but from my angle I couldn't see his face. He flipped a hand in a beckoning motion.

"Step out and I'll remove your cuffs, sir," the detective said.

I hunched down and leaned over toward the open door so I could see his face. "What about me?" I gave him what I hoped was an innocent smile.

He lifted his chin, indicating something on the other side of the patrol car. "She's going to read you your rights."

I whipped around just as Barnes appeared at my door.

A string of four-letter words streamed through my mind, but I managed to contain it behind my clenched teeth as the detective formally arrested me.

At the downtown Supernatural Crimes station—a building that ironically was within my Demon Patrol beat—I sat in a tiny cube of an interrogation room. It was just like on TV shows, me facing Barnes and Tall Detective across a banged-up table. His name was Lagatuda, I remembered. Like on a police procedural, except the chair I sat in was charmed to prevent me from using magic. Not that my magic was much of a threat. But they'd taken my actual weapons—my whole service belt, in fact—as soon as we'd arrived.

"So let me get this straight," I said. "You arrested me because I'd been in the houses at two crime scenes, but you have zero evidence that I was involved in any crime."

"We don't have direct evidence that you were involved, though we aren't ruling it out. But we *do* have evidence that indicates you have some connection to the perpetrator," Barnes said. Her short blond hair was held back with a black leather headband. She was actually rather cute in a perky, petite, head cheerleader sort of way. If you ignored the snarl on her face, that is.

"I'm sorry, but I'm confused. How can you know that I know the perpetrator if *you* don't know who it is?" I asked. I ignored Barnes, or at least refused to look at her, trying to appeal to Lagatuda instead. She'd clearly already settled on her suspicion, but I sensed I might still have a chance to gain a little sympathy from him.

"Our scans picked up likeness between the signature left by you and the signature left by the person we believe committed the crimes," Lagatuda said.

Barnes shot him an irritated look as if she didn't want me to know that detail, but he gave her a steady, cool gaze. My regard for him jumped up a notch or two.

My heart thumped. They hadn't mentioned maroon magic yet, so there was probably something less specific in their crime scene data.

"What was it?" I demanded.

They exchanged a look. "We don't have specifics."

I relaxed slightly. I could tell they hadn't fully deciphered whatever their scans had detected.

"That's a completely random thing, though," I said, trying my best to sound reasonable. "Even if there is a similarity, it doesn't mean I know him."

"Him?" Barnes leaned forward with a predatory gleam in her eye. "How do you know the perpetrator is male?"

"I don't. It's just a generic pronoun," I said through clamped teeth. I was losing patience. "But your argument is like saying, 'Well, you're tall, and we know the perpetrator is tall, so you must know the perpetrator.'"

"It's obviously not that simple. And regardless, we are within the law," Barnes said. She stood and her chair scraped the floor with an unpleasant screech. "Since you're not going to help us, we're going to have to monitor you."

"What?" I spat. I felt my blood pressure spike, and my face began to heat with the flush of anger.

She nodded at the mirrored window, and a second later the door opened. A female SC officer appeared with what looked like a thick white plastic bracelet. Two male officers were right behind her.

"We'll be monitoring your movements as well as your use of magic in real time," she said.

"No!" I tried to spring to my feet, but the two officers smashed down on my shoulders, preventing me from standing. "That is a complete violation of my privacy, and you don't have cause. You can't do this. I want a lawyer!"

I couldn't believe they were treating me like a criminal. It was humiliating.

"You're welcome to get a lawyer," Barnes said. "But that won't be of much help to you. As of now you're no longer under arrest. You're under surveillance. And trust me, we've got supernatural law on our side here."

I tried to shake off the hands clamped over my shoulders, but looking around the room, I realized it was five against one. I wasn't going to get past all of them even if I could escape the iron grips holding me in place.

"What if I refuse the monitor?" I asked.

Barnes crossed her arms. "We'll arrest you as a suspect, and you'll go to jail until we can determine the extent of your involvement in the crimes," she said, her tone maddeningly calm. "*Then* you might want that lawyer, though your refusal of the monitor would pretty much hamstring any further legal maneuvering."

"Fine," I said through gritted teeth. My head was starting to pound from all the jaw clenching, and I needed to get the hell out of there before I lost my temper and made things worse for myself. "Just get it over with."

The female officer knelt next to me, lifted my pant leg, and wrapped the white monitor around my ankle just above my boot. It was more rubbery than it looked, and I felt a whisper of elemental energies over my skin as it briefly glowed with strands of green earth magic and yellow air magic. Tightening slightly of its own accord, it molded to a snug fit.

"Don't go anywhere you can't easily justify," Barnes said. "And don't use any magic beyond—well, I guess I don't really have to warn you about that, considering your aptitude level."

The shadows edging my vision writhed as if they too were outraged by the constraint—and the insult. A new thought occurred to me, and my stomach dropped as I eyed Barnes sharply.

Did they know I was a necromancer? Deb had said that such skills were highly prized in the supernatural community, that my reaper soul, ability to wield magic even a little, and necromancy made me a "unique configuration" that certain people would love to control. By force, if needed. I was beginning to suspect she might be right. Most necromancers weren't crafters, and I assumed the reaper soul was even more rare.

Surely it wasn't within the purview of Supernatural law to force me to use my abilities for their benefit . . . was it? Even if it was, the joke would be on them. At this point, I could barely do any necromany, my magical aptitude was unimpressive, and the reaper soul was equally bent on killing me as assisting me.

My chest felt like it was wrapped in rubber bands. I needed to get out of this damn box of a room. With six people stuffed into it, it felt like there was barely enough oxygen to go around.

Barnes handed me off to the female officer for processing, and twenty minutes later I was standing outside in the gold-toned October afternoon sunlight, waiting for Damien and feeling like a criminal on an invisible leash. I'd tried Johnny first, but he'd been called away to a job.

When my partner's Lexus eased into the Supernatural Crimes precinct parking lot, my insides loosened a little. I suddenly felt empty, since my adrenaline had worn off and my anger at the whole stupid situation was calming to a dull ache in my temples. My ire flared again, however, when I got in the car and lifted my pant leg to wordlessly show Damien my new jewelry.

He let loose with the dirtiest language I'd ever heard from him, which actually amused me enough to lift my spirits for a moment.

"This has got to be a violation of your rights," he said.

"Apparently, it's not. How's Deb doing?" I asked.

"She's upset," he said. "She and some of her friends are at your place now. They're waiting for you."

I tried not to wince. I wanted to comfort Deb, but the thought of a bunch of weeping witches gathered in my living room made me a little twitchy. Outpourings of emotion—not exactly my comfort zone.

When we arrived home, I was relieved to find that although there were a lot of red-rimmed eyes, the mood was more quiet determination than hysterical grief. I was surprised to see Lynnette Leblanc, the powerful exorcist witch with the charter to the coven that Deb and her friends were trying to get into. Roxanne was there too, huddled on the sofa with Loki, her hands pulled inside the sleeves of her hoodie. Under Deb's mentorship, Roxanne had also been training with Amanda, the woman who'd been murdered, and other witches. Deb was skilled enough to guide Roxanne in all of the basics that new crafters needed to learn, but Deb thought it would be good for the girl to learn from multiple women, especially considering she didn't have a female role model at home. The young witch looked dazed and pale.

I cleared my throat as everyone turned to me.

"I'm so sorry about the loss of your friend," I said. I nodded at Lynnette. "I'm sure you've already talked about the connection between the killing and what happened at Jennifer's."

She blew out a heavy breath and nodded, her usual attitude seemingly deflated in the wake of tragedy.

I moved to join them, sitting on the floor next to Deb, and Damien perched on the sofa arm. No one seemed to mind that he was there.

"My first suspicion was that someone was targeting your

coven hopefuls out of competition or jealousy," I said to Lynnette. I paused, considering how much to reveal. "But I have reason to believe we're dealing with a man. Any idea why a man would take an interest in your coven?"

Only female crafters formed covens. It was a unique quality of feminine magic that allowed women to combine their abilities. When done in a well-bonded coven, the collective magic was much more powerful than the sum of the individuals' abilities.

Lynnette peered at me sharply with her kohl-lined eyes, and a couple of the other witches exchanged glances. I waited for someone to demand how I had such knowledge. I hadn't even had the opportunity to tell Deb about what I'd seen through the demon's eyes. But Lynnette just nodded again.

"Deb told us you'd sensed similar magic at both crime scenes, and that you sometimes have visions," she said.

I gave a small nod.

"What we need to figure out is one, how to prevent anyone else from getting hurt," Lynnette said. "And two, how to catch the son of a bitch who took Amanda from us."

The other women started talking, but my breath caught in my throat as the image of Amanda's body came rushing back to me. My gaze settled on my best friend.

Deb. She could be next. I watched her, sitting cross-legged with one arm crossed protectively over her lower belly. She wasn't showing yet, but for the past couple of months her pale cheeks had a new rosy flush and her eyes a sparkling brightness. If anything happened to her or her baby, I couldn't live with it.

Pressing my fingers against the smooth curve of the rubber ring around my ankle, the extent of my limits really began to sink in. A plan began to form in my mind. Instead of waiting around for the next attack, I wanted to draw the killer out. But with my independence severely pinched between the petite fingers of Detective Barnes, I was going to need some help if I had any hope of doing it without SC interference.

For the next hour, I fidgeted as the witches expressed their worries and tried to come up with a plan for protecting themselves. They decided that none of them would stay in their own homes, since Jennifer and Amanda had been targeted in theirs. When the party started to break up, I held Deb back.

"I don't want you going home by yourself, even just to get your things," I said. "Can you tell Keith you're staying here tonight?"

"I was going to ask you if I could anyway because he's out of town." Her shoulders inched a little higher and rounded forward. "I have zero desire to be alone right now."

I nodded, relieved. I didn't want to have to try to persuade her. "Good. Do you need anything from the house?"

"Eh, I can get by for a night."

"I'm going to your place either way," I said. "So I can pick up some stuff if you want."

Her brows drew together. "You don't need to do that."

"I'm going to draw him out," I said.

"What?" She shook her head once, her face scrunched in

confusion.

"The killer. I'm going to pose as you and bait him. But I'm gonna need some help."

"Ella, this is insane," Johnny said after I explained my plan. He'd shown up about the time the last of Deb's friends had departed.

"You mean you can't do it?" I challenged, one brow arched. I needed him to use his gadgets and doohickeys to mask what I was doing so Supernatural Crimes couldn't track my location or actions.

"I *can*, but I'm not going to." He folded his arms. "It's too dangerous. Not to mention that if we got caught disarming your ankle monitor, we'd both go to prison."

My nostrils flared as I planted my hands on my hips and looked off to the side, trying to keep my frustration under control. Johnny seemed to be developing a habit of calling me crazy—or at least calling my ideas crazy—and it was starting to piss me off.

When the discussion between Johnny and me had started to get heated, Deb had moved into the kitchen. I heard her rummaging around putting clean dishes away, but I knew she could still hear us. She'd already expressed her strong concerns about my plan before Johnny arrived.

The door opened, and Johnny and I both whipped around as Damien strode it. He stopped short, his glance ping-ponging between the two of us.

"Uh, should I come back later?" he asked, edging half a step toward the doorway.

"No," Johnny and I said in sharp unison.

Damien had taken Roxanne home to the apartment she shared with her brother, and I'd asked him if he'd be willing to come back and stay overnight. I wanted him to protect Deb while I tried to lure the maroon magic man out into the open.

"Please, stay," I said to Damien, softening. "Just give us a sec."

Sidling past us as if we might suddenly pounce and try to drag him into our face-off, Damien beelined for the kitchen.

I turned back to Johnny. "If I catch the killer, you and I won't have to worry about going to prison."

He dropped his chin to his chest, hiding his eyes, and exhaled. When he raised his head, his dark eyes shone with concern. "I can't put you in that position. You don't even know exactly who or what you'd be facing. Besides, how do you expect to overpower someone who can slip by wards and murder skilled witches? I can't do something that would put you in that kind of danger."

A series of bleeps came from the pocket of his leather jacket. He pulled his phone out and checked it.

"It's a job, and I've got to go. I'm sorry." He stepped forward and planted a kiss on my lips and then turned for the door. One side of his expressive mouth quirked up as he flicked a glance at me over his shoulder. "I dig your crazy, woman. But I don't want you to get hurt. Just let SC handle it."

I snorted a laugh and rolled my eyes, feeling slightly less resentful about his lack of support. But still, I had to do something.

I couldn't just wait around for the killer to continue to take out more witches—not when one of the victims could be Deb.

Absently scratching Loki's head as I stared out the front window, I tried to come up with something . . . *anything*.

"I could probably do it."

I turned at the sound of Damien's voice.

I perked up. "You could turn off my stupid ankle monitor?"

"Pretty sure I could at least freeze its state for a while," he said.

I narrowed my eyes, peering at him. "Why would you be willing to do that?"

"If I don't, you'll try to do something anyway and probably get arrested by Supernatural Crimes." He raised his hands and shrugged. "Lesser of two evils."

A slow grin began to spread over my face. "But I know you're not really comfortable breaking the rules."

He dipped his chin in acknowledgement. "True, but Barnes really ticked me off when she put us in cuffs. It's personal now."

My grin widened, and I pointed at him. "Okay, I've got a witness." I tipped my head in Deb's direction. "No take-backsies on your offer."

He gave a low, warm laugh. "No take-backsies. But I'm not just going to jam your monitor and send you out there. I want to stir up a defensive charm that'll help protect you. And you'll need something to incapacitate him."

Deb's face was scrunched up as if she were in pain. "Ella, this guy is really dangerous. I don't like the thought of you going alone. Can't Damien go with you?"

"No, I want him to stay with you," I said sharply. I glanced at Damien and back at Deb and then spoke more slowly. "Besides . . . I'm pretty sure he can't kill me."

Her brows rose.

"I'm not saying I'm immortal or anything," I continued. "But ever since the reaper, uh, *joined* me, I've been healing faster and faster. I can practically watch a scrape disappear before my eyes." I held out my arms. "At Amanda's I fell into some rosebushes, and look, now you can't even tell. Honestly, the reaper soul may get me in the end, but I feel pretty certain that in the meantime it's going to do its damnedest to keep me alive. It wants my body and mind. In a fight, it's going to be on my side. For now, anyway."

A few seconds of silence passed, and then Deb gave the tiniest of nods. She glanced at Damien. "How about an amulet that will tell her when someone with magical ability is nearby?" she suggested.

"Good idea," Damien said, giving her a professorial look of approval. "And why don't you help me with how to design the protection charm?" He turned to me. "You should listen in. I'd planned on starting to integrate charms into your training soon, anyway."

He pulled his notebook from his Demon Patrol pack, and the three of us gathered around the coffee table. I fought the antsy feeling stirring in my chest. I didn't want to sit around and talk and plan—I wanted to get out there and find the bastard who killed Amanda. But he was dangerous, and I knew I needed to go into this fully loaded with whatever protection I could get.

While Damien and Deb talked advanced magic, most of

which was way over my head, I watched Damien, wondering if he'd been in contact with his mage family back East. He'd come out here knowing no one, and in the months since he'd arrived, a good portion of his free time had been tied up in my little adventures, helping me hone my magic skills, or engrossed in his research. But what about his social life? I knew he was gay, and he knew I was perfectly comfortable with it, but I realized I hadn't even asked if he'd started dating. I vowed to make an effort to show more interest, maybe introduce him around a little. You know—if I was still alive in the morning.

During a pause while Damien wrote notes in his neat print, I shifted to the edge of the sofa cushion.

"We're doing this tonight, right?" I asked, looking back and forth between the two of them.

Deb's forehead creased with worry, but she lifted a shoulder and let it drop. "I don't think it's going to help anything to wait."

"Good," I said.

I didn't just want to protect Deb and the other witches. I had my own reasons for wanting to find the man with the blood-red magic. If there was any possibility that he was like me, and he'd figured out how to survive with a reaper soul, I needed to know his secret. I was still me, but I could feel the reaper's hold tightening, expanding. The sensation was hard to describe, but my dark companion seemed to breathe with me, watch the world as I watched it, and anticipate my movements. Before, the reaper soul had alternately emerged and hibernated, like a creature that preferred to shy away from the world. Now, it felt present in my every heartbeat.

I quietly stood and paced away into the dark kitchen under the pretense of needing something there. Leaning against the counter, I pressed a hand to my chest and drew a slow breath. I was changing. *We* were changing. Remembering the power of holding the cloud of souls in my left hand and the reaping blade in my right, exhilaration rushed through my veins. Part of me longed so strongly to feel it all again, it sent a knife of fear slicing through me. The soul-hunger stirred in my middle, and I actually *salivated* a little. Every muscle in my body tightened with the effort of pushing the sensation away.

"Hey, Ella?" Deb called. "Do you have something I can use to make the amulet?"

I drew a sharp breath in through my nose, trying to pull myself back into the moment. "Yeah, I've got a ring that you can re-spell."

I went to my room and dug around in the top drawer of my dresser where I kept what little jewelry I owned. I found the ring I was looking for—a thick-looking thing with a band made of a silver and copper alloy specially formulated for holding spells— that had belonged to my mother. The inlaid quartz crystal had turned milky, indicating whatever spell the ring last held had gone stale.

I brought it to Deb.

She turned it over in her hand. "I don't suppose you have any bloodroot on hand? Even some angelica root would do. I really need some sulfur, too, to make this work. And some nettle, now that I think about it."

I gave her a sheepish look and shrugged. "Sorry, I don't stir spells."

She stood. "I'll run to Crystal Ball Lane and pick up supplies."

"Huh-uh, you're not going anywhere," I said. "I'll go."

She let out an exasperated huff. "No one's going to try to kill me in broad daylight on the Lane."

"Fine, we'll go together," I said, my tone leaving no room for debate. I went to get my keys from the table under the front bay window and turned to Damien, who was still absorbed in his scribblings. "Need anything from Cauldrons R Us?"

He looked up, his sky-blue eyes distracted, and then cocked his head. "Is that a real store?"

I snorted a laugh. "No."

"I think I've got what I need, thanks." He made a vague gesture at his backpack and bent over his notebook again. Then he looked up again. "Wait—take my car."

He tossed me his fob, and I caught it with one hand. "Thanks."

Normally I would have refused, but I knew why he wanted us to take his Lexus. It had the modern upgrades that shielded against demon entry, and I'd bet a paycheck that he'd added some other fancy custom protection to his vehicle as well. My pickup and Deb's Honda were too old for the demon shields or any other magical protection to have come standard when they were manufactured, and neither of us could afford the retrofit, let alone any expensive upgrades. At least if something happened while we were in the Lexus, we might be protected. And Damien's wards on the vehicle would get tripped, and he'd know we needed help. Or maybe not, considering how the blood magic man had snuck past Jennifer's wards.

"I'm texting Roxanne to see if she wants to meet us. I'm starting to teach her some basic spells," Deb said as we left my apartment.

"You sure you want her with us?" I asked.

I slid into the smooth leather seat of Damien's car. The vehicle still had that fresh-off-the-lot smell.

"I refuse to let this asshole control my life," Deb said stubbornly as her seat belt automatically slid into place. "Besides, you're going to catch him tonight, and then the danger will be gone."

I gave a wry laugh. "I appreciate the confidence."

When the key fob came in proximity of the control panel, sure enough, a bunch of lights illuminated, indicating the activation of several magical shields and wards.

It was a short drive to Crystal Ball Lane, five minutes tops, and I found a parking spot on the curb a block down from the building that housed Roxanne's apartment. She emerged from the alley next to her building just as Deb and I got out of the car.

Roxanne was just coming into her magical abilities. She was a strong Level II like Deb. The girl lived with her brother, Nathan, and I'd met her when her brother had run into some trouble a couple of months back. He'd gotten caught up in a triple-species lockup—possessed by a demon and somehow trapped inside a gargoyle. I'd called in a ton of favors to get him free, and it had become quite the operation. Two international agencies had to get involved to help us rescue Nathan—and the gargoyle—from the clutches of Gregori Industries. The notorious corporation was headed by my biological uncle, my dead father's brother, but no one except Deb and Terrence, my old Demon Patrol partner before Damien, knew I was related to the infamous Jacob Gregori.

Since the incident with Nathan, Deb had taken the role of Roxanne's mentor to help cultivate her abilities and learn the basics of the craft of magic.

Roxanne hugged Deb and then wrapped her arms around me. After a second she stiffened and stepped back. She looked up at me, her round eyes wide.

"Whoa," she breathed. "There's something different about you."

She scanned me up and down, squinting, and then reached out and grabbed my wrist.

"What's this?" She brushed her fingertips over my arm and the faint pearly sigils that were barely visible, like faded white tattoos. With a sharp inhalation, she pulled her hand away as if my skin had given her a little shock.

"I don't know, exactly," I said honestly. "They appeared not long after my little brush with death."

Deb and I exchanged a quick glance. Roxanne knew I'd died temporarily after an accident on the job, but I'd never told her about the reaper soul.

Hesitantly, she touched some of the markings again. This time her eyelids lowered partway in concentration.

"They were put there by someone," she said softly, barely above a whisper. "By . . . by . . . something in the gray place."

She blinked several times and looked up at me. One of her emerging magical talents had to do with being able to touch an object and read things about it—sometimes who it belonged to, or who'd recently used it. I'd never seen her sense something like this before, and from the look on her face, it was a new experience.

Her eyes clouded with apprehension. "Did a ghost give you these tattoos?"

I gave her what I hoped was a reassuring smile. "Maybe. That's as good a guess as any. Don't worry about it, though. They come and go, but otherwise they're not causing me any trouble."

"We'd better get on with our errand," Deb said, putting a gentle hand on Roxanne's back and coaxing her forward.

While Deb shopped for herbs, spell candles, and other witchy doodads, explaining how to choose the right items and what they could be used for, Roxanne kept flicking furtive looks at my arms. She seemed more curious than fearful, so I tried to appear nonchalant.

I paid for the haul, and we walked Roxanne back to her building.

She started to turn to the metal staircase leading up to the second floor where her apartment was but stopped and came back to us.

"Ella, I just realized something," she said, her face bright with excitement. "The marks on your arms feel like something else, something familiar. They feel like ley lines."

"Really?" I said. Roxanne's apartment was right on top of the ley line that ran down Crystal Ball Lane, so if anyone would know what it felt like, it would be her.

She nodded vigorously. "I didn't recognize it at first because

I'm used to feeling ley lines within the earth, not on a person. But yeah, that's what they are. Or something *like* ley lines, anyway." She turned to Deb. "You need to teach me how to tap into ley line power."

Deb smiled. "That's a little advanced, but we'll get to it, I promise."

"Okay. Bye!" Roxanne gave us a little wave and trotted to the stairs.

Walking in silence, Deb and I went to the Lexus and got in.

Instead of starting the car, I turned to her. "Is there anything to what she said?" I asked.

Big surprise, I knew very little about ley lines, the underground veins of potent magic forming a web in the earth. One of the many ley lines in the Boise area followed Crystal Ball Lane before veering off into the foothills. I knew it was no coincidence that a street of magical shops had sprung up along an invisible river of supernatural energy, but I didn't really know much beyond the fact that a crafter's magical power got a little boost near a ley line. I'd heard of crafters who were able to draw ley line magic directly, but it was dangerous and very difficult to control.

Deb tipped her head to one side, her gaze lifted at an angle for a moment as she thought. "Considering everything else that's happened to you, I'd say it's not out of the question."

"Good point," I said.

For a breath or two, I sat with my hands on the wheel and stared through the windshield at the row of maples beginning to shed their flame-shaded leaves. I started the car, and steered us back to my place.

Damien had been busy.

"Okay, I've got the protection charm ready." He held up a plain round metal pendant on a leather cord. "I need a few minutes to probe the magic in your ankle monitor so I can figure out how to temporarily freeze it."

He patted the sofa cushion beside him, indicating I should take a seat.

"While you do that, I'll be stirring up the spell for the amulet," Deb said. She took her bag of supplies to the kitchen. Loki followed her, his nose in the air as he sniffed the trail of scents left by her purchases. A second later, I heard the sounds of drawers and cabinets opening and closing.

"Put your foot up on the table," Damien instructed.

I did as he asked, pulling up my pant leg to expose the ring clamped around my ankle. He moved to kneel on the other side of the table and then wrapped his hands around the monitor and closed his eyes in concentration.

A tingle of magic in the air washed over my face, neck, and arms, and the glow of yellow air magic illuminated around his hands. I sat still as he used his magical senses to examine the device. Seconds ticked by. Then minutes. I tried to keep my breaths quiet so as not to disturb his focus.

Finally, he opened his eyes and sat back on his heels with a sigh. His face looked drawn, and I realized he had the beginning signs of magical exhaustion.

"Don't tire yourself too much," I said quietly, my brows

pinching. "I don't want to leave you here defenseless."

He brushed off my worry with a shake of his head. "I'll be okay."

Maybe Deb could do some rudimentary healing to restore some of his energy. Though I didn't really want her to wear herself out either, especially if I wasn't going to be around for a few hours.

"The device isn't as sophisticated as Barnes probably wants you to believe," he said, lifting his chin at my ankle monitor. "I'm pretty sure I can freeze the signal and get it to communicate something boring for a while. A signal that makes it look like you're taking a nap, maybe."

"So getting it completely off my leg is out of the question?" I'd figured he wouldn't be able to remove it, but I had to ask.

His mouth pressed into a grimace. "I can tell how the locking mechanism works, and I could release it, but I'm not confident I could stop the alarm in time."

"That's all right," I said. "As long as I don't have Barnes up my ass while I'm trying to engage the killer."

He shook out his hands and blew out a loud breath like a gymnast mentally preparing at the start of a routine.

"Keep still, and no matter what, don't draw any magic," he said. He wrapped his hands around my ankle again. "Ready?"

I nodded.

A shock of heat, ice, and electricity jolted through me, and I clamped my arms against my sides to keep from squirming. The sensation strengthened, as if I'd grabbed a live wire and couldn't let go. I ground my teeth and watched Damien through slitted eyes.

Magic swirled so brightly around his hands, I couldn't see them through the furious flashes of yellow, red, and green.

Then it was over. We stared at each other, both a little breathless. Then he pushed slowly to his feet.

"You should be good to go," he said.

"I've got your amulet." Deb appeared at the end of the sofa, holding out the ring I'd loaned her. "The stone will turn red if anyone with magical aptitude is within about three hundred feet of the ring."

"Awesome, thank you." I took the ring and slid it onto the middle finger of my left hand.

Damien sat heavily next to me and reached for the charmed necklace he'd been working on. "This is a one-time thing, but it's powerful protection if you need it. To activate the charm, yank the necklace to break the cord, and then throw it at your attacker. It doesn't have to hit the person. It's just a directional thing so the magic knows which way to go. It'll give a blast that should stun strongly enough to incapacitate for a few seconds, similar to what our stun guns do to minor demons but a whole lot more powerful. But like I said, it's only got one charge. I also souped up my Demon Patrol net launcher for you. It'll trap and hold things much bigger than minor demons now."

"You guys are the best." I slipped the cord over my neck and settled the pendant under my shirt, the metal cool against my skin. "I don't know how to thank you."

"Don't die. That'd be thanks enough," Damien said wryly.

"I won't," I said, my tone sober.

I glanced out the front window. The sun had set, and it would be dark enough to sneak out soon. My fingers tightened into loose fists as anticipation began to churn around in my stomach.

If things went the way I hoped, I'd soon come face-to-face with the only other person in the world I knew of who might hold the key to my survival, and I'd end the threat to Deb and the other witches.

"Just pull the trigger like normal." Damien was holding out his modified service net launcher. He'd juiced it so I could use it to trap not a demon but a man. I intended to net the killer and turn him in. Only after I'd had the chance to do some questioning of my own, of course.

The last order of business was my disguise. Even Damien wasn't a strong enough crafter to make me look exactly like Deb, who was eight inches shorter than me and a good deal curvier. He managed an obfuscation spell that made my hair appear to be Deb's strawberry blond color, but the best I could do otherwise was to change into the most Deb-like clothes I owned and hunch to try to look shorter.

I wore a knee-length jacket to conceal the weapons I carried, and flat slip-on shoes I'd worn to a wedding reception a couple of years back but hadn't touched since. A light gray wool sweater and jeans were the best I could do for a Deb outfit.

Before full darkness fell outside, we dimmed all the lights in my apartment. Deb handed me the key to her Honda, and I checked one last time to make sure I wore the charmed pendant, the amulet ring, and had Damien's net launcher and my whip.

"Take this too," Deb said, producing a little fabric drawstring bag from her pocket. "Spell salt. It's simple, but it's powerful. You never know when you might need it."

She'd always tried to get me to carry salt, but I told her that even if I had some on me I'd probably forget it was there. It was handy for dissolving small amounts of magic and used in combination with a magic circle could offer protection.

I took the bag and slipped it in the front pocket of my jeans. "Thank you."

Deb gave me a quick hug and then went into my bedroom so she wouldn't be visible when I opened the front door.

Damien touched my shoulder. "I really think I should go with you. I can tail you in my car."

I shook my head firmly. "No, stay here with her. If we left Deb alone and something happened to her, I'd never get over it."

I reached down to give Loki's head a pat, and then I was out the door.

After sitting around in the itchy wool sweater, the cool fall air was like a refreshing splash on my face. As I made my way to Deb's Honda at the curb, I kept my head bent, my shoulders hunched, and walked with my knees flexed to try to appear shorter.

When I started the car, 80s rock blared from the speakers. I turned it down with a faint smile. Deb tended to listen to music by decade, and she'd get on a kick that would last for weeks.

With frequent glances in the rearview mirror, I steered across the west end of downtown and caught the connector ramp to the freeway, heading west to Meridian and Deb's house. I suddenly realized I had no idea how long I would be away pretending to be my best friend. I'd stay overnight if I had to.

By the time I pulled into the familiar driveway and the garage door sensor activated, I was keyed up with unspent energy. I parked in Deb's garage and went into the house. Before I turned on the light, I pulled out my phone to send a quick text to her and Damien to let them know I'd arrived.

Deb and Keith's place was a two-level family home in a sprawling neighborhood development built about five years ago. She'd always wanted a house like this, which I never really understood. To me, it looked the same as the bazillion other houses that surrounded it, and I couldn't see the draw.

Inside, the place felt cozy, the thermostat turned up and the air infused with the faint smell of herbs and flowers that I always associated with Deb's things, but it also somehow emphasized the warmth and scratch of the wool I wasn't used to wearing.

Turning on a couple of lights as I went, I headed upstairs to Deb and Keith's room to look for something to change into. I stripped out of my sweater, found a pink t-shirt with a flowery peace symbol silkscreened on the front and pulled it on. It was too short on me, but it was better than the wool.

With my hands on my hips, I glanced around the room. It was too early to pretend to go to bed. What to do?

I tapped my lips with the end of my index finger, considering. I spotted the book on Deb's side of the bed, a nonfiction title about circle casting. I grabbed it and headed back down.

Tea and reading, that would be a very Deb-like way to pass the evening. I heated up water in the microwave, found some boxes of tea in the pantry, and picked a pouch of the least gross-sounding one.

A few minutes later I settled on the overstuffed sofa with a steaming mug smelling of cinnamon and oranges in one hand and the book in the other. After a few pages I gave up trying to read and flipped the TV on with the sound muted.

When my eyelids tried to drift downward, I realized the warm tea and flickering screen were too comforting. With a shake of my head, I stood and set the mug on the side table, intending to turn the thermostat down several degrees. I'd have a better chance staying alert if the house were chillier.

When I straightened and turned toward the front hallway, I realized the crystal on my ring was glowing angry red. A shadow moved across the carpet. My pulse jolted. I wasn't alone.

It was him. The blood-magic man I'd seen through the demon's eyes. He was taller than I'd expected. Maroon magic surrounded him in a faint corona.

My heart lurched, but the flash of panic I expected didn't come. Instead, there was a stirring in my chest, whether mine or my reaper's I wasn't sure. But I knew what it was: recognition.

"You're better as a brunette," he said, his voice calm, surprisingly smooth and resonant. He stood with his feet planted wide, his elbows slightly bent. In his duster he looked like an old West gunslinger.

I felt myself automatically shifting into a similar posture. Readiness. Expecting a fight. The pulse of the reaper grew in the center of my forehead, spreading rapidly until my entire body seemed to thump with its rhythm. The shadows gyrated around the edges of my sight, and my right eye blurred and then revealed the room in the necro-vision tones.

With my necro sight, I could more clearly see the blood-red aura of magic that surrounded the man.

"Who are you?" I demanded. My fingers twitched with the urge to reach for the net launcher at my hip.

A cold smile tugged at the corners of his lips. "Ah, humans, always wanting to put names to things."

My eyes narrowed. "You're not human?"

"That depends on your definition." He sounded almost bored.

"Why are you trying to kill witches?"

His face turned dark. "I'm not a killer, and I don't care about the coven witches and their fascination with darkness. I'm not here for them. I'm here for you."

Hell no, I wasn't going anywhere with this guy. But so many questions swelled in my mind. He saw my distraction, and I realized too late it was what he'd been waiting for.

With a blinding-quick flick of one wrist, a disc of blood-red magic sprang from his hand. The disc grew arms, turning into a whirling spiral as it flew.

My reaper took over, gifting me reflexes beyond my human capabilities. In a flash I dove to one side, and the disc only kissed one shoulder. On the floor with the sofa between me and the man, adrenaline surged through me. My vision changed again, revealing the gray mist of the *in-between*. This time, there were no reaping knife or cloud of souls in my hands. And the sofa—my cover—was absent in this realm.

My chest clenched when I realized I had no net launcher, either. Damien's pendant was gone from my neck, too.

But for some unknown reason, my whip remained. I pulled it from my belt, gripped the handle, and sprang up to a crouch.

The man I faced was no longer a man. He was a specter, a skeletal nightmare with glowing blood-red orbs for eyes, clad in the clothes, boots, and duster he wore in the living realm.

His face had an eerily familiar quality. It looked like what I'd seen in Jennifer's scrying mirror. *My* face when I'd learned that the soul of an angel of death was feeding off me.

I pushed the horror of it aside, and without even consciously thinking of it, I drew magic. Not soothing green earth magic, but sickening dark red magic. Just before I snapped my wrist in a practiced motion, sending the whip and a bolt of blood-red magic blurring toward him, I registered that he was hesitating.

My whip, fueled by magic, found its target and wrapped around his exposed neck above the collar of the duster like a little bloody boa constrictor. It happened so fast, and I wasn't sure I'd directed my own actions or if it was my reaper controlling me. The man's skeletal hands flew up to clutch at it.

The mist suddenly cleared, and we were standing back in Deb's living room. In a lightning-quick motion, I switched the whip to my left hand and yanked it hard, pulling him off balance. I gripped the net launcher, aimed, and shot him.

My breaths fast and shaking on a tide of adrenaline, I strode to where he lay paralyzed within the trap. The net was alive with strands of magic of all four elements pulsing and writhing like a light show at a rave. For a split second I marveled at the sheer volume of magic Damien had infused into it.

I loomed over the man as if he were my trophy kill. "Who *are* you? Who's paying you to kill witches?" I yelled down at his still form.

For a moment I wondered if I'd knocked him unconscious. I wanted to nudge him with my boot, but I hesitated. He was on his side, and I couldn't see through the flashing magic well enough to tell whether his eyes were open.

"I was called Atriul," he said. "I have killed no witch."

I took a breath, intending to call him a liar, but lights through the front windows caught my eye. Blue and yellow bubble lights.

Shit. Supernatural Crimes had shown up. Had my ankle monitor given me away? I wasn't going to wait around to find out.

I sprang toward the hallway leading to the den with the door that let out into the back yard. Before I turned the corner, I glanced back over my shoulder. The net was crumpled on the floor—empty.

Scrabbling at the deadbolt, I turned it just as someone banged heavily on the front door. I closed the door as quietly as I could behind me, having no choice but to leave it unlocked, and raced across the dark lawn.

Damn, more fences. My attempt to scale a fence earlier hadn't ended very well. I angled toward the pine in the corner and heaved myself up into the prickly boughs, fighting through needles until I could reach for the top of the wood slats and throw myself over. I landed on my side with a rib-cracking impact, but at least my fall was partially cushioned by a strip of grass next to the sidewalk that lined the west side of Deb's property. Hissing a breath out through clenched teeth, I pushed to my feet and tried to ignore the pain along my ribcage.

Pumping my elbows for all I was worth, I raced away from the house and into the cover of night.

Once I was a few blocks away, I dropped to my hands and knees next to a minivan, trying to listen for approaching cars over the pounding of my pulse and heaving of my breaths.

I peeked around the bumper to look back the way I'd come. Just when I thought the coast was clear, a Supernatural Crimes cruiser rounded the corner from the next street over, moving fast and heading straight toward me.

When a hand clamped around my upper arm, I barely held in a shriek. I tried to whirl around but couldn't yank free of the iron grasp.

"This way," a voice hissed near my ear.

For a wild, illogical moment I expected to see the man with the blood-red magic. But instead of a duster my would-be rescuer wore a familiar leather jacket.

"*Johnny*?" I said in disbelief as I allowed him to tow me at a sprint around the side of the dark house that presumably belonged to the minivan owners.

He pulled me with him into the tight space between a hedge and the house's siding. The bushes scratched at my bare arms and caught on the thin fabric of Deb's pink t-shirt. The thing was going to be in shreds by the time the night was over. We slid to the ground, our knees pulled up tight against our bodies and our backsides pressed into the dirt. Cold moisture began to seep through the seat of my pants. I clamped my arms around my torso, trying to hold in some of my body heat.

"You didn't think I'd leave you by your lonesome, did you, sugar?" His lips moved at my ear, and even though he barely mouthed them loud enough for me to hear his words, I could tell he was smiling. "I had a hunch you would try to find a way to go after the killer."

"But how did you know where I—"

His hand pressed over my mouth, silencing me just before a

Supernatural Crimes cruiser rolled slowly past.

I grasped his wrist and pulled it away.

"My monitor," I said urgently, my teeth starting to chatter. "Damien thought he froze it, but maybe it didn't work. If they figure out I was at yet another suspicious scene, I'm screwed."

"If they were tracking you by the device, they'd already be on top of us."

"Then why did they show up at Deb's while I was there?" I squinted through the thick hedge. Was that the sound of another car approaching?

"Neighbor probably called it in," he said. "That's why I came. Supernatural Crimes sends me alerts on my phone. When I realized it was Deb's house, I headed straight here."

I peered at him, trying to read his face, but it was too dark. How would Johnny have recognized Deb's address? Surely he'd never been to her house before. They only knew each other through me, and it was barely more than a casual acquaintance. And his explanation didn't account for how he found me crouched behind a minivan blocks away from Deb's house.

"I like you as a blond," he said, again with the smile in his voice.

I snorted a laugh and shifted so I could pull Deb's bag of salt from my pants pocket. I loosened the drawstring and poured some into my hand.

"Eh, I don't think it suits me," I said, sprinkling the salt over my head and whispering the words Damien had told me would reverse the obfuscation spell. I used my fingers to comb the grains through my hair.

A warm shiver of dissolving magic passed over my scalp. I lifted a strand and held it up close to my eyes. Satisfied that my hair had returned to its natural color, I brushed off my hands and stuffed the tiny sack back into my jeans.

We both went still as another car passed—an SUV this time.

After a few minutes Johnny pulled his phone out and checked something.

"I think we can make our move," he said.

We crawled out from behind the hedge, and I shivered as I stood next to him in the deep shadows between two houses. My adrenaline had long ago subsided, and my body dragged with the beginnings of magical exhaustion, which I hadn't noticed in my efforts to escape Supernatural Crimes and another possible showdown with Detective Barnes.

"I parked two streets over," he said. He took off his jacket and threw it over my shoulders.

Taking my hand, he led me through the quiet neighborhood to his Mustang. Once I was settled in the passenger seat, I texted Deb and Damien to let them know I was okay and headed back home.

The ride was quiet as I sank into my thoughts, replaying what had happened. Atriul. That's what he'd said his name was. He'd insisted he wasn't a killer. I had no concrete reason to believe him, but I felt an uncanny certainty that he was telling the truth.

Back at home, Deb and Damien came to the door along with Loki, greeting me with anxious expectant looks. Damien's expression shifted to surprise when he caught sight of Johnny behind me.

"I'm fine," I said. Deb grasped both my hands and pulled me into the middle of the living room, looking me up and down as if not quite convinced I was unharmed. She eyed her pink t-shirt, which exposed an inch or two of my midriff. The shirt was singed on the shoulder where Atriul's magic had nicked me and torn in a couple of other places. "I'm sorry about your shirt. And I had to make a quick exit and leave your car there."

I went to the sofa, sinking gratefully onto the soft seat, and started giving them an account of what happened.

"Wait," Johnny interrupted. "You didn't tell me you actually confronted the guy."

I shrugged. "I didn't really have a chance to tell stories while we were hiding from Supernatural Crimes in the bushes."

His jaw muscles flexed as if he wanted to argue, but he let me continue.

"Does the name Atriul mean anything to any of you?" I asked. "That's what he said his name was. And he was pretty insistent about not being a witch-killer."

"I'll look into the name," Damien said. His blue eyes unfocused as if he'd already begun his research in his head.

"Of course he wouldn't confess," Johnny said. "People who commit crimes rarely do."

My gaze slipped off to the side as I mentally replayed my exchange with Atriul again.

"He said he didn't care about witches," I said quietly. "He said he was there for me."

When no one responded after a moment, I brought my focus

back to the room to gauge their reactions. Damien's eyes were still thoughtful. Lines of concern etched across Deb's forehead. Johnny looked kind of pissed, his brows drawn low and his expressive mouth pinched.

"You don't believe him, do you?" Johnny asked with thinly disguised incredulity.

"I don't know. But I'm not ruling out the possibility that he's telling the truth."

He glanced down at his phone in his hand. "I need to take off, but I should do another scan first."

I nodded, and he rose and went out to his car to get his scanner.

Deb scooted closer to me. "What's eating him?" she whispered.

I lifted a shoulder and let it drop. "He didn't want me to go out looking for the killer in the first place. Maybe he's just irritated that I did it anyway."

"Maybe," she said.

Johnny came back inside holding his tablet, and I got up and led him into the kitchen. I would tell Damien and Deb the results but didn't want an audience for the scan. Johnny's face was unreadable as he held up the device and aimed it at me.

"How are you feeling?" he asked.

"It's eaten more of my soul, hasn't it?" I said flatly, ignoring his question.

His dark eyes softened into intent worry and focused on me. "Another couple of percent."

"Well, shit."

"No solutions yet from your friend?"

I raked my fingers through my hair, and a few grains of salt rained softly onto the floor. "I haven't really had a chance to talk to her. I got distracted by the murder."

"I'd get in touch." He started fitting the tablet into a protective rubber sleeve.

I propped my hands low on my hips, watching him. "Why does it tick you off so much that I might believe the guy—Atriul?"

Johnny's face briefly tightened before he could smooth his expression. He gave an exasperated sigh. "You just keep taking these risks, one after the other, doing things that put you in serious danger."

"None of them are going to kill me, though." I gave a short, humorless laugh. "The reaper isn't going to let me die by someone else's hand."

"You don't know that for sure. But in the meantime you're acting like you're indestructible."

"I'm *acting* like I don't want my friends to die," I shot back. Irritation prickled through me, but I didn't really have enough energy to get riled up, which only annoyed me more.

With a swift movement, Johnny stepped into my space and slid his hand up the side of my neck until the tips of his fingers tangled into my hair. The pressure of his palm along my jaw tipped my face up, and our eyes locked for a moment before he covered my mouth with his. The kiss was warm and lingering, and I let myself sink into it.

He pulled away and rested his forehead against mine. "I just wish you'd stop taking chances. Just do what I say, would you?" he said with a low laugh.

I couldn't help a smile. "Good luck with *that*."

"I gotta go." He drew away from me reluctantly. "Call your witch friend."

"I will." I followed him to the door.

He turned and planted another kiss on my lips. "And call me if anything else happens."

"Bye, Johnny," Deb called from the sofa.

He waved at her and Damien and left.

"I need to remove my spell from your ankle monitor," Damien said, suppressing a yawn.

I sat down on the sofa and put my foot up on the table.

"Do you mind staying here with us tonight?" I asked. It wasn't for my own benefit. I wanted as much protection as possible for Deb.

"I was planning on it," he said, his voice already distracted as he began to focus.

I pulled out my phone and quietly started typing a text to Deb. She was sitting on the leather chair only a couple of feet away, but I didn't want to mess up Damien's concentration.

I'm starting to think Johnny is pissed because I won't let him push me around.

Out of the corner of my eye, I watched her tap a response. *From what you've told me, he doesn't tend to spend much time on any one woman. This is probably all new for him. What did the scan say?*

I suppressed a little sigh. *Could you call Jennifer for me? If she has anything at all, we probably need to try it.*

Deb glanced at me and nodded, her lips forming a thin line, and then went into my bedroom and shut the door. A moment later, I heard the low murmur of her voice.

Loki hopped up onto the sofa and curled up with his rump pressing against my thigh. I absently petted his back and watched Damien. Just as my mind began to drift back to my encounter with Atriul again, a dark tingle deep in my brain told me a minor demon was nearby.

In the blink of an eye, Loki went from heavy-lidded dozing to head up and ears perked. A feline howl and a clatter from the back of the house told me the gargoyle that often roosted in my yard had probably just learned of the visitor, too. Loki jumped down and trotted into the kitchen. I itched to follow him, but Damien wasn't done yet.

Trying not to squirm, I silently willed him to magic faster so I could go investigate, but he was still deep in a trance. In spite of Loki's yips at the window and the gargoyle's yowls outside, the demon stayed. Pulling within, I focused on the point of connection between me and the demon and followed it to the pulsing center at the other end—the creature's consciousness. Forcing past the stomach-turning sensation that accompanied this mental proximity to a demon's mind, I gently pushed inside.

Linking my own mind with that of a Rip spawn was like entering a tight underground cavern filled with cobwebs and the touch of creeping unseen creatures. Everything inside me strained to run the other way, and every time I emerged I seemed to carry a thicker film of demon-darkness that settled in my brain and around my heart. It seemed to act as a mental lubricant, making it easier each time to link my mind with a demon's. It wasn't something I cared to dwell on.

I knew right away it wasn't my demon, but it seemed to expect me and willingly presented the image of Atriul. My breath caught in my throat. He was standing outside somewhere. It was dark, but I could see hills in the background. The image lurched and swung around, showing city lights filling the valley below and stretching into the distance. It turned again with a nauseating swing. The demon was looking back at Atriul, and I recognized the spot where he stood. It was Tablerock, a small mesa in the foothills that provided a spectacular view of the city, with glimpses of the Boise River winding through the trees.

The demon replayed its flight from Tablerock to my yard. It perched in a bough that hung over my fence and angled its head down, giving me a view of the ground. A bundle dropped to the ground below.

The demon had brought something from Atriul.

Damien took a deep breath, snapping my focus back into my living room. He pushed up to his feet.

"Okay, I think I've put it back the way I found it," he said.

I stood and squeezed his forearm. "You're a miracle worker. I'm going to go check on that racket in the back yard."

"Be careful," he said and followed a few steps behind.

I opened the door, and Loki bounded out ahead of me to antagonize the gargoyle. The shy creature turned to stone, quickly putting an end to my dog's attempt to play with her.

I crossed the small cement slab of a patio and then the swath of grass. A glance up told me what my senses already knew, that the demon still perched above. Perhaps waiting to see what I'd do so it could report back to Atriul? Or maybe he was in the demon's mind, watching in real time.

I squatted and reached for the pale bundle, picked it up, and turned it over in my hands.

It was the net I'd used on him. He must have returned to Deb's house for it.

Something crinkled in the middle. I unfurled it to find a folded piece of paper.

Even in the semi-dark, I recognized a sheet from the fat pad of paper that Deb kept on her kitchen counter. Cream background adorned with a frame of intertwining vines and delicate little flowers. The handwriting looked hurried.

> *I didn't kill anyone, and I mean you no harm.*
> *Meet me tomorrow night at midnight. Come alone*
> *and unarmed—I'll have eyes on you. I can help you,*
> *but if you attack me again, you're on your own.*

Attack *him* again? He'd tried to slice me in half with a chunk of blood magic. I'd only been defending myself.

I read the note again. What help was he offering, exactly? My heart jumped to the possibility that he knew something about my brother Evan's location, but I knew that was unlikely. Maybe Atriul recognized the reaper soul I carried, and as I'd hoped, he could tell me how to keep it from killing me. Or perhaps, as he'd claimed multiple times, he wasn't the witch killer. Maybe he knew who it was.

I folded the piece of paper and tucked it into the seat pocket of my jeans. The demon still perched above. I moved back a couple of steps, tipped my gaze up until I found it, and gave it a single nod.

Inside, I shoved the net into a cabinet in the kitchen. If Damien saw it, he'd ask questions, and I was a shitty liar. If I told him about the note, there was no way he'd let me go alone to meet Atriul. And I wasn't going to let anything stand in my way. Despite Johnny's distrust of Atriul's claims and the fact that he'd tried to zap me with maroon magic at Deb's, a part of me believed he wasn't responsible for Amanda's death. Or maybe I just wanted to think he was one of the good guys—or at least not one of the really bad guys—because . . . why? We had something in common? Because I hoped he was the key to saving my life? Regardless of the answer, I knew I had to meet up with him.

I tried to relax my face into a neutral expression before continuing to the living room. I found Damien bent over his notebook.

"It took off, huh?" he asked distractedly.

"Uh, yeah. I didn't think it was worth trying to kill it," I said.

There was something about minor demons I'd noticed since I'd gained enough necromancy skill to probe into their minds— something I didn't particularly want to acknowledge. But there was no denying it. Minor demons weren't all alike. Some seemed craftier than others, more interested in living among humans than just causing trouble.

Deb straightened when she saw me.

"Jennifer said she and Lynnette have been working up a couple of spells," she said. "But with no way to test them, and not having any experience with how magic affects a double soul situation, let alone what it might trigger, they're hesitant to have you try them. For all they know it could accelerate the process. They've been distracted lately, obviously, but Jen said she intended to re-focus her efforts. I'm sorry I don't have better news."

I nodded, trying not to let my disappointment show.

"I've set several wards around the house. I tried some different things, but based on what Deb told me, they may not work with the killer," Damien said.

His face was pale and drawn, and I realized he was magically tapped out after the work he'd done on my ankle monitor, the charm he'd made, the enhancement to the net I'd launched at Atriul, and the wards he'd put up.

I gestured at my dog. "Loki might be our best bet at an alarm system tonight," I said. He thumped his tail at the sound of his name.

It was nearing midnight, and all of us had work the next morning. Damien crashed with a blanket and pillow on the sofa, and Deb and I settled in my bed.

I fell asleep easily but some unknown time later opened my eyes. I wasn't sure if a sound had awakened me or something in my dream. With a glance at Deb's slumbering form, I sat up and swung my feet to the floor. I paused, holding my breath and listening.

After several silent seconds passed, I stood. I might as well check the house since I was awake. I made it a few steps out of my bedroom when a sharp ping in my mind signaled a presence. I froze mid-step and then whirled and sped back to my room to snatch my whip from the top of the dresser.

The pulse of the reaper's awareness in the center of my forehead kicked up along with my own heartbeat. My right eye shifted to necro-vision but revealed nothing of interest in my dark living room.

"Damien?" I whispered.

Loki came to stand beside me, his eyes two dull points of orange. A soft growl rumbled low in his throat. He took a few steps toward the kitchen and growled louder.

My awareness pinged again, and this time I recognized the dark presence but not the usual Rip spawn. It was something large. Sharp-minded.

I hurried toward the kitchen, unfurling my whip as I went. I almost reached for earth magic but instead pulled at my newly discovered maroon power, and the sickening sensation of its dark magic filled me in a nauseous rush. It tingled down my arm and into the whip, which sent little reverberations back at me.

Maybe I should have been more afraid, but since I'd died, demons wouldn't come near enough to harm me. Even the arch-demons kept their distance. I snapped the deadbolt back, opened the back door, and stepped down to the freezing-cold patio in my bare feet. I pulled the door closed so Loki couldn't follow me out.

With every muscle tensed and my hands half raised, I swiveled left and right, scanning the yard. Nothing out of the ordinary, except . . . something in the grass. I focused more fully through my necro-vision and it revealed the dull glow of something dark pooled near the fence. I started toward it but then stopped when a blob fell from above.

With my heart in my throat, I looked up. High in the maple where Atriul's small demon had been hours before sat a great winged creature. Coal-black smoke—no, *magic*—also seemed to lick the air around the creature, like dark flames. Neon blue sparked within the smoky magic here and there. The dark magic that dripped from it was what I'd spotted on the ground.

At first I relaxed a little. This thing wasn't nearly as big as the arch-demon that had killed me. But then I focused on its face, and my eyes widened as the chill of horror rose up my spine.

It was a winged demon, yes, but not like the arch-demons I'd seen before. This one had a rounded head and a twisted human-like face. It raised its wings and revealed a humanoid body. From each index finger a scythe-like claw extended several inches.

Revulsion filled me as I tried to reconcile this creature that appeared half-human and half-demon. What *was* this thing?

Loki's growling changed to a loud snarl, and he rose up on his hind legs as his snarls became punctuated with barks. The man-demon's lips parted, and its mouth stretched into a sharp-toothed grin.

I didn't have time to further contemplate how this nightmare creature could exist. With unexpected grace, it sprang from its branch and spread its wings for a gentle descent into my yard and landed in a crouch.

In a reflex, I pulled magic, grasping at earth energy in addition to the maroon magic. The two energies clashed, jolting my insides so hard it felt like lightning burst inside my ribcage. White noise filled my head as the powers mingled within me.

The creature rose, a horror of gray flesh and wing that stood taller than me.

Its lips peeled back to reveal its sharp teeth again. "Give me the blond witch," it hissed. "She'll be the next to die. One by one, they'll all fall."

Deb. This thing wanted to kill her. My skin crawled at the sound of its voice, but I held my focus. I opened myself to earth magic, and green-laced maroon spun around the whip handle and shot down the length of it. I barely had time to register that I'd managed to pull the two types of power at once.

I twisted my upper body to get maximum momentum and lashed out with the whip with cobra-strike quickness. The end of it caught the demon down one shoulder, ripping flesh and tearing a hole in the leathery wing attached to its arm. The wounds knitted themselves before my eyes, and the creature cackled at me.

"Such tame little magic," it hissed, mocking my use of earth and fire. Part of me could hardly blame him. My elemental power was barely worth acknowledging.

I tensed to strike again, and the creature opened its mouth in a silent scream. Dark flames edged in neon blue blasted from its throat as I struck out, stopping the forward progress of the whip as if it had hit a wall. The brush of the unfamiliar neon-edged magic washed over me, stinging my skin like a thousand ant bites. It was all I could do not to fall to the ground and writhe around in agony. My magic recoiled up the whip, to my hand, and into my body, and I nearly dropped it. I lunged and fell into a roll, barely avoiding the lick of fiery demon breath as it arced out. The smell of sulfur and burnt meat filled the air.

That was how this thing killed—by distracting its prey with stinging magic and then slashing it to ribbons with its knife-claws.

The dark magic pouring from its mouth petered out, giving me an opening. Rising to one knee, I summoned blood-red power, swept my arm out, and sent the end of the whip flying with as much magic as I could bear.

The creature balked at the sight of the maroon magic, and that split second of hesitation gave me the upper hand. The whip seemed to elongate, stretching beyond its physical length to reach the creature. Under my direction, the whip roped around its neck, doubling and then tripling in a blur. I stood and heaved back on it, yanking with both hands. Blood-red magic surged through me with blinding pain, but I kept my hold as I pushed the power down the length of the whip.

Through squinted eyes, I saw the creature scrabbling at its neck as its eyes bulged. Any second I would deplete my capacity to sling magic. I bore down and sent one more pulse—as much as I could draw—through the whip. Shaking with the strain, I heaved back as hard as I could.

The collar tightened around the demon's neck, and with a sickening pop that I heard as well as felt down the length of the whip, its head severed from its body. It rolled a couple of feet in the grass while the headless body collapsed forward.

My eyes fuzzed over, and I fell to my hands and knees, sucking wind. I looked up at the sound of an angry sizzle. The white liquid spilling from the severed neck was forming a smoking puddle in the grass. The stench of rotted flesh reached my nose, and I slapped a hand over my mouth as bile rose up my throat.

"Ella." Damien was at my side, his hand curled around my shoulder.

My head still hanging, I turned so I could peer at him. I was too nauseated and drained to respond. All at once I was frozen to the bone. Every muscle began to shake as if my blood sugar had just taken a dive off a cliff.

He bent to slide his hands under my arms and then straightened, pulling me up to my feet. I nearly pitched forward onto my face when his grip slipped.

"Come on, we need to get you inside," he said. He grunted with the effort of keeping me upright as I listed weakly to the left. My legs felt like limp spaghetti as he half-carried me into the house.

Loki was alternately whimpering at me and running to the back door to snarl at the demon corpse.

I swallowed, trying to work some moisture back into my throat. "That stinking thing is going to ruin my lawn," I said hoarsely. My vision was fuzzing and narrowing to a tunnel as lightheadedness washed over me.

Damien chuckled wryly. "We'll reseed it."

The living room light flipped on, and I squinted in the painful brightness. Deb let out a high-pitched squeal of alarm and ran to help Damien get me to the sofa.

"Oh my god, what *happened*?" Her voice was already ragged with the threat of tears. "Ella, you've got severe magical exhaustion. We've got to get her warm. Hurry, lay her down here."

"That thing wanted Deb," I murmured. "It's the killer. It said it's going after you one-by-one."

Everything seemed to fade to a pleasant, faraway buzz. I knew they were saying things but hadn't the energy to try to make out the words. Through the freezing numbness, I felt my body move under their hands, the softness of a pillow behind my head and the weight of heavy covers over me.

A pleasant hum of magic washed my skin from scalp to feet, and it drove away some of the cold. I wanted to speak, to tell them I knew now that Atriul wasn't the killer, but my mind grew too heavy, and the world dissolved into darkness.

I awoke to the sharp smell of singed herbs and Loki's wet nose nudging my wrist.

The smell wasn't unpleasant, but it seemed to overwhelm my brain momentarily. I cracked my eyelids open. My attention automatically drifted to the group of spell candles burning on the coffee table, as they were the only source of light in the room. Someone moved in front of them, and I blinked.

"Ella?"

I winced as the sound of my name seemed to knock around inside my head, though Deb's voice was gentle and quiet. The rustling of her clothes felt like a cheese grater across my eardrums.

"Your senses have been damaged, and pretty much everything is going to hurt for a little while," she whispered. "After-effects of magical depletion."

I groaned, and the vibration of my own voice in my throat made me want to vomit. Squeezing my eyelids closed, I waited for the sensation to pass and then carefully nodded.

"Time?" I croaked.

"It's almost three thirty," she said. She touched my forehead as if checking for a fever. "In the afternoon."

My eyelids popped open as my heart lurched.

"Damien's at work. He told your supervisor you wouldn't be in today."

I started to groan again but then thought better of it.

I heard Deb settle on the leather chair. Sounds were growing slightly less offensive.

"I made him go to a healer before his shift," she said. "He was too drained to help you fight that nasty thing out there. He felt horrible about it. I shouldn't have let him get that depleted."

I wanted to protest. He had no reason to feel bad, and neither did Deb. I was the one who'd pushed to track down the witch killer last night, and if anyone was at fault for Damien's weak state, it was me.

"We had to call Supernatural Crimes to come and pick up the body of that demon thing. Barnes didn't show up, but the guy, Lagatuda, came."

I swallowed hard, wanting to ask if they still thought I was involved.

"They want you to come in as soon as you're able to so they can get your account of the whole thing," Deb said before I could form my question, as if she'd read my mind. "I hope by then they'll have done whatever magical forensics they need to do to that will prove that creature killed Amanda and you had nothing to do with it."

Irritation simmered under my skin. How could they still think I was involved? The killer had come to my house with the aim of murdering my best friend, and I'd done SC's job for them by taking it out. And I'd nearly gotten myself killed in the process.

"Lynnette and some of the others came over and tried to clean up the mess on the lawn, but they're afraid that spot where the thing bled out might be permanently damaged," Deb said, already moving on to a different topic.

She appeared to believe I didn't have anything to worry about with Supernatural Crimes, but I wasn't so sure. SC could have removed the device from my leg if they really thought I was innocent.

"They left a big bunch of flowers. Desiree tried to do some healing—one of her specialties is treating magical exhaustion—but she couldn't do much. I'm not sure if it's because you were too far gone and couldn't handle it yet or if the reaper interfered."

Deb paused and let out a long breath. "They're so grateful, Ella." She giggled softly. "Lynnette practically teared up. I've never seen her get emotional."

My cheeks flexed in a small smile. I kind of wished I could have seen the exorcist witch all teary-eyed over little old me.

I cleared my throat, determined to get my vocal chords up and running again. "Did anyone know what that thing was?" I asked hoarsely. I shifted so I could peer at her. My head swam with dizziness at the movement, but my hypersensitivity seemed to be settling down a little.

Her face grew serious. "Supernatural Crimes was very tight-lipped, and they were in and out *really* fast. If I had to guess, I'd say they'd never seen anything like it around here. Maybe ever."

My eyes slid to the spell candles, which had burned down to just an inch or so. By the array of crystals, incense burners, and other items, it looked as if Deb had been working healing magic for hours. I hoped she'd at least taken a break to sleep.

"How are you feeling?" I asked, my voice still just a scratchy whisper. "Do you need to rest?"

Her hand moved to her belly. "Feeling good. Don't worry, I wouldn't do anything that would harm the baby."

I gave a slight nod. My eyelids felt weighted, and I couldn't resist the downward pull. I closed my eyes, intending only to rest them for a moment, but sleep tugged me under.

The next time I awoke, my heart was thumping as if something had startled me. I blinked several times, trying to clear my eyes, before I realized the living room was bathed in darkness. I sat up and waited for vertigo to slam me back down, but the world gave only a small tilt before my equilibrium righted itself.

My stomach felt like it had been hollowed out with industrial cleaner, and there was an uncomfortable pressure in my sinuses and behind my eyes. But I felt . . . *good*, all things considered.

I looked to the leather chair. Damien was sleeping there. My fingers slid over my pockets, searching for my phone, but I was still wearing the cutoff sweats I'd slept in the previous night. Yep, I'd battled the man-demon in my pajamas.

I needed to figure out what time it was. I intended to keep my midnight appointment with Atriul, magical exhaustion and ankle monitor be damned.

As quietly as I could, I pushed the covers away and placed my feet on the rug. The reaper seemed to stir, sending the shadows dancing through my vision and its presence pulsing in my forehead. With a determined set of my jaw, I pushed to my feet. My head swam for moment, and I breathed through it. I kept my knees flexed, ready to sit back down if my legs didn't want to hold me up.

Seconds passed, and my head settled. I straightened and took careful steps toward my dark bedroom. Loki rose and followed me, the tags on his collar making soft metallic clinks. I glanced back at Damien, but he didn't stir. The bedroom door was open, but I couldn't tell if Deb had crashed there. I waited for my vision to adjust to the darker room.

The bed was made, and the covers were flat. She must have tagged out and gone home when Damien came back.

The red numbers on the digital clock next to the bed said 10:58 p.m. *Yes.* I could make it.

I pulled clothes from the hamper to avoid the noise of drawers opening and closing and changed out of my pjs and into dark gray cargo pants, a sports bra, and a black sweatshirt with the Demon Patrol logo on the chest. Socks, boots, and a heavy jacket to combat the lingering chill of magical exhaustion, and I almost felt like a real human being. Now I just needed my keys and phone. And some water and food. I was *starving* all of a sudden. I'd have to stop somewhere—I couldn't afford to make a racket in the kitchen.

I lifted my service belt and held it while I crept back into the living room, where I swiveled my gaze, trying to make out objects in the dark. I found my phone on a side table next to the sofa, my keys where I'd left them near the door, and my whip coiled next to them. Atriul had said no weapons. I'd leave everything in the truck when I reached Tablerock, but I wasn't leaving the house completely unarmed.

I slipped the front, feeling triumphant about my escape but also guilty for sneaking out on Damien. On the front porch, I hesitated. Damien had set multiple wards around the house that would magically signal us if someone or something unwanted passed through them. Would I set them off, or would I pass through the wards like a ghost as I had at Jennifer's house?

Only one way to find out. I took a deep breath, held it, and sprang across the porch, down the walkway, and zipped to my pickup as fast as my still-weak legs would take me.

My stomach rumbled along with my pickup's engine as I pulled away from the curb. I glanced in the rearview mirror, expecting to see Damien trying to wave me down, but the sidewalk in front of the four-plex was empty. I made a quick left at the end of the block, as if getting out of sight of my house would help me escape his notice.

I took another turn at State Street, heading toward a nearby fast food taco place that I knew would still be open. I ordered at the drive-through, paid at the window, and then parked for a couple of minutes so I could wolf down part of a burrito and drain one of the three bottles of water I'd purchased.

With my gnawing hunger somewhat satiated, I got back on the road and drove with one hand while I finished my first burrito and guzzled more water with the other. I kept checking my phone, wondering if maybe I should at least send Damien a text to let him know I was okay. I knew it would wake him up, though. I compromised by deciding to send him a message as soon as I reached Tablerock.

While I drove, I tried to take stock of my condition. I still felt weak and achy, as though I'd spent the past several days laid up with a nasty flu bug, but my strength was starting to return. I hoped the food would speed up the process. The swollen sensation in my head had subsided somewhat, but I now recognized it as one of the signs of magical drain—one that warned of the brain damage that would happen if I repeatedly exhausted my magical energy. I needed a strong healing session, and sooner rather than later.

But I'd get through the next few hours. I blasted the heater to combat the late fall chill in the air and the cold still sitting deep in my bones.

As I wound my way through Foothills East toward the dirt road that would take me to Tablerock, I felt unexpectedly buoyant. The killer was dead, and if the universe had any love for me at all, I would soon have a solution to my reaper problem, something to freeze it in its tracks. Hell, by tomorrow life might be almost back to normal. And most important, I could funnel some real effort into figuring out where Evan was being held.

The pickup's tires left the asphalt and crunched onto gravel. The uneven road bumped me along as I ascended the back face of Tablerock and rose above the city. When I reached the plateau, there were no other vehicles. Apparently it was too cold for teenagers looking for a spot to make out or drink beers they'd stolen from their parents' refrigerators.

I eased partway across the natural plateau and killed the engine. A sliver of moonlight faintly highlighted the angles of the rocky formations, and the city lights stretched out in a wide twinkling river below.

A glance at my phone showed it was eight minutes till

midnight. I got out of the truck, leaving my whip and service belt on the passenger seat, and a flicker across my senses drew my attention to the sky. High up, a minor demon circled. I couldn't see it against the dark background of night, but I knew it was there. Probably Atriul's minion, checking to see I'd kept my word about coming unarmed.

A gritty whisper of shoe sole over rock behind me strung my muscles tight and sent a little punch of adrenaline into my bloodstream. I whipped around to find Atriul approaching. I couldn't see his face, but I recognized his stride and the duster that billowed a little around his legs.

I held my hands away from my body, fingers wide, to show I wasn't hiding anything.

"I trust you won't try to slice me in half this time," I called.

My pulse kicked in anticipation.

He approached until he was about eight feet away and then stopped and regarded me for a moment before he spoke. At least, I assumed he was looking at me. His eyes were hooded in shadow, though the bit of moonlight revealed the planes of his cheekbones and jawline.

"I wasn't aiming for you," he said.

I crinkled my nose. "What?"

"I was aiming for the Baelman behind you. You're lucky I hit it, too, or you wouldn't be standing here. I injured it badly enough to halt its attack. Then it must have realized you weren't its target." His voice had a pleasant baritone timbre to it, and the hint of an accent I couldn't place.

"What the hell is a Baelman?"

"That thing you finished off. Nasty creations, aren't they?" He shifted, slipping his hands into the pockets of his jacket. His stance was wide but easy, and I relaxed a little.

"That demon-man I killed last night was—wait, *creatures*? Plural?" Suddenly all that Tex-Mex fast food wasn't sitting so well.

"Unfortunately for your friends, yes."

I felt the blood drain from my face. "Oh, shit. There are more killers." Deb. She was still in danger. I started digging in pockets for my keys, but I couldn't seem to find them. "My friend, she went back home. I can't leave her alone."

"The witches are safe for the moment," he said.

I inhaled sharply, and my head whipped up at the near sound of his voice. He'd moved closer, only three or four feet away.

"Only one Baelman at a time can exist in this dimension. It will take some time for another to come through." His mild tone implied no urgency, but somehow his calm amped up my agitation.

I licked my dry lips. "How can you be sure?"

"I've been dealing with them long enough to know. Odd that I haven't caught wind of any for the past few months, though. In any case, the replacement for the one you killed can't enter our world until the next new moon."

I hesitated, considering whether I should believe him. "What were you doing at Jennifer's house, if you weren't there to kill her?" I demanded.

"Tracking the Baelman."

"Why?"

The soles of his shoes gritted against the sandy dirt as he shifted slightly, his only subtle display of discomfort so far. "We don't have time to get into that now."

I filed it away to probe later.

"Those things, they have some kind of blackish-blue magic," I said. "The one in my yard last night tried to fry me with it, like a fire-breathing dragon."

"They contain a good quantity of one type of underworld magic, yes, but they can't wield it, only vomit it out as you saw. They've got too much demon DNA and not enough human in them to truly craft magic, thank the devil for small favors." He made a derisive noise that wasn't quite a laugh.

Underworld magic. It wasn't a term I knew, and it piqued a spark of interest.

"You've got blood-red reaper magic, too. Is that also underworld magic? How'd you get yours?"

"Yes, the blood-red magic is necromancy energy. But most necromancers don't have magical aptitude, so it's rare." Then he gave me a strange look, as if I were a child who'd asked a foolish question. "Reapers don't possess or wield magic. The maroon energy is a type of underworld magic that comes from where death and life aren't supposed to touch, but they do anyway. When life and death meet in unnatural ways, sometimes underworld magic emerges, sometimes skills of necromancy. In rare cases like yours and mine, both. "

I shoved my fingers into my hair and gave it a little tug. The blood-red magic didn't come from my reaper? I'd been assuming this new power came from the reaper. But it didn't. It was *mine*, earned from my near-death experience. And if I somehow managed to exorcise the reaper soul? The magic would remain. It put my situation in a new light. I wondered how many of my other assumptions might be wrong.

I had so many more questions, but I had to reorder them in my mind since I knew the threat to Deb and the others wasn't gone. "I need to know more about this Baelman. How do we get them to stop targeting Deb and her friends?"

"We?" He quirked an eyebrow.

"Me. Whatever." I made a frustrated noise in my throat. "Okay, I need information. Are you a Baelman hunter? Why is that thing targeting witches here? Why did you want to meet with me in the first place?"

He lowered his lids partway, and I thought I detected the hint of a smile in the twitch of his lips. "I'll make you a deal. A question for a question."

I made an impatient wave of my hand. "Fine. Whatever."

He turned and began strolling toward the side of the plateau that overlooked the city. I watched for a second, confused, until he looked over his shoulder and beckoned me with a flip of his fingers.

At the stone bench near the edge, he sat and eased back, crossing one ankle over the other knee as if settling in to watch a movie. As if we had all the time in the world. My hands clenched as irritation rose through me. I *didn't* have time. Deb and her friends were still in danger. I needed to find my brother and get him out of the vamp feeder den while there was still something of him left. And, oh yeah, there was a ticking bomb inside me.

But I contained my frustration and sat down next to Atriul.

"What kind of name is Atriul, anyway?" I asked.

"*That's* the question you want me to answer first?"

"Uh, no. Start with the others." And for the love of life, talk *faster*. I had people to save and shit to do.

"I'm not a Baelman hunter, not in the sense you're implying. I track them for . . . my own purposes." His gaze slid over to me. "Now your turn. What reaper are you?"

"No idea. The thing eating my soul didn't exactly introduce itself. Why, did yours?"

He straightened, and his head whipped around at me. "You're still human?" He said it so vehemently it sounded like an accusation.

My eyes wide and my heart thumping, I returned his stare.

"Yeah. At least mostly." I swallowed. "I take it you're . . . not."

He was still staring. "I've inhabited this body for over five decades."

This man was not more than fifty years old. He couldn't be much over thirty. I shook my head. "I don't understand."

"I'm not human. I'm a reaper walking around in a human shell in a dimension I don't belong in," he said with bitterness edging his voice.

It struck me that he was disappointed. He thought we were alike, but apparently we weren't.

"So Atriul is . . . ?" I trailed off.

"The name I was given when I came into being. As an angel of death."

My chest seemed to cramp. "How did you come to inhabit a human body?" The words came slowly, reluctantly. I had to ask it but dreaded the answer.

"I don't know, exactly. A glitch when I went to cut his soul free." His voice had gone flat, dead. "Suddenly I was in the body of a man, and over time . . ."

"You ate his soul." I drew away from him as my insides felt like they were plummeting.

"It's not as if I wanted to. I couldn't stop it from happening." He plucked at his jacket with his hands as if he loathed the thing. "I don't want to be here, stuck in this body. I don't know how to get back."

I jumped at his defensive anger. Swallowing the revulsion I felt at the knowledge that this reaper next to me had dissolved an innocent man's soul into nothing, I tried to keep calm.

"That's why you sought me out? You thought I'd know how to get back?" I asked.

His face still and hard, he didn't answer.

"Back, or . . . gone," he finally said. "Or at the very least, I figured you *wanted* to get out of here. I thought we could find the answer together."

I couldn't help cringing at what he might be suggesting. Some sort of mortal double-suicide that would release two reapers back to the *in-between*?

I jammed my fists into the pockets of my jacket and hunched

my shoulders against the cold, looking out at the lights of the city. So this was what happened to me. It must have been. I'd died, a reaper had come to claim my soul, and some cosmic glitch had joined us instead.

"What's the name of the man you killed?" I asked, not caring if the question offended him.

"I didn't kill him. He was already dead, and I came to reap his soul." He took a breath as if trying to calm his own agitation. "His name was Rogan."

I couldn't help wondering how Rogan had felt when a reaper had invaded his body. Did he have any idea what was happening to him? How long had it taken for the end to come? Was there any pain when his soul was extinguished?

"He was a mage," Atriul said.

I looked at him in surprise. "Did you retain any of his abilities?"

He nodded, looking uncomfortable. "But I only have the knowledge we shared before he . . . It's not like I have his complete set of skills or experience."

I blew a harsh breath out through my clamped teeth. "I'm not going to let my reaper kill me. I can't. I have to find my brother." I stood. "If you get any bright ideas about how to stop—well, how to stop what you did to Rogan, you know where to find me."

I started trudging back toward my truck, suddenly too drained and disappointed to try to carry on any more conversation with the reaper who'd killed an innocent mage.

"Ella, wait."

I turned to see him hurrying toward me, his duster billowing.

"What?" Alarm pinged through me as I watched him speed up.

He grabbed my wrist and pulled me toward the south edge of the mesa. "A Supernatural Crimes cruiser and an unmarked car are coming this way."

Damn. My ankle monitor.

I started to run with Atriul, but then pulled up short, twisting my wrist out of his grip.

"Go ahead," I said when he turned in question. "I'm not doing anything wrong, and running away will just make me look guilty."

He gave me a short nod and then sped over the side of the plateau, disappearing into the dark as if he'd leapt off the edge. I angled toward my truck, ambling casually, as the two vehicles came into view.

They crunched to a halt nose-to-nose with my pickup.

The doors popped open, and two SC officers stepped out of the cruiser. I recognized Barnes's blond hair and Lagatuda's tall frame in the unmarked car.

Great.

I leaned my back against the driver's side of my truck.

"You didn't bother to show up when I nearly died taking out the killer for you, but you follow me up *here* in the middle of the night?" I called as Barnes marched toward me.

"Relax," Barnes said. "Your friend called us. He said you disappeared."

Oh, shit, I'd forgotten to let Damien know I was okay, and I'd left my phone in the truck. He'd probably been frantically trying to reach me for who knew how long. I swallowed a groan as I realized I'd brought this headache on myself.

"Uh, well, thank you for your concern," I said. "I was just about to head home."

Barnes planted her hands on her hips, scrutinizing me. "Seeing as how you seem to have made a fast recovery, we look forward to interviewing you at the station first thing tomorrow."

"I have to go to *work* in the morning," I said, feeling petulant about this entire situation.

She pointed at my boots. "You want that thing off? Show up at the station." She gave me a hard look and then turned on her heel.

Lagatuda had stayed by the car, and the officers had kept back too. The tall detective flipped his fingers in a little wave, and he and Barnes got in. Both vehicles flipped U-turns and disappeared.

Heaving a sigh, I pulled open the pickup's door and reluctantly picked up my phone. Seven missed calls—from my friends and from Lagatuda. A bazillion texts from Damien and Deb. I sent them a message saying I was fine and on my way home.

I tipped my head back against the headrest, let out a long moan, and then started the ignition and bumped back down the dirt road.

When I arrived at my apartment, Damien was stalking the living room with his phone in his fist.

"Ella—" he started and then just rolled his eyes, passed a hand over his brow, and blew out a loud, exasperated sigh. "I'm glad you're safe. Now tell me where the hell you were and what the hell you were doing."

After everything he'd done for me and the scare I'd given him, I owed him the truth. I told him everything I knew about Atriul. I also repeated what he'd told me about the Baelmen, and how the threat wasn't gone.

"Do you have any way to contact this Atriul again?" Damien asked.

"No," I said sheepishly.

"If he's tracking the Baelmen, we need to work with him. He can tell us when another one appears. Maybe even where it'll come through. If we know ahead of time, we can take the offensive." Damien's eyes took on a gleam. I knew that look. It meant he wanted to dig into his research.

I pulled the palm of my hand down the side of my face, feeling stupid for not thinking of it myself. I really should have gotten the guy's phone number. "Yeah, you're right. My bad. I'll figure out how to contact him."

"Okay. Let's get to bed. It's going to hurt when the alarm goes off." He sat down heavily on the sofa and turned to fluff the pillow I'd left there, obviously planning to spend the night. He looked up at me. "Actually, you should take another day off. I can tell you're still weak."

I shrugged. "Eh, I'll be fine."

I hated missing work. I needed to be on the move. The thought of calling in sick to lie around my apartment recuperating made me want to yank my hair out.

I tossed my keys on the table near the door and rubbed my eyes as I headed toward my bedroom.

"Seriously, Ella. You've been through a lot, and you've got more sick time."

"We'll see in the morning," I called and then closed the bedroom door before he could protest.

My alarm went off at my workday wake-up time, but instead of taking a jog and running through my calisthenics, I dressed, hollered through the door at Damien in the shower that I was going out for a quick errand, and then stepped through the front door into the cold morning.

White puffs of my breath fogged the windshield of my pickup, and I shivered as I waited a minute for the engine to warm up. I knew Barnes would be pissed I didn't come in, but I needed to take care of something else more than I needed to get grilled by her. Even more than I needed to get rid of the damn monitor strapped to my ankle.

I drove to the nearest Supernatural Primary Care Clinic—it was a national chain that had gotten its start on the East Coast, and lately it seemed like there was one popping up every few miles around here. Deb would be horrified that I went to a doc-in-a-box instead of someone she referred, but I needed a boost of healing, and this would do until I found a regular healer. I tried not to groan at the thought of the additional expense of routine healing. I'd never used magic enough to reach the point where I was accumulating the negative effects. But at least the insurance I had through work would cover part of it.

I pulled into the parking lot in front of the clinic, which was in the strip mall next to Albertsons. A man and woman sat next to each other in the waiting room, both of them wolf shifters by their wild tawny eyes and the way my magical senses tingled in their presence.

I checked in at the counter and then picked a chair on the opposite side of the room from the couple. Shifters tended to make me edgy, and I knew they wouldn't appreciate me crowding them anyway.

A few minutes after the shifters were called back, a nurse came for me. In the exam room, we quickly ran down the usual questions about my general health and possible symptoms of the damage caused by crafting. I had to skirt around some of them—I wasn't about to try to explain the reaper soul.

The witch who came in to heal me was a strong Level II. She was young, not much older than me. She asked me about the extent of my recent magic use, and I gave her as much information as I could without actually mentioning the Baelman. She had me lie face-down on a contraption that was like a souped-up massage table while she lit a few spell candles, and then she explained that next she would place various crystals along my spine. I could hear her moving around me and whispering the words of healing spells.

Still exhausted from too little sleep and lulled by the pleasant warmth of healing magic, my gaze on the tile softened as my muscles seemed to melt into the padding of the table.

When she was finished, I turned over and sat up. Energy surged through me, and I felt like I could go outside and sprint ten miles. But there was something else, too. The soul-hunger I remembered from standing over Amanda's body with her soul still tethered gnawed at my insides like acid. It was so strong I could barely focus on anything else.

"You're an unusually fast healer," she said. "I expected a lot more damage from the recent crafting you described."

I could see the curiosity in her eyes—she'd probably felt something unfamiliar within me. I stiffened as the world flashed over to the gray of the *in-between* and then dissolved back to the world of the living. A ghostly aura seemed to glow around her, and I felt the reaper thump with excitement inside my head. It wanted to reach out and . . . oh shit, I was seeing the woman's soul and the reaper wanted it. *Badly.*

"Yeah, I'm a fast healer," I echoed, forcing my eyes away from her and down to the floor. I edged toward the door and grasped the handle. "I should run, or I'll be late for work. Thanks so much for the healing."

I checked out and nearly sprinted outside.

In my truck, I sat gripping the wheel hard and taking deep breaths.

"You can't do that," I gritted out harshly through clenched teeth. "You can't go after the souls of *living people* like they're your own personal buffet. We're not going to hurt the innocent. And we're not going to add any more souls to your little collection, so you can just get rid of that hope right now."

I glanced to the left out of the corners of my eyes when a car pulled up next to my truck. I probably looked deranged, sitting there muttering to myself—well, muttering to the *reaper*, not that it made me seem any less crazy—with my white-knuckled grip on the steering wheel.

I kept focusing on my breath. When the hunger finally subsided to a dull ache deep in my stomach, I nearly went limp with relief.

Back at home, Damien was sitting at the tiny kitchen table drinking coffee and reading something on his phone.

His eyes widened slightly when he caught sight of me. "You look worried," he said.

I went for the coffee pot with one hand while the other hand rummaged in the cabinet above for a mug. I sloshed brew into the cup, gulped without letting it cool enough, and winced as it burned all the way down.

"I went to a clinic. The healing went well, but the reaper wants to, well, reap," I said. "But not just souls of the dead. It was eyeing the soul of the healer like she was a Christmas dinner prime rib roast. It's not as bad now, but I still feel like I want to scarf down every soul on the block. It's like this awful, insatiable *need*." My mouth twisted with revulsion.

He drew back a little, his brow furrowing.

I gave him a withering look. "Relax, I'm not going to snatch your soul and eat it for breakfast. I can control it. I think, anyway."

"Maybe you just need to . . . reap, every so often," he said. "Only souls that *need* reaping, of course."

I grimaced at the thought. "Maybe you're right. I'm not crazy about the idea of moonlighting as a reaper, though. I mean, doing the work of an actual angel of death?" I shuddered.

I didn't know anything about angels of death beyond what I'd personally experienced the past few months. They were mostly the stuff of fables. They couldn't be trapped and studied like demons. At least, I didn't think so. I needed to know more about them, and since I'd met Atriul I could.

The time on the stove's clock caught my eye. Damn. I really was going to be late if I didn't leave the house in ten.

"You can go ahead to the station if you want," I said over my shoulder as I headed to my room. "I'm just going to change, and I'll be right behind you."

"Okay, but no shenanigans. You'd better come straight to work."

"Promise," I called to him.

I heard his chair slide back against the linoleum and a moment later the sound of the front door opening and closing.

I quickly put on my Demon Patrol uniform and added a patrol-issue jacket over the getup. I tightened my service belt around my waist, attached my whip at my left hip, and grabbed a hair elastic and tucked my Patrol baseball cap under my arm. In the summer I wore the visor instead, but it was cool enough now for the hat. Another month or so, and I'd trade it for the ski cap.

I let Loki in from the back yard, refilled my mug, and then I was out the door. At a stoplight I pulled my hair back into a long ponytail and fitted my cap on my head.

My shift hadn't even started yet, and I already felt antsy to turn my attention to other things. I had to find a way to contact Atriul. Another Baelman was coming with the new moon on Halloween, and I recalled what Damien had said about Samhain this year—it would be a crossroads of events that he suspected would give a big boost to dark magic. And if a Baelman wasn't a thing of dark magic, I'd eat my next paycheck.

So basically, the next Baelman would be born on the most powerful dark magic day in decades, and it would be looking for Deb and her friends.

We'd have to intercept and destroy it, but there was something else that kept poking at the back of my brain. I still didn't know *why* the Baelmen wanted to kill the witches.

I pulled into the lot at the station and eased into my parking spot. When I walked through the double doors, I nearly crashed into Sasha Bowen, a fellow officer, coming the other way.

I brightened. "Hey, Sasha, how are you? We should get a drink sometime."

She grabbed my forearm and pulled me off to the side. "Sergeant Devereux is looking for you, and there are two Supernatural Crimes suits with him."

My smile folded into a grimace. "Blond lady and a tall guy?" I asked.

"Yep."

I groaned. "Thanks for the heads up."

Seriously? Had they really chased me here to my place of work? I knew they wanted to ask me questions about the Baelman. Barnes had all but promised to remove the monitor if I showed up at the SC precinct and succumbed to their grilling. In retrospect, I supposed it was a little petulant of me to refuse to comply with her agenda just on principle.

Part of me wanted to turn around and go right back out to

my truck, but I knew I'd have to face whatever was waiting for me. Would have been nice to keep my sergeant from finding out about the ankle monitor, though. I was already on his shit list, and this would just be one more giant mark against me. It wouldn't matter that I hadn't actually done anything wrong.

I headed for Devereux's office. When I stopped in the doorway, he and the two detectives went quiet.

"Hey, it's three of my very favorite people, all jammed into five square feet. My lucky day!" I knew I shouldn't have said it, or at least not with quite so much sarcasm, but it slipped out anyway. Actually it was unfair to Lagatuda. He seemed all right. It wasn't his fault he had to partner with Barnes.

Devereux and Barnes both reacted with similar red-faced irritation. For a split second I wondered if Barnes was single. I was pretty sure Devereux was. Maybe the two of them could get together and exchange pissy glances over a candlelit dinner.

"Officer Grey." Devereux's southern accent always made him sound nicer and gentler than he was. At first, anyway. "These detectives have been telling me about how they came to know you and how they expected you at their station this morning. Yet here you are."

He paused, clearly waiting for me to say something in my own defense.

"Yeah, well, I'm really dedicated to my job," I said quietly. It was the truth. I detested my boss, but I did think the work was important, and I knew I was good at it. I tilted a look at Barnes. "Maybe you haven't heard that I received a commendation recently.

Not to mention the fact that I did *your* job, too, by killing that Baelman the other night."

I wasn't trying to brag. I was just sick of being treated like a criminal by Barnes and a delinquent by Devereux.

Barnes's eyes narrowed when I mentioned the Baelman, and uncertainty crossed her face for a split second before she composed her expression back into her usual pinched distaste. I swallowed a groan. Maybe I shouldn't have called the thing out by name. Barnes didn't seem to like that.

"You and the detectives can discuss that further at Supernatural Crimes," Devereux said. "You'll be on leave until you can resume your duties here."

My mouth dropped open. Wait, *what*? They should have been giving me a medal for killing the man-demon. What the hell were they going to accuse me of now?

The stares of the other Demon Patrol officers tracked me as I walked through the station hallways bookended by Barnes and Lagatuda, but at least Barnes didn't slap cuffs on me. I almost wished she would have. Then at least they would have had to explain what the hell was going on.

They insisted on driving me to their station, so I had to leave my truck behind. Once there, they shuffled me into the same tiny interrogation room as before.

My anger flared as the two detectives sat across from me. I leaned forward. "You're costing me wages, and if I get any more grief from my Sergeant over this, I'm going to sue. You have no proof of any wrongdoing on my part, and keeping this monitor on me is harassment."

I was punctuating my words with hard jabs of my index finger on the surface of the scratched table. They waited until I'd finished and leaned back with my arms crossed.

"You're not going to be arrested," Barnes said. "And we'll remove the monitor."

My eyes went wide as the gathering storm of my mood paused.

"Oh, really? Why the change of heart?" I asked, making no attempt to hide my bitterness.

They glanced at each other.

"We did some more magic forensics on the crime scene data after we claimed the body of the—the Baelman," Barnes said, tripping a little over the thing's name. "We know now that *it* was the killer, and we believe you played no part in the crimes, in spite of your suspicious behavior and the similarities between your signature and the signature found at the scenes."

"Well, hallelujah," I said sarcastically, but tiny wisps of relief began to inch through me.

I didn't want to get too excited yet, though. They could have just removed my monitor in Devereux's office and let me go. Instead, they'd brought me here, so I knew there was more.

Barnes looked at Lagatuda, and silent signal seemed to pass between them.

He fidgeted in his seat, adjusting one side of his open slate-gray sport jacket. "We, uh, need your help," he said.

I quirked a brow at them. Well, this was certainly a turn of events. Not that I was necessarily going to agree to anything.

"We have no record of this Baelman, as you called it," Barnes said. "We think it could be a newly spawned species."

"Spawned? Like from the Rip?" I asked.

"We don't know," Lagatuda said with a small shake of his head. "We were hoping you could tell us something about them."

I narrowed my eyes and shifted forward, resting my folded arms on the table. "Take my monitor off and get me a guarantee that I won't lose any pay, and I'll tell you what I know."

Barnes rose and left, presumably to fetch someone who could

remove the damned ankle device.

I had no reason to keep my limited knowledge about the Baelmen from them. After all, they were Supernatural Crimes and much better equipped to deal with a new supernatural threat than I was alone—even if I *had* single-handedly disposed of one of the creatures. I didn't actually have much to say about the Baelmen, but they didn't know that.

"We got permission from your sergeant to borrow you for a period of time," Lagatuda said, speaking quickly in a clear attempt to reassure me. "When he said 'leave' it only referred to the fact that we'll be paying you while you're working with us. If you choose to, that is."

I snorted. "You could've told me that at the station."

"We wanted to keep it quiet."

"So you marched me through my place of work like a fricking criminal? Gee, thanks for the subtlety and the careful preservation of my dignity." I huffed out a loud breath and massaged a temple with the fingers of one hand, trying to get my irritation under control.

We had a common goal, I reminded myself. We all wanted to keep the Baelmen from killing anyone else. From killing my best friend.

Lagatuda lifted his hands in a small gesture. "Sorry, Ella. Wasn't my call," he said in a low voice.

"That I can believe." I gave him a wry look.

We both went silent as Barnes returned with an SC officer, a meaty guy with a horseshoe of thin reddish hair around his balding crown. With some effort, he got down on one knee next to my chair. I pulled up my pant leg, and he touched a white fob to my monitor. His little tool looked like it was crusted with crystals—spell salt, I guessed. The flexible ankle monitor glowed with the pale blue of water magic and then opened and fell to the floor.

I pushed my cuff back down, suddenly feeling about twenty pounds lighter.

Barnes took her seat, watched the officer leave, waited until the door was closed, and then turned to me.

"What do you know?" It was barely a question, bordering on a demand.

I pierced her with a hard look for a beat. Her people skills could really use some work. She stretched her lips in what was probably supposed to be a conciliatory expression.

I repeated what Atriul had told me about the Baelmen, including the part about how another one would be making an appearance at the upcoming new moon.

"No one can say for sure that the next one will be going after the same targets, but for the safety of my friends, I'm going to assume that's the case," I said. I locked eyes with each of them in turn. "Don't you think that's the best approach?"

"How do you know all of this?" Barnes asked, ignoring my question.

My jaw muscles flexed in irritation. Her condescending attitude was getting really fricking old.

"An associate who would prefer not to be identified," I said, my voice frosty. I gave my head a shake to cut her off before she could ask. "I'm not going to tell you who it is. Don't push me on this, if you want my help."

She pursed her lips for a beat. "If your information is correct, then we know approximately when it will appear. But where?"

Oh, now it's "we," huh?

"That's what I aim to find out next," I said. "But I need assistance from my Patrol partner, Damien Stein. He's got some working theories about the Baelmen."

Barnes started to brush me off with a little flick of her hand. "We don't have authorization for—"

"Damien Stein. Look him up," I interrupted. "He's a scholar, one of the brightest minds in the country when it comes to theories about magical shifts as they relate to location, time, and other influences. We need him."

I was thinking fast, and to some extent making it up as I was talking, but I was pretty sure Damien's credentials would back up my claims well enough.

"Why would a renowned scholar be on Demon Patrol?" Lagatuda asked. To his credit, he didn't sound too incredulous.

"Part of his studies," I said. "He moved here specifically to research the local supernatural phenomena."

Damien had more or less told me that this was true, but he'd remained mysterious about the details. When we'd first met, I'd been less curious about his vague explanation, but I realized the past several weeks had slowly piqued my interest in his work.

"Look him up," I said again. "You'll see it's all true. If you can afford to cover me, you can afford to take him on, too. We have, what, less than two weeks until the next new moon? You saw the thing that killed Amanda. We need every advantage we can get. It's not going to hurt anyone to put Damien on the SC payroll for a few days. Better that than more deaths on your hands and living with the knowledge you should have used every resource when you had the chance. Right?"

With her lips pressed into a thin line, Barnes blew a noisy breath out her nose, and I knew I'd won. I held back a triumphant smile. Didn't want to jinx anything before it was official.

She stood, her chair scraping back loudly as if it, too, were annoyed that she had to give into my request. "Fine. We'll make the arrangements. In the meantime, we expect you to get to work figuring out where the Baelman is going to appear and learning anything else you can. Detective Lagatuda will be working with you."

I shook my head. "No, I work alone or with Damien. I don't need a Supernatural Crimes babysitter."

She gave me a little narrow-eyed smile. "That's not your call to make. You're on our payroll now, Officer Grey."

Damn.

Well, at least I had Damien, too. And since the monitor had been removed from my leg, it should be a fairly simple task to slip away from Lagatuda when needed.

Barnes left, and Lagatuda took me to an office with a desk and chair where he gave me a tablet with legal paperwork, waivers, and contracts to read and sign. I noted with interest that I was classified as an independent consultant, and the fee they'd be paying me was almost three times what I made on Patrol. It also meant that technically I *wasn't* a Supernatural Crimes employee, contrary to Barnes's jab, but another document I had to sign basically spelled out that I had to agree to whatever logistical terms my SC supervisor dictated. And who was I reporting to? Of course—Barnes.

Next, Lagatuda got me an SC consultant badge. And I didn't like it, but the contract also said I was obligated to allow him to install an SC app on my phone.

"Keep the badge and your phone with you at all times," he said. He opened the app and pointed to a red dot the size of a dime. "This is a panic button. If you get in trouble, hold your finger on this dot for three seconds, and we'll respond immediately."

I eyed my phone, suddenly feeling like it might betray me since it had a piece of SC installed on it. Keep it with me at all times? Right. Unlike the ankle tracker, the phone wasn't attached to my body, and just because I was on the SC payroll didn't mean I was going to let them monitor me 24/7.

Lagatuda gave me a ride back to my truck.

"Change into street clothes, and come back to the station at one for a briefing. Then we'll go from there," he said.

"Will you be able to get Damien into the briefing, too?" I asked.

"We'll try."

I got into my pickup, and feeling a little unsettled about ditching Demon Patrol, I headed to my apartment. I briefly wondered how Devereux would get coverage for me and Damien on such short notice, but that wasn't my job, and I couldn't afford to worry about it. There were plenty of officers trained to do catch minor demons, but only a few people in a position to help give the next Baelman a deadly welcome to our dimension.

At home, I considered the contents of my closet. The other detectives all wore button-down shirts and suits or nice pants with a blazer over a solid t-shirt. I didn't own any blazers, and I sure as hell didn't have anything resembling a suit. I pulled out a pair of black stretchy pants that were styled with pockets and details to make them look like regular pants—about as close to slacks as anything in my wardrobe.

A pale green t-shirt and a cropped, lightweight silver down jacket would have to do. A blazer would never work over the bulk of my service belt, anyway. And there was no way I was going anywhere without that—Barnes would have to physically fight me for it if she tried to force the issue.

I got dressed, re-did my ponytail, and put on a little blush and mascara for good measure.

I sent Damien a text to see if he'd been called in by Devereux for his new assignment and then went to let Loki out and make myself a ham sandwich.

By twenty till one I still hadn't heard from Damien, but it was time to head back to Supernatural Crimes.

With a faint stir of anticipation stirring in my stomach, I grabbed my service belt and headed out.

The Supernatural Crimes briefing room looked more like a small university classroom than the scuffed-up and overcrowded space I was used to for Demon Patrol briefings. Supernatural Crimes was the governmental policing and investigative arm for the supernatural world. The department housed at my own station, which included Demon Patrol and Supernatural Strike Team, was technically under the same branch of government as Supernatural Crimes—under the umbrella known as Supernatural Law Enforcement and Public Safety—but there had always been a division and rivalry between our two departments. The separation was literal, in that we had different facilities, but there were also marked differences in the work culture. And the difference in funding between us and SC was painfully obvious.

Demon Patrol and Strike Team were seen as blue-collar, military wannabes who enjoyed waving our weapons around and frying Rip spawn. That was true of some of us but not enough to make such a sweeping generalization.

Supernatural Crimes had a lot more resources and reach within the government, and their detectives drove fancy cars and wore nice clothes to work. SC was the governmental policing and investigative arm for the supernatural world.

We protected the population from the demons that came through the Rip. They investigated crimes involving supernatural people like shifters and vampires, arrested crafters for magic violations, and generally held themselves above the outright killing, the so-called dirty work we did on Demon Patrol and Strike Team. There were also other Departments in the governmental branch of Supernatural Law Enforcement and Public Safety that conducted research, cataloged supernatural creatures, issued the implants that turned vamps docile—probably more departments that I didn't even know about.

The SC briefing room had tiered seating with cushy upholstered swivel chairs behind long rows of tables. As I took a seat next to Lagatuda, I noted there was not a coffee stain in sight. The floor was carpeted—and clean—in contrast to the dingy linoleum of the Demon Patrol briefing room.

More detectives and SC officers were filing in, so much more orderly and subdued than the start-of-shift Demon Patrol meetings. I missed the noise and raucous jokes of my co-workers.

I had one eye on the door, still hoping Damien would make it. Lagatuda's vague assurances weren't exactly convincing me that SC was truly following through with getting my partner on this case. I hoped the delay in getting Damien here was just due to red tape. I really wanted another ally in the room.

A man I recognized from the news as Orestes "Rusty" Garcia, the head honcho of the local division of Supernatural Crimes, took the lectern.

He was a little paunchy and round in the face with a heavy-lidded gaze that made him look like he was always on the verge of a nap, but I remembered him seeming sharp-minded and articulate.

He ran through some department business, not unlike the types of items Devereux and the other sergeants presented at the start of our Patrol briefings—local supernatural crimes activity, as well as some national news. Then Garcia stepped away and nodded at Barnes, who was sitting in the front row. She took his place, tablet in hand. Using the device, she brought up an image that stood out against the white wall behind her.

I straightened as I recognized a picture that had been taken in my own back yard. It was a rotating three-dimensional holographic image that showed the corpse of the beheaded Baelman from all angles.

"These are the remains of the creature that was retrieved from the yard of Demon Patrol Officer Gabriella Grey two days ago, after she killed it," Barnes said. She gestured to me. "We have Officer Grey working with us for the next couple of weeks, as she has unique knowledge of the creature."

Those were the nicest words Barnes had ever said in my presence. No accusations, no pinched-faced looks. Maybe she and I would turn over a new leaf.

Most of the faces in the room had swiveled my way, so I raised my hand in acknowledgement.

"News of this heretofore unknown species hasn't been released publicly, and details are not to leave this room," she continued.

The image changed to a shot of the creature—and its detached head—laid out on a stainless steel table, the type you'd find in a medical examiner's autopsy lab. The Baelman was hideous but also disturbingly human-like in its build.

"We have unverified information that another of these creatures will transit into our dimension upon the next new moon," she said.

She didn't have much more to say about the Baelman after that and moved on to another investigation involving rumors of new black-market, magic-laced drug that supposedly produced the same euphoria as vampire bites. The mention of such a drug brought a sudden pang in my chest. Evan had gotten mixed up with illegal drugs before he'd disappeared.

I pushed aside sad thoughts of my brother. I was anxious to find Atriul so I could get more info about the Baelmen, and by the time the briefing was over, I'd fidgeted one of my shoelaces into knots.

While Lagatuda and I were waiting for the detectives on either side of us to file out of our row, I tapped him on the arm.

"I understand we're working together on this, but my contact who knows about the Baelman isn't going to talk to me if you're hanging around," I said. "No offense, but I need to be alone if there's any hope of getting his help."

He rubbed the back of his neck and slid a glance over at Barnes, who was talking with Rusty Garcia.

"I'm really not supposed to let you go out on your own," he said.

Remembering the SC app, I pulled my phone out of my pocket. "You'll know where I am at all times. Is there an open mic setting on the walkie or something?" I flipped through the menus on the device. "When I make contact I can turn it on so you can listen in, if you want."

At this point I was less concerned about independence and privacy than contacting Atriul again.

He took my phone and tilted it so I could see what he was doing. "I'm setting up a quick-connect channel between the two of us, and then you just have to make sure it's active when you want to use it. You push and hold this symbol for a couple seconds to turn it on. If you contact me on this channel, I'll be sure to keep myself on mute. It's like wearing an old-fashioned wire."

"Great. Perfect. Thank you."

I took my phone and shoved it into my pocket and began moving toward the aisle. I wanted to get out of there before he changed his mind about letting me go off on my own or Barnes came over to poke her nose into things.

"I'm going to try to make contact tonight," I said over my shoulder. "You'll know if I'm successful."

I practically speed-walked out of the SC station and to my pickup. I tore out of the parking lot.

When I was halfway home, my phone jangled with an incoming call. I glanced at the I.D., ready to hit ignore if it wasn't a number I recognized. I could almost hear Barnes's voice demanding I return to the station. But it was Damien.

"Hello?" I answered.

"Hey, we just missed each other at the Supernatural Crimes precinct," he said.

I felt a grin forming. "So you're on board, too?"

"Yep." He laughed. "Devereux tried to block it, but somebody higher up must have pulled rank."

I let out a relieved breath. "I suppose they've got a pile of paperwork and stuff for you."

"Yeah, I'm waiting for all that right now."

We arranged to meet at my place later so we could dig into some heavy-duty research for anything that might give us more information about the Baelmen. Or more likely, Damien would be doing the academic work while I tried to find Atriul.

I was glad for some time to myself at home. I eased up to my usual spot on the curb next to the four-plex, shut off the engine, and went into my apartment.

I left the back door partway open so Loki could go in and out as he pleased and then settled cross-legged on the sofa.

When I closed my eyes, I turned my awareness outward. With swiftness that made me gasp, my necromancer senses stretched wide, beyond the room, the house, the block. My heart pounded as I tried to get my bearings.

Like dots appearing on a sonar readout, I felt the presence of the Rip spawn in the surrounding area. It was way beyond anything I'd ever been able to do before. There were three minor demons within about a five-block radius. I could sense even more of them beyond but kept my focus narrowed to the nearest ones.

I picked the nearest one and concentrated my awareness along the invisible line that connected us. Probing into its brain like a chopstick sliding into Jell-O, I took control. While I sighted through the creature's eyes, I steered it toward the foothills to the east, aiming for Tablerock.

I didn't expect Atriul to be just hanging out there waiting for me to come looking for him, but I wanted to investigate the area and take a closer look at the spot where he'd jumped over the edge when Barnes and her crew had interrupted us. He'd seemed, I don't know—*comfortable* up there overlooking the city, as if he went there a lot. It seemed as good a starting place as any.

I kept the demon flying high so anyone glancing up from below would think it was a bird. It was still full daylight, though the sun wasn't too far from the horizon in the west. We circled Tablerock. Finding a couple of vehicles parked there, I angled the creature out toward the undeveloped hills so we could swoop back under the plateau and out of the line of sight of anyone enjoying the view from above.

As I drew the demon closer to where Atriul had jumped over, I sensed through the creature that there was life hiding nearby— Rip-born life. The one I controlled seemed interested in its kin but also wary about approaching. I didn't want to instigate some sort of demon turf war, so I didn't force it too close. But there was something on the rocky side of the plateau . . . there. A narrow slit of an opening that would have been invisible to any hikers below and positioned on a nearly inaccessible vertical face. Well, inaccessible to all who didn't have wings. A flock of minor demons were roosting there, and something about them felt familiar. Not friendly, exactly, but perhaps a bit less wild.

It was the same sensation I'd noticed when Atriul's messenger demon had appeared in my yard with the net and the handwritten note.

I didn't think he was hiding in there, but I'd bet my paycheck—yep, even the fat Supernatural Crimes one—that the demons in the cave belonged to him. As much as Rip-spawn can belong to a person, anyway.

Now, how to signal that I wanted to meet?

I'd follow Atriul's lead.

I turned the demon west, bringing it to me. While it made its transit, I opened my eyes and rose and went to the cabinet in the kitchen where I'd stuffed the net. I scribbled a note on the back of a flyer that sat on top of last week's mail I still hadn't sorted. I didn't have any pretty pads of paper like Deb. I bundled the note into the net, tying it tightly with a piece of twine I found in the junk drawer. I suppose I could have sent just the note, but I wasn't sure how dexterous—or how careful—a minor demon would be with a single piece of paper. The net seemed like it would be easier to keep hold of.

As I did these small tasks, part of my awareness stayed with the demon, making sure my hold on its mind was firm enough to keep it on course. It felt almost natural to do so, an observation I didn't particularly want to dwell on, but my thoughts kept circling back.

Was I destined to keep a flock of demons and hide away from society like Atriul?

I grimaced down at the bundle I held. Probably not. My reaper would likely kill me before it got that far.

The demon I was driving arrived and alighted in the tree in

the back yard. If I hadn't sensed it, I'd have known of its arrival by Loki's growls.

I went outside.

"It's okay, boy," I said, snapping my fingers to get Loki's attention. He came over to stand at my left side, fur spiked along his spine. "This one's not dangerous. He'll be gone in a sec."

I communicated my intention to the creature and then moved closer to where it perched. With a gentle toss, I sent the net up into the air. The demon jumped from the branch, spread its wings, and swooped to catch the bundle in its sharp talons. It sped away into the twilight, back toward Tablerock.

Now, I just had to wait for Atriul.

I let Lagatuda know that I expected to make contact with Atriul sometime that night, if things went my way. He was cool about letting me pursue the meet-up without trying to bust in on my plans. For his part, he was making the rounds to check in with Deb and her circle of friends. He genuinely seemed to care about how they were doing, but as he mentioned, we still didn't know why the Baelman was targeting her group.

Each time I recalled that the nasty creature had been standing right behind me at Deb's house as I'd faced off with Atriul, I got the willies. Deb had been the Baelman's third target. If I hadn't taken her place that night, she'd probably be dead. I pushed the thought away. Deb was fine, and I needed to focus on next steps.

Damien showed up with his backpack, and he set up camp on the coffee table where charts, notebooks, and his laptop took up the entire surface. I let him know about my attempt to summon Atriul.

"I'll wait till it's full dark and then take a drive up to Tablerock," I said.

I headed into the kitchen to put on a pot of coffee. It was going to be a late night.

When the percolator finished, I carried two steaming mugs

into the living room.

I knew better than to interrupt Damien when his brows were this pinched in concentration, so I idly pulled one of his lunar charts closer to get a better look at it. It was an oversized piece of paper crisscrossed with a lattice of creases like a map. The current year was at the top, and it showed tables and dates with little drawings of moons in various states of ebb and flow plus a ton of other notations I didn't understand. The sheer amount of information the chart contained was enough to give me a headache.

After a while, Damien looked up.

"You know, it's possible that the Baelmen originate somewhere far away," he said. "Just because one of them turned up here doesn't mean they come through a local rip."

"Do we even know for sure that they come through a dimensional rip?" I asked. "Or are we assuming that because they have wings and magic and look demonic?"

The tip of his tongue appeared at the corner of his mouth as his gaze unfocused. "Good question," he said faintly. He pulled his computer onto his lap and began furiously typing.

My phone vibrated on the side table. I picked it up to see a text from Johnny.

Hey sugar, just got a call for a high-priority case. Flying to Nashville tonight. I'll probably be gone a week, maybe more, maybe less depending on how it goes. Let's catch up when I get back.

I gazed at the message, realizing that he could very well be gone when Samhain and the new moon arrived. I knew Johnny couldn't help from a magic perspective—he didn't have any ability—but he'd helped me so much in the past I didn't like the thought that he'd be clear across the country at such a critical time.

I texted back. *Good luck with the case. Safe travels. Talk soon.*

I chewed the inside of my cheek for a moment, looking absently down at my phone. I stood and stretched. I needed to move.

"I'm going for a drive," I said.

I put on my Patrol parka and strapped on my service belt under the jacket's cropped waistband. I shoved my phone into my pocket, grabbed my keys, and went out into the cold evening.

It wasn't quite cold enough to see my breath, and the air was still fragrant with decaying fall leaves, but something about the chill had turned sharper in the past week, as if hinting at winter.

I looked up and my boots scraped to a halt as my heart tried to jump up my throat. Someone was leaning against the side of my truck.

Atriul. The shadows swirled around my periphery, and the pulse of the reaper bumped between my eyes, as if in recognition.

He straightened, pushing away from the rail of the truck's bed and letting his folded arms drop to his sides. I wondered how long he'd been waiting. He wore only his duster over a t-shirt and jeans. Maybe bodies occupied by reapers didn't feel the cold.

"Ella." He stepped forward. "You paged?"

"Yeah." I stopped a few feet away, my mind oddly blank though it had been swirling with questions all day. "Thanks for showing up."

I shoved my hands deep in my jacket pockets, the fingers of my right curling around my phone.

Did he expect to get invited in? Somehow I doubted that was his preference. I couldn't really picture him sitting with me and Damien in my living room, bouncing around theories about the Baelmen while we drank coffee from my mismatched mugs.

Atriul might look human, but what I saw was only a shell. The human originally inside had been extinguished long ago.

I nodded at my truck. "Want to take a ride?"

"Yes."

We got in, and I started the engine.

"Any preference for destination?" I asked.

"Let's go to the edge of town. Federal Way," he said, naming a road that skirted the edge of a canal for some distance and then veered out into the boonies south of the city.

I nodded and pulled away from the curb. Acutely aware of my phone in my pocket and my promise to Lagatuda, I hoped he wouldn't try to call. I was sure he saw that I was on the move, but I didn't want to allow him to listen in on me and Atriul just yet.

"I take it you got my message," I said, glancing at his shadowed face. In the light of passing street lamps he looked older than I remembered.

"I was informed," he said. He didn't look at me, but there was a lilt of amusement in his voice.

And then with a jolt, a realization struck me. It was something he'd said last time we'd met, but it hadn't really sunk in at that moment. "How long ago did you say you ki—took over the body of the mage?"

"Over five decades ago."

"You're . . . immortal? I mean, not just impossible to kill, but *ageless*? There's no way you're that old."

He heaved a heavy sigh, as if it were something tragic. "That's right. This body stopped aging when my soul replaced its original owner's."

"I don't mean to sound self-involved," I said, the words coming reluctantly. "But does that mean I've stopped aging, too?"

I spoke the question, but I couldn't bring myself to truly examine the implications of it, not yet.

With a flick of a glance at me, he gave his head a small shake. "Your situation is different. I can't say for sure."

"Since the reaper joined me, I've begun to heal very quickly from injuries. I recovered fast from the Baelman attack, too," I said. I could tell he wasn't enthusiastic about discussing these things, but I couldn't help myself. Who else could I talk to?

"The reaper has a vested interest in keeping you whole," he said.

"That's what I figured." I paused. "You really can't die?"

I pulled up to a red light and watched him out of the corners of my eyes. He was drawing random lines through the condensation on the passenger side window.

"Nope. I've tried, believe me."

"You're that unhappy?" I asked quietly.

"This isn't my world. This body doesn't belong to me."

I gripped the wheel. "I suppose I'd feel the same way if I got stuck in the *in-between* and couldn't ever leave."

"The in-between?"

"Yeah, the gray, misty place. Where the souls wait to be reaped. That's where you want to get back to, right?"

"Yes." He pointed ahead. "It's green."

I took my foot off the brake and drove through the intersection. We'd reached Federal Way. "Should I keep going?"

"Yes, a little farther."

"You can go there, though, right?" I asked. "You can still reap souls?"

"Yes and yes, but I can go there only as a visitor, as you can. I can't dwell there in this form. And I don't reap anymore."

"But you must want to," I said, thinking of the soul hunger.

"I feel the pull, but I resist. When, or if, I make it back to the in-between as you call it, I'll resume my duties as an angel of death." He said it heavily, and a realization struck me.

"You punishing yourself?" I asked. "For Rogan?"

He sighed as if he didn't want to answer, but after a moment said, "I suppose that's the best way to explain it, yes."

I saw the first sign for Gregori Industries and gave him a sharp look. "Is that where you wanted to go?"

He nodded. "This is where the last Baelman was born."

Ice-cold fingers seemed to grasp my heart, and I couldn't respond right away. I drove a few more yards and then pulled off to the side of the road opposite the corner of the Gregori Industries campus, shifted into park, and killed the headlights. I left the engine running.

I twisted so I could face him. "You mean those creatures are *created* here? In a—a lab?"

His brows rose. "You didn't know?"

"I thought they came through the Rip!" My voice had slid up half an octave.

"Baelmen were eradicated centuries ago." He gestured up ahead to the main entrance to the Gregori grounds. "But recently someone in there figured out how to bring them back."

Someone.

That someone had to be Jacob Gregori—my uncle, though only a couple of people knew I was related to the infamous tycoon. It wasn't a fact I cared to broadcast. Gregori Industries had been engaged in cutting edge work that intersected technology with magic when the original Rip tore through Manhattan and spilled demons into our world. Though the conglomerate had never been proven responsible in court, everyone knew something had gone awry in the Gregori labs that caused the permanent inter-dimensional tear in New York and later in a few other places, including here near Boise.

"At least they haven't discovered how to make more than one appear at a time," Atriul continued. "Thank the devil for small favors."

My phone was vibrating a specific pattern my pocket. I recognized it as the SC app, and suspected it was Lagatuda calling. I pulled out the device and hit ignore but then quickly held the symbol that would open our channel, hoping that would keep him from another call attempt—or worse, coming out to check up on me.

"Something wrong?" Atriul asked.

"No, I'll call him back later." I stuck the phone back in my jacket. "Can you tell me how you know the Baelman I killed came from Gregori Industries?" I asked.

"Through my network," he said.

My eyebrows inched up. "Network of . . . people like you?" I didn't need to give away too much about Atriul to Lagatuda.

"In a sense. Necromancers and others who have unique abilities in that area."

"So is this a project that was approved at the top, or did it come from someone else within Gregori—a rogue scientist perhaps?"

It was as close as I could get to naming Phillip Zarella while Lagatuda was listening. Zarella was a scientist and the most notorious human rights criminal since Hitler, and most of the world believed he'd been killed several months ago in a prison escape attempt. But I knew Zarella was living right here on the Gregori campus under Jacob Gregori's protection. Yet another fact I had no desire to reveal. If I did, I'd have to explain how I knew he was there, and I couldn't do so without exposing way too much about myself. It wouldn't do any good, anyway. Gregori had special status for his campus that prevented police and military forces from storming the place. And from what Jacob had implied, the government knew he had Zarella there and were willingly permitting the arrangement.

Atriul gave a humorless laugh. "Oh no, it's all approved at the highest levels."

So Jacob *was* behind the creation of the creature.

"Why, for the love of all that's good in the world, would anyone want to unleash the Baelmen?" I asked.

It didn't make sense, from what I knew of Jacob Gregori. I didn't agree with a lot of his practices, but his mission in life was to close the Rip, to save humanity from the scourge of demons. Even if the Baelmen weren't Rip-spawned, bringing them into existence seemed counter to Jacob's aim.

"A Baelman is the perfect assassin," Atriul said. "Like you, others would assume they were some new type of demon and most likely wouldn't even think to look for a human culprit. And if by chance a Baelman is killed, a new one will be ready to take its place within a month on the next new moon. A steady supply of untraceable killers."

Except the Baelman *had* been traced—back to Gregori Industries.

I firmed my mouth into a hard line.

My mind spun, thinking of alternate possibilities. Maybe Jacob was hiring out the Baelmen as assassins? Some of the things Jacob did were reprehensible, but I didn't really see him going into the business of hiring out hits. He must be the one ordering the kills.

"We know the next one is coming on Halloween, with the next new moon," I said. "And you're saying that it will originate here, from the Gregori campus?"

"I believe that's correct."

"How do we stop it?" I asked.

"You know that better than I do, having killed one yourself."

"Yeah, but I almost died doing it. I might not be so lucky next time."

"Sorry, I don't have any tips for you there."

"Wait," I said. "I thought you told me you've been tracking Baelmen."

"Yes. Tracking. Not trying to kill."

I looked at him in confusion, trying to read his expression by the glow of the numerous Gregori Industries security lights. I thought I caught the mournful look I'd seen on his face a couple of times before and had a guess as to why he would want to try catching up to a Baelman. He'd been looking for a way to end his human existence, to kill the body he inhabited so he could be released back to the place he considered home.

Atriul straightened and leaned forward. "Someone's coming."

I squinted into the semi-darkness. He was right. Three people were approaching at a fast jog—men, from their bulky, tall builds—and it looked as if they carried weapons.

I flipped on the headlights.

I recognized the uniforms. Three of Jacob's men were headed straight for us.

I reflexively reached for earth magic and touched my stun gun, though I knew my service weapon wouldn't be much use against the assault rifles Jacob's men carried.

I felt the tingling flow of Atriul summoning his magic next to me.

I could have started the engine and sped away, but I didn't. Jacob already knew it was me, and his men weren't going to gun me down on the side of the road. I didn't think so, anyway.

"Stay here," I said to Atriul and carefully swung open my door and stepped out with my hands raised. They were well-trained men and not likely to be too jumpy with their triggers, but I didn't want to give them any excuse.

"Hi there," I called. "You know me—Ella Grey. I have a stun gun on my belt, but I'm not going to draw it. And, uh, these aren't the droids you're looking for. Does that work on you guys?"

Atriul snorted a laugh, and I almost cracked a small grin. Maybe he was more human than I'd assumed.

The soldiers weren't laughing, but at least they weren't pointing their guns at me. They'd stopped several feet away.

"Mr. Gregori sent us to escort you onto the campus, ma'am," one of them said in that formal, staccato speech style common among military men. "He'd like to speak to you."

I felt myself harden. If Jacob had sent the assassin, he had a hell of a lot to answer for. Could he know that I'd discovered he was behind the Baelman? He wasn't stupid. Atriul had been tracking the Baelmen and might have already drawn Jacob's attention for that, and Atriul was sitting right here in the passenger seat of my truck. Jacob was more than capable of doing that math.

Regardless, I wasn't going to walk into a trap.

"Sorry, but I prefer neutral ground," I said, my voice chilly.

The lead guy nodded, and the three of them turned and jogged back toward the entrance to Gregori Industries.

Just as I slid back into the driver's seat, something hit me: my channel with Lagatuda was still open. I could only imagine what he made of Jacob's invitation. The way the crew-cut guy had spoken to me left no doubt that there was some familiarity between me and Jacob Gregori. My only hope was that with the phone stuffed into my pocket and the men several feet away, Lagatuda had missed at least part of the exchange.

I turned off the open channel between me and Lagatuda.

When my phone vibrated, I jumped.

It was Jacob. I answered.

"I know it's you behind the Baelman. Now Supernatural Crimes knows it, too," I said, irritated by his boldness and my own carelessness with the SC app. "Your fences aren't going to protect you from a murder charge."

"I care about you, Ella, and I'm only trying to warn you," he said, ignoring my accusation. His smooth voice only pissed me off more. "Your blond friend and her witches are dabbling in things they can't control. They're going to tear the Rip wide open, and I can't let that happen. But I'll make you a deal. I'll spare your friend if you promise not to interfere with the rest. It's an offer you should take. You can't protect them."

I was yelling, telling him where he could shove his deal, when he broke through my tirade with his icy calm.

"The creature brought me the scrying mirror, Ella. I know all about you."

My blood ran cold as words died in my throat. I took a breath to resume my hollering, but he'd already disconnected. I stared down at the phone in my clenched fist, my pulse pounding in my temples.

I slammed the heel of my other hand into the steering wheel. He'd *admitted* to it. He'd already killed one woman and attempted to murder two more. I'd nearly lost Deb.

And he had Jennifer's scrying mirror. That meant he knew everything about who I was—my necromancy, the reaper soul, and probably the underworld magic I could command.

My head swam as anger pounded through me. I squeezed my eyelids closed and tried to get my breathing under control.

Deb. She'd sworn to me that she and the other witches weren't involved in anything dangerous. No black magic, just a few dark-edge practitioners in the group. It wasn't like her to lie outright. But since she'd told me, I'd thought it odd that she was friends with dark-edge witches. That didn't seem like her, either.

Trepidation quelled some of my anger. I needed answers. I

tapped call under Deb's name.

"Hello?" Her voice sounded groggy with sleep. I hadn't realized it was so late.

"Deb, we need to talk, and it can't wait," I said.

"Okay." Her voice sharpened. "I'll be at your place in thirty."

"See you soon." I disconnected.

She hadn't asked what I wanted to talk about. Maybe she already knew. Maybe she'd been expecting it.

I blew out a long breath and turned to Atriul, who'd been watching and listening to it all—my exchange with Jacob, my little outburst, my call to Deb.

"You and Jacob Gregori have exchanged phone numbers?" he asked, seeming to choose his words carefully.

I stared straight ahead for a moment. "We've had run-ins before."

I pulled away from the side of the road and flipped a U-turn.

He made a little noise of interest but didn't ask any more questions. I definitely wasn't going to offer additional information.

"Had enough human drama for one night?" I said wryly.

"I've lived among you for long enough, nothing really surprises me anymore."

"I bet," I said. "Speaking of human things, I want to be able to get in touch with you. You know, preferably with a method from this century that doesn't involve using demons as carrier pigeons. Any chance you have a phone?"

"No," he said. "Thus far I've found such a device unnecessary."

"Just how isolated are you?" I tossed him an incredulous

look, but he ignored my question. "In any case, I think we need to remedy that."

I pulled into the brightly lit parking lot of a gas station and left the engine running.

"I'll be right back," I said.

I ran in and bought an inexpensive burner phone plus three months' worth of basic service. Back in the truck, I tore the package open, activated it, and showed him how to use it.

"See, you can go on the internet, too." I peered at him. "You know what that is, right?"

He barked a laugh. "Just because I've had no use for a mobile device doesn't mean I don't know what it *is*."

"How do you keep in contact with the network you mentioned?" I asked.

"Necromancy. Demons," he said. "Occasional face-to-face meetings."

I wanted to know more, to fire off a bunch of questions about underworld magic, but Deb would be arriving at my place soon.

"Where can I drop you?" I asked. I took the turn off Federal Way that led to Broadway, a street that would take us most of the way back to my part of town.

"The end of Reserve is fine," he said, naming a street that led up into an older neighborhood of the East Boise foothills.

I pulled over to let him off where he'd requested.

"Don't forget to keep the phone charged, and carry it will you," I said as he stood with one hand ready to close the passenger door.

He lifted the phone in a little salute and dipped his chin once.

As I drove away, glancing at his duster-clad figure in the rearview mirror, I couldn't help a stab of curiosity about his living situation and what his home was like. Did he rent? Where did he get the money to pay for housing? Did he have any decorative flourishes, or did he prefer to be strictly utilitarian? Did he have a jar of mayo in his fridge? What was in his medicine cabinet?

Somehow it was really hard to picture him doing mundane household things like sitting in front of the TV pairing socks from a pile of clean laundry, or balancing on a ladder cleaning leaves out of the rain gutters.

But he'd laughed at my Star Wars reference. Maybe he was a movie buff.

When I reached my apartment Deb's Honda was already there.

My insides tightened. I'd never *not* wanted to see my best friend. She was the one person in the world whose presence I always preferred over my own solitude. But I couldn't imagine why she'd tied herself up with a group of dangerous witches, and I dreaded her possible answers to my questions.

I killed the engine and sat there for a moment gathering myself and then got out and trudged up the walkway to my front door.

A cozy billow of air greeted me inside, and Damien stopped talking mid-sentence when he looked up and locked eyes with me. He and Deb both looked at me in that guilty way that made me pretty sure I'd been the topic of discussion.

She gave me a tiny smile. "Do you want to go in your bedroom?"

I shook my head as I peeled off my jacket. "Damien might as well hear this, too."

I sat down on the leather ottoman, wrapped my arms around my middle and hunched forward.

Sucking in a small breath, I fixed my best friend with an unblinking look. "What have you and your friends been doing to draw the attention of an assassin?"

I didn't want to reveal Jacob Gregori's connection just yet. It was more important for me to first get the information I needed from Deb.

She pulled a square decorative pillow into her lap and partially imitated my posture, wrapping her arms around the pillow in a sort of hug.

"It's not what it seems. Really, there's nothing—"

"Deb, I need to know the truth," I cut in quietly. "All of it."

"Okay." She settled back into the sofa and gave me a resigned look. "But first I need to explain a few things about the inner workings of a coven."

I gestured with my palm, inviting her to keep talking.

"Covens aren't just magic clubs or some sort of witch sororities," she said. "They're businesses. Most covens are made up of members who can offer specific skills or services. Some coven memberships are built around a theme of skills. Healers, for example."

I'd seen ads for services offered by covens, but I had to admit it had never occurred to me to think of them as legitimate businesses.

"Lynnette's charter is for a coven with unique services," Deb continued. "She's one of the only witch exorcists in the world, and probably the strongest, and that's the basis of the theme for her coven—supernatural services that deal with those kinds of things.

Not black magic, but problems that most people would consider dangerous or at least unpleasant."

"Dark-edge magic, like you told me," I said.

She nodded. "There's no other coven in the world with someone like Lynnette at the helm. She's looking for members who complement her theme. And once the membership is set and the coven hangs out its proverbial shingle, we have high hopes we'll be able to command *serious* fees for our specialized services."

She gave me a pointed look that sent my mind spinning in a new direction. I was beginning to see why Deb wanted to be part of Lynnette's coven. Money had always been a huge issue in her marriage. Her husband had a bit of an addiction to get-rich-quick schemes, to put it lightly. Somehow he always talked her into investing in just one more, promising that *this* one would be the pot of gold at the end of the rainbow, while Deb barely made anything on her teacher's salary. They were in debt up to their ears, and Deb was three months pregnant.

"Back up a sec. You're no dark-edge witch. How do you fit into her plan?" I asked.

It would have made more sense to me if Deb were vying for a place in a coven full of healers. That was much nearer to her supernatural talents than what Lynnette Leblanc seemed to be focusing on.

"No, I'm not. Far from it," she said. "But she wants a couple of healers on board, in-house witches with not just medicinal talents but emotional healing abilities who can take care of the others in the coven. And possibly also help any victims that hire our services.

Some of them are bound to be traumatized if they've experienced things like demonic possession or black-magic attacks."

I started to breathe a little easier, realizing that Deb wasn't dabbling in anything dark. But she'd said "we" a few times. Maybe Lynnette was close to making the coven membership official.

"Okay, that all makes sense," I said. "But still doesn't explain why someone would want all of you dead. There's gotta be more to it than that."

She raised her palms and shrugged. "That's it. I can tell you more about the specialties of the women involved, but none of them are practicing black magic. I swear I'm not hiding anything, Ella. I can't think of any reason someone would hire out hits on us. There's competition for Lynnette's coven, but no one would stoop to *murder*. In fact, some of the witches who wanted in but won't get picked have already applied for their own charter. Word is they're bringing in a witch from Europe who is almost as powerful as Lynnette to lead it."

I knew she was telling the truth. But I was equally sure there was more to the story, and there was only one person who could give me the full picture: Lynnette Leblanc.

"Why don't you stay here tonight since it's so late," I said to Deb.

"Yeah, I will, thanks. I'm going to hit the hay now, I'm beat."

Rising from the sofa, she yawned so wide her jaw cracked. She came to give me a hug and then went into my bedroom.

I turned to Damien, who'd been silent through the entire exchange.

"Lynnette," he said in a low voice.

I glanced toward my bedroom and then nodded at him. "I'm going to track her down first thing in the morning," I said, quiet enough so Deb wouldn't hear.

Lynnette was hiding something, and it had killed one witch and nearly cost Deb her life, too. What could possibly be *that* important? I wouldn't leave the exorcist witch alone until she gave me answers.

Early the next morning, I called Lynnette and she answered on the first ring.

"I really need to talk to you about the murder," I said. "I've learned something that puts a new spin on things."

"I'm available now," she said quickly, her voice sober. "Where do you want to meet?"

"Text me your address, and I'll come to your place."

I was curious about Lynnette's home. She was a powerful witch, and she made quite a visual impression, too, with her piercings, heavy eyeliner, faux leather pants, and obvious confidence.

It turned out she lived only about half a mile from Amanda, the witch who'd been murdered by the Baelman. The woman whose soul I'd reaped. My reaper stirred at the memory, obviously delighting in it, and my scalp crawled. The intense temptation of collecting the soul instead of reaping it, and then the rush of cutting it free, tried to crowd into my senses. I pushed it firmly to the back of my mind.

I eased to a stop in front of an updated Victorian-style house with a four-foot-high black iron fence around it. It was quite grand by my standards, and I recalled what Deb had said about the business of the coven. It appeared Lynnette was already doing quite well as a freelancer. Not that it surprised me. Her services were in high demand, and from the sounds of it, she traveled for jobs almost as much as Johnny did.

As I got out of my truck, I recalled Lynnette's command of verbal magic—a rare magical skill that let her manipulate people in subtle ways, especially if the person she was speaking to was unaware of her ability. When we'd been working to rescue Roxanne's brother, I'd carelessly allowed Lynnette to rope me into a promise, one that she had yet to call in. She'd agreed to help Nathan free of charge, saying she would do a trade with me instead. Only, I hadn't pushed to define the details at the time. I had a feeling I'd soon come to regret that oversight.

Lynnette opened the door before I could knock.

"Thanks for making time on such short notice," I said, glancing up at the gothic chandelier that hung in the small vaulted entry.

"Of course." She closed the door. "This is highest priority. Come on in."

She led me through a short hallway that went to what was likely supposed to be a small formal dining space, but instead of table and chairs, there were only built-in bookshelves lining the walls. Another chandelier, a variation on the one near the front door, hung just overhead. She angled off to the right into the kitchen.

"I was just about to make tea," she said. "Have a seat if you'd like."

I pulled out a black-leather-covered bar stool but then thought better of it and remained standing. I needed to stay alert.

The countertops appeared to be made of black marble, or

some other dark stone with flecks of silver winking here and there. Slate tiles covered the floor, and the neutral scheme finished with white-painted cabinets.

She glanced at me expectantly, her face tense with concern, as she went about filling her electric kettle with water.

I was mentally prepared for a confrontation, but her inviting manner disarmed me. I realized too late that it might have been better to set the meeting in a more neutral location.

"Whatever you and the other witches are dabbling in, Jacob Gregori believes it's worth murdering all of you to stop it," I said. She stiffened, her hand still on the kettle, and her body and expression seemed to freeze for a second or two. I paused for a moment to let my words sink in. "I need to know what you're involved in."

She pressed the start button on the kettle's handle, her attention still on me. Then she moved to stand across the island from where I stood and placed her palms on the countertop. Her face had paled.

Her kohl-lined eyes narrowed and then widened. "Jacob Gregori killed Amanda?"

"Not by his own hand, but yes. And he wants the rest of you dead. Why?" I pressed.

She looked down at the darkly reflective countertop and frowned.

After a couple of seconds ticked by, I leaned forward. "Lynnette, another Baelman, that creature I killed in my yard, is coming with the new moon. Jacob's not going to let this go."

"But if he admitted it, we can go to the police. They'll arrest him, and he'll have to call it off."

"You know it wouldn't be that simple. He'd find a way to delay things and probably slip the charge completely. Meanwhile, we only have a few days until the next new moon." I felt my face harden as the heat of impatience and a small jolt of adrenaline flowed through me. "Stop avoiding my question."

She gave me a sharp look, her jaw clenching, and for a moment I thought she might try to stonewall me.

"We're not doing anything that warrants murder," she said, her tone even but her eyes flashing defensively.

"Clearly Jacob doesn't agree. I need details."

She shifted her weight to one hip and looked off to the side, her nostrils flaring as she inhaled slowly before meeting my eyes again.

"We're working with underworld magic," she said. "Specifically, the magic that's produced around the edges of the interdimensional rips. But we're very careful, and we've *never* gone beyond dark-edge practices. I've been extremely clear with the women that we are *not* black practitioners and never will be. I've never practiced black magic myself."

It seemed we'd touched a sore spot, and I guessed by her tone that she'd probably been accused more than once of practicing the darkest of the magical arts. People probably looked at her goth-chic appearance, her great power, and the services she offered, and assumed that she dipped into black magic.

But her mention of magic around the rips was what really caught my attention. I had a lot more questions about what they were doing with the underworld magic, not to mention the fact that Atriul was the only other person I'd heard use that term. But first I wanted to understand how Lynnette was getting rip magic in the first place.

"What do you mean?" I said. "You can't just walk up to one of the permanent rips and collect the magical energy there. They're heavily guarded and completely inaccessible to civilians."

Her eyes flicked to the side, and then the button on the kettle popped, and she turned away to get a couple of mugs. She filled them and brought them over to the counter, producing little wicker basket of assorted teas from a cabinet. Ugh. Witches and their tea.

Ignoring my mug, I watched her, waiting.

"We're making our own rips," she finally said with obvious reluctance.

My mouth dropped open. "You're *what*?"

"We know how to do it safely, and we close them immediately after we harvest the magic. The whole thing only takes a few seconds at most."

Surprise mixed with anger, and a tendril of fear curled through it all. I struggled to find a response.

"Deb doesn't know about this," she added quickly. "Only a few do at this point."

That gave me a tiny measure of relief. At least I knew Deb hadn't been concealing this from me. But if she knew what Lynnette was up to, I wondered if my best friend would still be so enthusiastic about joining the coven.

Shaking my head slowly, I reached for one of the packets of tea without bothering to read the label, tore it open, and dunked the bag into my mug.

Well, at least I had a pretty good idea about why Jacob would want Lynnette and her witches dead. Opening new rips went against everything he claimed he was devoted to. I wondered how he'd even found out about what they were doing. And had he brought the Baelman to life just for the purpose of assassinating the women, or had he done this sort of thing before?

"Jen and I are using rip magic for your charm."

I looked up, my mind chugging for a second as I pulled away from my thoughts of Jacob to refocus on Lynnette. "What charm?"

"We think it'll help with your reaper," she said. Her eyes glinted as she placed her hands wide on the counter, regarding me. "But if we're correct, you're going to need a continuous supply of rip magic."

Ah, so this was her safety net? Trying to make me dependent on her dangerous rip magic dabblings in exchange for not interfering with what she was doing? I wasn't sure I even believed there *was* a charm. It might just be another manipulation tactic.

"Not sure I like the idea of being dependent on rip magic," I said. "And now that you know it's responsible for the death of one of your friends, as well as a threat of more murders if you don't stop, how can you continue what you're doing?"

I was genuinely curious. It was clear she didn't believe that what she was doing was wrong, and it sounded like she intended to keep doing it.

Her eyes went round, and she gave a quiet little laugh. "We're not the only ones in the world using rip magic. The government is collecting it. Jacob Gregori is collecting it. But someone like me? I don't have the connections or the money to gain access to the big rips. I believe what I was taught by my mentor. Magic belongs to *everyone*. Not the rich. Not the government. *It flows freely from nature, available to all*," she said, paraphrasing one of the handful of magic tenets handed down from mentor to pupil for hundreds of years.

My lips parted as I took a breath to argue, but I hesitated. Maybe sending the Baelman after the witches wasn't about Jacob's supposed lifelong pursuit of closing the rips. Maybe it was really about money. Just another capture in the chess game of corporate gluttony.

Shit. Now I didn't know for sure. Murder was murder either way, but to me it changed things if he was doing it out of greed rather than a desire to end the nightmare of the rips.

"Even if your charm keeps the reaper from killing me, that's not reason enough to put all of you in danger," I said. "Not to me. I'd rather let the reaper consume me."

"You don't think we have the right to all magic?" she challenged, her voice taking on a harsh edge.

I lifted my shoulders and let them drop. "I don't know enough about rip magic to say whether it's a good idea to make it freely available. The tenet you quoted was written long before the first Rip tore Manhattan in half. Maybe some types of magic do need regulation. But that's not really the point. Instead of ripping more holes in our world, you could find another way to gain access to rip magic. Go public, stir up support, and start a movement. You're a natural leader. People would listen to you."

I couldn't help thinking of Rafael St. James, the well-known activist who'd also played a part in rescuing Roxanne's brother. He was a master of using the media and public pressure to call attention to his causes.

But I already knew Lynnette was no activist. She was too powerful, and she used her power to press people and maneuver through situations. I was starting to understand that her abilities had probably always gotten her what she wanted, eventually. The realization sent an icy ripple up my spine.

"I disagree completely," she said. "I think access is *exactly* the point. If we allow government and industry to start controlling and regulating magic, what's next? Where do they draw the line? How long before all crafters are under restriction? How long before the government decides who can use what magic, and to what extent. Or who should be stripped of their abilities?"

Her cheeks were reddening as she spoke, and her face was growing more pinched with anger. But when I felt the brush of magic through the air as she reached for her power, my pulse jolted.

"Obviously I can't answer any of those questions," I said, purposely lowering my voice to a soothing register. Going against my instincts to tense for a fight, I sat down and tried to look placating. I had to keep this from escalating. "For now, can we focus on preventing more murders? Don't you think that's most important?"

Even as I attempted to loosen the tension stringing through me, I fought to keep from slipping my hand down to my whip or drawing a thread of earth power. Lynnette would take it as a challenge, and although I'd come a long way in the past couple of months, I still wouldn't be much of a match against her in a duel, even with my blood-red magic. I couldn't fully align myself with Lynnette, but I couldn't afford to turn her into an enemy, either. I certainly wasn't stupid enough to engage her in a magic battle.

There was another invisible whisper of power across my bare skin as she released her magic. I took a slow breath in through my nose. Her eyes were still flashing.

"Yes, we need to prevent more murders," she conceded.

I gave a tiny nod of acknowledgement. "Okay. We have to stop the next Baelman. We've got, what, eight days until Halloween?"

"Yeah." She shifted her weight and leaned a hand on the counter, propping herself on her palm. The tip of her tongue touched the corner of her mouth as she paused, thinking.

"Collective magic is the safest way to go," she said.

The term referred to the joining of abilities, the type of group crafting that covens were known for. Only female crafters could magically link with each other. It took a lot of practice and ideally close bonds between the women. It was the traditional basis for forming covens in the first place. Collective magic created power beyond the abilities of the individual practitioners, and sometimes produced some unusual powers depending on the mix of the people involved. It was as unpredictable as it was powerful, which was why group drills and training were essential.

"I know your coven isn't official yet, but if you think the group is ready for this kind of challenge, I trust your judgment," I said.

"I'll support you any way I can. I dealt with the last Baelman, so I'm the logical choice for backup. Unfortunately I'm going to have to loop in Supernatural Crimes, but I'll figure out how to keep them from interfering with you."

My mind was spinning ahead, planning. I was babbling a little, and it took me a second to notice the look on her face. It was something between amusement and triumph, and the darkness in her eyes made me want to draw back.

The air changed as something trickled through the room and silently scratched across my senses like a dry branch across a window pane. At first I thought she was reaching for her magic again, but this was different.

"You owe me a favor, Ella Grey."

Her voice was pitched low, with a melodious quality that was anything but pleasant. The image of a snake charmer flashed through my mind's eye.

"I gave my aid when you were in need, and to this trade you freely agreed," she incanted. "With the universe as witness to the promise you made, join my coven and your debt is paid."

I opened my mouth to protest, but the words seemed to stick at the back of my throat like tar and die there. My hands tightened into fists as I struggled to fight it, but I only achieved a weak strangled sound. With my lips curling back as I threw all my effort into my attempt to speak, and sweat popping out on my forehead, I strained to voice my refusal.

The corners of her mouth stretched in a little smirk of a smile that made my blood turn cold.

I lurched to my feet, bumping the stool back. It toppled and clattered onto the tiles.

She gave the tiniest shake of her head. "No use resisting."

My breaths grew ragged as my mind raced to look for a way out. But I had no experience with verbal magic. There had to be some loophole or counter to what she was attempting to force upon me, but I had no idea how to challenge her demand.

My alarm began to dissolve after a few seconds, transforming into churning hot anger as Lynnette and I stared each other down.

"I agree . . . you scheming bitch," I finally ground out through clenched teeth as every four-letter-word laden phrase I'd ever heard screamed through my mind.

Whatever power had held me captive disappeared with my next breath. I whirled, nearly running into the fallen stool. I stomped out of Lynnette's house, got into my truck, and slammed the door so hard my ears rung.

I'd allowed her to trap me. I knew how powerful she was, and I should have guarded against her manipulation. I should have been better prepared. I no longer even trusted that she and Jennifer had developed some sort of rip-magic charm that might help me.

What had she said about the charm? It all depended on her exact words, but I couldn't remember. A strangled noise swelled at the back of my throat. What did it matter? Either the charm wasn't ready, or she was withholding it for some reason. Regardless, I was locked in to her scheme.

I wanted to slam my hands against the dash and throw back my head and yell, but I knew she was watching, and I refused to give her the satisfaction. Instead, I jammed the key into the ignition and drove away, but a few blocks away I had to pull over.

My stomach was still roiling with unspent tension and the infuriating knowledge that I was backed into a corner. Something else was bubbling up, too—rapidly heating to a raging boil. The yearning to reap, the urge that constantly gnawed at the middle of my stomach, was exploding into blinding need. Lynnette's verbal magic incantation had somehow slashed at my control. The soul hunger was emerging so strongly within me, and for a terrifying second, I felt like an observer in my own body.

For a minute I considered going back in, begging for her help. She was powerful, and she might know what to do. But I didn't trust her. And in my agitated state, the reaper might feed on my anger and force me to take her soul. With my head spinning, I gripped the wheel hard and pulled away from the curb. I needed to get home. Damien should still be there, and if anyone could help me, he could.

I struggled for a few seconds to free my phone from my pocket, and finally dialed him with shaking fingers.

"You're at my place?" I asked when he answered.

"Yeah, how'd it go with Lynnette?"

"Could've been better," I said. "But that's not my biggest problem at the moment. Something's happening. With the reaper. I don't know exactly what."

My words were starting to come haltingly, as if I'd forgotten how to smoothly link them together in a sentence.

"She used verbal magic on me. When we were trying to save Roxanne's brother." It was like my vocal chords had lost interest in working, and my voice had taken on a strange, guttural tone. "I didn't know it until later, but she roped me into a favor. She called it in just now. I th—think it triggered—"

I winced as a surge of dizzying disorientation swept over me. I felt like I was drowning. Or dissolving. My heart lurched and then sped.

Was this it? Was the reaper finally consuming me?

The phone slipped from my hand and fell to the floor as the world paled, transforming into the misty gray of the *in-between*. The other cars on the street turned ghostly, colorless and silent as they pushed through the fog and left curling eddies in their wakes. Somewhere in the back of my mind I realized the vehicles appeared driverless here in the realm where souls waited and reapers freed them.

In fact, there were no other people in sight.

I looked down at my hands and saw nothing more than delicate bones clutching the steering wheel.

Some of my panic lessened when I realized *I* was still there, too—my frantic thoughts, my observations. Ella had not been pushed out completely, not yet. But I was no longer in control. The reaper had taken the wheel in every sense.

Damien's alarmed voice had cut off when I entered the *in-between*.

We were heading toward downtown, and it seemed the reaper had been paying enough attention to understand the rules of the road and how to operate my truck. It creeped me out, thinking of the foreign presence within me silently observing, taking it all in, probably waiting for the moment to make its move. I wondered what I looked like to the people in the regular world as the reaper drove us along. Maybe just a zoned-out woman with a thousand-yard stare.

Hope leapt in my chest when the reaper steered onto State Street, and I realized we might be heading back to my place. But instead of taking a right into my neighborhood, we went left on 15th.

Just as we made the turn, I noticed the sensation surging in my middle. It was the bone-deep, consuming hunger, the soul craving I'd felt when I'd come upon Amanda's spirit, still tethered to the body it used to inhabit. I let out a small, high sound of dread.

I knew where we were going: the ghost house.

The reaper shifted my right foot to apply the brake, and we stopped at the curb.

We'd arrived at the very place the reaper had taken me weeks ago, when it had commanded me in the middle of the night and marched me from my apartment to here. Loki had followed and somehow knocked the reaper's control loose, and I'd awakened scratched and bruised on the very sidewalk where I now stood.

The house was still surrounded by chain link and no trespassing signs. Even though it was full daylight in my world, you'd never know it by the ever-present fog of the *in-between*. The ghost house looked even more decrepit here, with ugly, jagged holes gaping through the walls and a roof that looked like it was molding away. The Ella part of me shivered at the sight of movement within—the stirring of the souls that still resided there. But the reaper looked on hungrily.

With quick movements that felt jerky and foreign, the reaper took us around to the left side, forcing me through the overgrown bramble of bushes and unkempt trees growing along the edge of the property next door.

The reaper and I both seemed to spot a way in at the same time—a place at the base of the fence where the chain link had been distorted to create a small gap underneath. Just enough space for me to drop to the ground and pull myself through.

When I stood up inside the perimeter, it struck me that it wasn't *just* the reaper. Our desires had become mingled, and I couldn't truly separate them. Some part of Ella-me knew I should be horrified by this, but instead we looked upon the house like a starving woman would drool over a loaf of bread.

Movement in the nearest first-floor window drew our attention, and any thought of resisting what was about to happen fled from my mental grasp like dandelion fluff in a windstorm.

I went up a set of steep concrete steps to a side door. A tattered, barely recognizable scrap of police tape had snagged on the skeletal, leafless bush next to the steps. Odd that police tape would be present in the *in-between*, but I didn't yet know the rules of what carried over here and what didn't. A rattle of the knob proved the door locked, but it seemed flimsy and looked as if it had been broken into and repaired before.

I moved back as far as the small concrete landing would allow, took aim, and jammed my heel at the spot just below the knob. Something snapped but the lock still held. I kicked again, with gray mist stirring in my movements. The third kick freed the door and it gaped wide, inviting us in.

I'd vaguely wondered what I'd find inside, how the souls would look. With Amanda, her soul had still been near her body. Here, of course there were no bodies. Maybe I expected the souls would appear decrepit, as if they'd decayed along with their long-removed physical remains.

But there was no soul decay, only hologram-like specters of the children who had died in this house years ago that stared vacantly at me—three of them visible from where I stood. The house was like some sort of macabre photography display that captured the tragedy. The children's souls were still attached to their mortal forms, or whatever was left of them, by cords stretched hairline thin off into the distance to some unknown point where their remains must have ended up.

The filament of a doe-eyed girl of maybe twelve sang to me as if an invisible hand plucked it in a siren song. I sucked in a breath as the reaping blade appeared in my right hand and the cloud of trapped souls in my left.

The ecstasy that flowed from the little points of light in my left palm rushed through me in a heady wave. I squeezed my eyelids shut, groaning through clamped teeth. The reaper wanted me to keep the little girl's soul, to add to the collection.

I jerked my head from side to side, trying to resist.

I tried to force my blade hand forward, but the reaper refused. Sweat sprang out on my forehead as we battled over control.

"We reap," I growled. "We set them free."

I pushed against the presence inside me, my eyes fixed on my blade hand. It was my hand. This was *my* body. I had been born into it. In my twenty-four years in this body, I'd nourished it and tested it and learned to live in the world in it. It displayed features handed down to me from my parents. It bore scars from missteps I'd taken as a child. Miscalculations I'd made as an adult. It was a living flesh sculpture of my DNA and my life.

The reaper had consumed more of my soul, but this body was still mine to command.

Mine!

With one final mental shove, I took control. The blade sliced the thread.

We reaped until every soul in the house was free.

When I came out of my stupor and found myself sitting on the cold concrete step outside the side door, I felt hollowed out and nauseous. I wasn't sure if the sick feeling was my human reaction to what I'd just done or the after effects of so much time in the *in-between*.

I wondered how the souls could have remained for so many years unreaped, but I didn't have time to get cerebral.

Two cars pulled up to the curb, bookending my truck. They both jolted to abrupt stops as if the drivers were in a rush. One was Damien's Lexus. My stomach dropped as I recognized the other as Detective Lagatuda's unmarked Supernatural Crimes vehicle.

Great. How would I possibly explain my presence here to my new Supernatural Crimes partner-slash-babysitter?

I started to trudge toward the fence to meet Damien and Lagatuda but then remembered how I'd gotten in.

"Ella!" Damien grabbed the chain link, looking half ready to scale the barrier. "Are you okay?"

Not wanting to further pique Lagatuda's suspicion, I waved and tried to smile, hoping Damien picked up on my silent plea to downplay my frantic call to him.

"Yeah, I'm super!" I chirped then winced. Too much forced enthusiasm. Even I wasn't convinced. I pointed off to the side. "I've gotta go through, uh . . ."

I trailed off and sidled toward the opening at the base of the fence. At least there was some coverage provided by a scruffy overgrown hedge to block my indignity of slithering under the fence like some delinquent garden snake.

On the other side, I brushed myself off, straightened my coat, and squared my shoulders.

Lagatuda stood with his arms crossed, peering at me while his jaw muscles worked.

"Your partner lost contact with you and called me in a panic," he said.

Shit. This was the second time Damien had called in SC when I went off air. At least it was only Lagatuda this time.

I tried not to look at Damien, but I couldn't help a slight widening of my eyes. I understood why he'd been so worried. I just wished I didn't feel like we were a couple of naughty kids who'd just been caught by Dad. Damien winced and sent me an apologetic look, but then had to smooth his expression when Lagatuda half-turned to glance at him.

I cleared my throat. "We got cut off mid-conversation, and I wasn't able to get him back on the line."

"So you came *here*?" Lagatuda made no attempt to hide his skepticism. He glanced past me, and I wondered if he knew the history of what had happened in the house.

"I was following up on a hunch, but it turned out to be nothing," I said brusquely. I pushed my hair back from my face. "Speaking of, I've recruited some associates who should be able to help us at the new moon."

"Oh? Who are they, and what qualifies them for involvement?" Lagatuda looked interested, but I could tell he was still trying to figure out what was really going on and why the three of us were standing in front of an abandoned house.

"The witches the Baelman was targeting. They're in the process of forming a coven, and the leader believes that collective magic is the safest way to deal with the threat."

He narrowed his eyes. "Supernatural Crimes already has covens we contract with for collective magic services."

"I don't doubt you've got superb resources at your disposal, but these witches are the targets. They're the bait and the solution wrapped into one," I said. "And their collective magic services include, uh, *me*. Seeing as how I'm the only one who's managed to kill a Baelman it makes sense, don't you think?"

"I'll have to run it by Barnes," he said. He seemed to dismiss the matter as something out of his purview. Then his forehead creased in concern. "Have you spoken with your friend Deb today? I meant to check in with her."

I felt one brow lift the tiniest amount. "You're checking up on Deb?"

He shoved his hands into his pants pockets. He was actually wearing jeans, the first time I'd ever seen him in something other than a suit. Damien must have caught him off duty.

"She seemed a bit rattled last time we spoke. I just wanted to make sure . . ." He trailed off and cleared his throat.

I pressed my lips together to avoid the knowing grin that was threatening to call him out.

"Right, right," I said. "I haven't talked to her this morning, but I'll give her a call and I'll be *sure* to let her know you were *very* concerned about her well-being."

I started toward my truck, but not before I saw the beginnings of a blush on his cheeks.

"I'll be in touch soon with more information about the coven's plans for the Baelman," I said, my hand on the driver's side door.

"Right," Lagatuda echoed, and headed toward his own vehicle.

I gave Damien a silent tip of my head, indicating I hoped he'd follow me home, and he nodded.

Five minutes later, I was back at my place with Damien crowding in through the door right behind me.

"What the hell happened?" He burst out as soon as we were inside.

I swiped my hand across my forehead, blinking hard as I tried to take stock of the past couple of hours. Suddenly lightheaded and off-balance, I knew I needed to get off my feet before I toppled into something.

"Sorry," I said, my equilibrium reeling. I went to the sofa and sat down. With my elbows propped on my thighs, I held my head in my hands. "Give me just a sec."

"What is it?" I heard him moving to my side, and his weight made the sofa dip gently next to me. "Ella?"

I raised my head and peered at him. "It's . . . gone."

Hope brightened his face. "The reaper soul?"

"No, *that's* still there." I pressed my fingers to my temple. I could still feel the faint thump in my head, the presence of the reaper. "But the crazy hunger, the preoccupation with reaping. Right now I can't feel it at all."

His expression sobered. "How many souls were in there?" he asked quietly.

I shook my head, looking down at the threadbare rug in between my boots. "I don't know. I can remember parts of it vividly, but I was very focused on—"

I halted, thinking of how to explain the pull of collecting the souls rather than setting them free, but not really sure I wanted to go there.

"Focused on?" he prompted.

I sat back, slouching into the cushions. "The reaper . . . my reaper . . . I don't think it was a, uh, good one," I said slowly. "I think it kept souls instead of cutting them free. When we come upon a soul, there's a very, very strong temptation to keep it instead of to cut it loose. It's hard to explain."

"But so far you've succeeded in overcoming the temptation, right?"

Sighing, I pulled a hand down the side of my face. "Yeah, but I can tell the reaper isn't satisfied with that. It's trying to find a way to force me to collect the souls instead of reaping them. With Amanda I didn't have too much trouble overcoming the temptation. This time it was a lot harder. Maybe when it's consumed a little more of me, I won't have a choice. It's learning, Damien. It's watching and observing, figuring out how to control me with more skill."

I clamped my arms against my sides, suddenly chilled.

"I say we take that up later," he said after a couple of silent seconds. "You're still here, you haven't done anything wrong, and you seem relatively okay."

I could tell he was just as worried as before but trying to make me feel better.

"I guess so." I nodded. I watched as he passed his hands over his face and then sighed heavily. "Hey, are you dating anyone?"

"Huh?" His expression tightened back into alarm at the abrupt topic change, and he searched my face. "Maybe I spoke too soon. Are you sure you're okay?"

"No, I've been meaning to ask you," I said. "You haven't mentioned anyone, and I just wanted to, you know, see how your love life was going."

He snorted a laugh. "It's not. Going, that is. But that's okay, we've got other things to worry about."

I echoed his wry laugh. "I guess you're right. But if you need me to introduce you around or whatever . . ."

"Maybe later." He scooted forward. "Okay, tell me what happened with Lynnette."

I recounted the entire story of my stupidity, starting with the first time I'd met the exorcist witch and inadvertently allowed her to magically bind me into a promise.

When I got to the part about getting forced into Lynnette's coven, I couldn't tell if Damien was more horrified or amused.

"You?" he said with a tiny giggle. "A coven witch?"

I did a slow blink and nodded miserably. "But only until I can get out of it. I don't trust her. I think we need her in order to deal with the Baelman, but beyond that I don't want anything to do with her, which means I've got to convince Deb to get out too."

Just at that moment, my best friend breezed through the front door. Damien and I both jumped.

"Did you lose your phone?" she demanded, hands on hips. "I've been texting and calling for the past two hours."

I smacked my skull with my palm.

"I left it in the truck." I stood and gave her a long-faced look. "I'm going to run and get it, and then I hope you've got a minute because I need to tell you a few things."

When I came back in and confessed that I was—at least for the moment—part of the coven, Deb sprang from the sofa with a squeal and actually danced. She did a full turn, shaking her backside and gyrating her arms in the air as if club music pumped in her head.

She caught the look on my face and flopped back down beside me. For a second she tried to suppress her broad smile, but she couldn't hold it back.

"The coven will be sealed soon," she informed me. "We'll have to do a circle ceremony to bind the members and then send in paperwork to make it official."

"Great, I can't wait," I said flatly.

I'd have to look into the process of un-joining a coven, but I'd do it quietly on my own later. No reason to stomp all over Deb's joy right away.

"Aw, come on." She punched my shoulder lightly. "It's a huge honor. In fact, I never *ever* would have guessed Lynnette would actually invite a Level I into the coven."

She sobered as she tilted her head and stared off across the room. Her expression pulled into an almost frown.

"Yeah, *exactly*," I said, guessing what Deb was thinking. "She has her reasons for wanting me, and whatever they are, they're for her benefit. Not mine. I know she's your friend, but she's used to manipulating people until she gets what she wants. I don't trust her at all."

Deb rubbed one of her temples, looking deflated. "I was so excited to have you in the coven, I guess I kind of brushed past the fact that she's forcing you to do it against your will. Sorry, Ella. That was kind of crappy of me."

I flipped a hand in the air, softening a little. "No need to apologize."

"You still haven't gotten to the part about the ghost house," Damien said from the leather chair, where he'd been watching us quietly.

She gave me a sharp look. "The house where the foster kids died?"

She reached for her necklace and wove it around her fingers in a nervous little gesture, seeming to shrink into herself.

I nodded. Deb hadn't been there at the time of the fire, but she'd lived in that house for a short period during the years she spent in the foster system. She didn't talk about her experiences much, but it didn't take a degree in psychology to understand where her deep longing for a happy home and big family came from.

In the briefest terms possible, I told her about the mass reaping.

She chewed her lip for a second and then looked at me. "I think it's really good all those little souls can move on now." One hand moved briefly to her pregnant belly.

We were all silent for a moment.

I gave her a little smile. "Oh, and Lagatuda asked about you. He seemed concerned about how you were doing."

I kept my voice neutral, wanting to gauge her response to see if she'd picked up on the detective's interest in her.

"That's nice of him," she said absently.

I flicked a look at Damien, and one of his brows arched.

Apparently Deb was oblivious. Not that I was surprised. She was so wholesome she probably couldn't even consider that a good guy like Lagatuda could have feelings for a married woman.

"When is Keith coming home, anyway?" I asked.

She took a loud, exasperated breath in through her nose. "Tonight or tomorrow." Her short tone made it clear she didn't want to talk about her husband.

My phone and Deb's chimed at the same time.

"Text from Lynnette," she said and then glanced over at my phone's screen. "It looks like you're on the distribution list now."

Hey witches! Mandatory gathering tonight. My house, 7 pm.

I tried not to sound like a sulky child when I asked Deb if there was anything I should do to prepare for the coven meeting. And I could tell she was doing her best to not seem too ecstatic that I would be attending. She headed home, and Damien also departed not long after.

Exhausted after the events of the past couple of days, I collapsed on the sofa and fell asleep for a few hours. When I awoke, it was full dark outside.

As I got ready, changing into warmer clothes after Deb's warning that we'd be outdoors for part of the evening, I tried to look on the bright side. If I had to do this, I could at least take the opportunity to try to discover more about the rip magic Lynnette was harvesting and any other questionable things she was up to. I hadn't mentioned the rip magic to Deb. I knew she'd be hurt that the exorcist witch had let me in on a coven-related activity Deb didn't know about. But more importantly I intended to use this fact and the danger of what Lynnette was doing as leverage to convince Deb to leave the coven. But first, I had to figure out how to get myself out of the binding agreement with Lynnette.

There was a tap of a car horn out front, and my phone buzzed with a text. Deb had arrived to shuttle me to Lynnette's.

I paused to scratch the spot between Loki's ears. "Wish me luck, boy." His tail thumped the sofa cushion a couple of times.

Halfway down the front walk, I could already hear 90s grunge blasting from the Honda's stereo. I angled myself into the low-slung front passenger seat, and Deb lowered the volume partway.

She squeezed my forearm, and even in the weak light from the dash, I could see the excited anticipation shining in her eyes.

"Aw, come on," she cajoled. "You look like you're going to your own execution."

I gave her an apologetic shrug.

"At least it gives us an excuse to hang out together," she said.

"True."

I leaned forward and turned the music back up as Deb's 90s playlist switched to Nirvana. I wasn't in the mood for chitchat or mustering up fake enthusiasm.

When we reached Lynnette's street, we passed by the cars already lining the curb. We had to park a block away and walk, kicking through the crunchy fall leaves. Considering we were only a few days from the start of November, it wasn't as bone-chillingly uncomfortable out as it could have been.

A car door slammed across the street, and I recognized Jennifer Kane, the vampire witch, getting out of her SUV.

Deb and I stopped to wait for her.

"Hey, how are you?" Deb greeted Jen with a hug. "Did you get your poor house put back together?"

"Oh yeah, good as new." Jen eyed me. "Welcome to the club, reaper witch." She let out her cackley laugh.

I rolled my eyes but couldn't help a small laugh of my own.

"The others don't know about the reaper, do they?" I asked, my voice low as we went through the gate in front of Lynnette's house.

"No, just me and Lynnette," Jen said. "But not for long. You can't keep secrets in a coven."

A few choice four-letter words streamed through my mind, but we were at the door, so I had to keep my displeasure in check.

Jennifer knew about my reaper because she'd more or less helped me confirm what it was using her scrying mirror. And she'd told Lynnette, hoping to get the exorcist witch's help with a possible magic solution to halt the reaper's chow-down on my soul. At the time, I'd figured letting Lynnette in on my secret was worth the risk. But I deeply regretted that she knew anything at all about me. In retrospect, I realized it had probably just made her bent on maneuvering me into her coven. And so far, she and Jen hadn't come up with anything to keep the reaper from killing me. Lose-lose for Ella Grey.

I suppressed an exasperated sigh as the three of us went inside, peeled off our jackets, and added them to the pile on the antique iron bench set against one wall of the entry.

The chatter of voices carried to us from farther back in the house. The smoky forms in my periphery gyrated a little, as if anticipating the gathering.

Every head turned our way when we entered the kitchen, where the overhead lights were dimmed and the flames of several candles warmed the stark neutrals of the finishes. Even though I knew we weren't late, it looked as if we were the last to arrive.

I recognized many of the faces from when most of the coven had gathered at my place after Amanda's death. As they watched me, some of them weren't exactly welcoming. It hit me that I was taking the place of their dead friend. Lynnette had her twelve for her coven—thirteen counting her—but then one had died. I felt stupid for not thinking of it before, and uncomfortable with the realization that my presence was made possible only through the loss of someone they cared about.

I nodded a cool greeting at Lynnette out of respect for her position in the group, but hung back as the witches shifted around. Most of them looked to their leader to take in her reaction to my arrival. Sensing the pause in the group, she quickly moved out from behind the island.

With a surprisingly kindly smile that I didn't trust in the least, she spread her arms in a welcoming gesture.

"Ella, we're so blessed to have you joining us," she said with a magnanimous tone. She beckoned with a rolling movement of one arm. "Please, come in, and I'll get you some mulled wine."

The tense pause in the room seemed to resolve itself back into the soft din of conversation, though there were still several sidelong glances my way as I followed our host to the Crockpot and tray of mugs set out on the counter.

Lynnette lifted the lid off the ceramic inset, and the smell of red wine and winter spices wafted out.

"Thanks for coming," she said casually as she ladled some deep red liquid into a mug.

"As if I had a choice."

I mustered up a fake smile for show as she passed the wine to me.

"For a while, they're going to be a little sensitive about you taking Amanda's place," she said, ignoring my tone and insincere expression. "That's to be expected. But it won't be long before they accept you as one of us."

I took a sip of the hot wine and tried not to pull a yuck face at the sweetness of it.

"Sounds like they're firmly under your control," I said pointedly. "Are they all here under their own will, or did you trick them into joining, too?"

Lynnette's face clouded for the briefest of moments. "No one is here under persuasion."

"Except me."

"There are plenty of benefits here for you," she said. "In time you'll thank me."

I let out a surprised bark of a laugh at her boldness. "I sincerely doubt that."

Something caught her eye, and I turned to see a couple of women were trying to get Lynnette's attention.

"Excuse me, it looks like I'm being summoned." She gave me a smile and touched my forearm, but again I knew it was just for the sake of appearance, and I caught the flinty flash in her eyes. "My home is yours, make yourself comfortable."

Right.

Deb saw me standing by the Crockpot alone and came over to fill a mug for herself.

"I don't think they want me here," I said bluntly. My feelings weren't hurt by it. I just wanted Deb to see this was a bad idea.

"Just give them a chance, Ella." She blew across her mug and scanned the room. "They're good people. They've been great friends to me."

"Including Lynnette?"

Her mouth scrunched to one side for a second. "She's not interested in friendship as much as building a strong, viable coven. And frankly, that's fine by me. I want a shrewd leader at the helm. This isn't just about warm fuzzies. I want this to be my livelihood for the long term."

I tilted my head, tuning into her face more sharply. "My, singular? As in you alone, without Keith?" I asked.

Her eyes began to well.

Before either of us could say anything, Lynnette moved a little apart from the group and raised her voice to get everyone's attention. "Let's get bundled up and head out back."

I turned back to Deb.

She shook her head and furtively swiped her fingers under her lower lids.

"Talk later," she whispered.

I kept near to her as we got our coats and herded out the dining room's glass-paned double doors to the back yard. It was more of a courtyard, with high stucco walls and neat borders of concrete curbing separating the grassy area in the center from the flowerbeds around the perimeter.

One of the women helped Lynnette light five modern-looking

stainless steel torches that were staked in the lawn. I could see the mark of a circle, a width of grass thinner and paler than the rest. The torches were spaced equally around the circumference. A narrow table that appeared to be from a set of metal outdoor furniture had been placed at the north-most part of the circle, just inside the border. It had some pillar candles and several small items on it, but Lynnette went to stand before the table, blocking my view of what it held.

In the dark, the wards around Lynnette's house were visible as faint traces of magic, like ropes woven of colored light. As I moved with the other women, the magic moved like plucked strings. The fact that I didn't trip them was masked by the group. I wondered if Lynnette had noticed that her wards hadn't reacted when I'd come to her house alone. Maybe Jen had already tipped her off that I could pass through wards like a ghost.

I guessed the circle was about twenty feet in diameter, enough room for all of us to gather within it. The women spaced themselves around the border, facing inward. I stood next to Deb, and Jen took the spot on my other side. It was intimate, but not uncomfortably crowded.

"Welcome, witches," Lynnette said, pausing as everyone settled. "This lunar cycle has visited upon us great tragedy and great fear. We've said our goodbyes to our sister Amanda, but we know that the pain of her loss will linger yet. We hold her in our hearts. Now let us open ourselves to the magic that is our birthright."

She closed her eyes and bowed her head slightly, and the other women followed suit. The tingle in the air told me everyone was drawing magic. I focused within and then reached down for earth energy. I was by far the lowest level crafter in the bunch, and I hoped we weren't expected to draw all the elements. I could manage earth for a sustained time and fire for maybe a few minutes. I could have drawn blood-red magic instead, but wasn't ready to reveal that power to a bunch of witches I didn't know. I decided it was best to stick with what was safe, so I drew only a wisp of earth magic and left it at that.

I kept my eyelids open a crack so I could watch Lynnette and observe the others. I felt like a little kid peeking during prayers at church, but I wasn't in the mood to be caught unawares.

After about five minutes, Lynnette took a breath in through her nose, raised her head, and opened her eyes. She turned to reach for something on the makeshift altar behind her, and the women all moved two large steps toward the center of the circle. I did the same, glancing at Deb who gave me a tiny encouraging nod. We were now shoulder-to-shoulder.

In Lynnette's hands I recognized a larger version of the drawstring pouch of spell salt Deb had given me and a slim crystal wand, probably quartz, about five inches long.

I sensed the women around me still holding their magic, so I kept contact with my little thread of earth energy.

Chanting an incantation, Lynnette began at the altar and moved clockwise, pouring out a thin line of salt around the circumference of the circle. The whispering tingle of magic nearby swelled slightly. When she completed the circle, she dropped the bag of spell salt on the table and started around once more with the crystal wand in her hand.

Keeping inside the border of the circle, she pointed the wand down at the line of salt. She whispered a ritual circle spell, her words obscured except for when she passed behind me, and then I only caught a fragment.

" . . . *protected within this space . . .*"

I watched in fascination as magic streamed from the point of the wand down just inside the salt line of the circle, the elemental colors twining around each other like little arcs of electricity.

She passed around a third time, and as she did, the magic circle spread upward forming a half-dome that enclosed us, and I realized the two steps forward were to make sure our heads would be within the ritual space. The protective orb also extended down into the earth to form a complete sphere.

Back at the altar, Lynnette began the classic directional blessings, asking each direction and the associated elements for their presence. North for earth. East for wind. South for fire. West for water. But in addition to the usual four, she added another.

"*Guardians of the place that kisses the space between planes, and the mystical element, I call upon your presence. Join us now and bless this circle.*"

The torches flared, and the pulse of the reaper banged against the inside of my forehead. I squeezed my eyelids closed in a wince, but not before I saw the beginnings of a jagged vertical line of blood-red magic. When I opened my eyes, my jaw dropped. The line had widened into a huge crack and maroon magic was leaking from it like mist. And there was something there, standing in the dull light of the opening. It was the silhouette of a giant winged form towering behind Lynnette, the orbs of its eyes bright with blood-red magic.

I didn't just see it, I felt it—the connection between my mind and the hulking demon's springing into existence out of nowhere. But this was no small-brained pest like the minor demons I'd linked with and controlled.

This one was intelligent.

I knew because it greeted me by my own name.

You are known, Ella Grey.

My heart hammered as I sucked in an alarmed breath, ready to scream a warning to the others. Deb was close enough for me to clutch at her forearm. My eyes flicked to her and then to Lynnette.

Surely Deb saw it, too. Surely Lynnette *sensed* the creature looming twenty feet high at her back.

But when I blinked several times, all I saw behind Lynnette was an expanse of lawn leading to a border with a low hedge and the stucco wall beyond.

Squinting into the darkness, trying to see past the flare of the torches, I searched for the enormous demonic shape.

"What's wrong?" Deb whispered without moving her lips.

I strained to find the thing, my glance darting around the yard, but I couldn't feel its presence anymore. Whatever had been there was gone.

I gave my head a slight shake.

"Nothing," I whispered under my breath.

But the creature *had* been there, I was sure of it. And if any question about the danger of Lynnette's dabblings with rip magic had lingered in my mind before, it dissolved into certainty that she was messing with something better left alone. She'd added that mystical element to the ceremony. That wasn't normal, even I knew that. And after, the giant creature had appeared and greeted me inside my own mind.

I shuddered. Maybe Jacob was right. Not about murdering witches, but about keeping some types of magic restricted.

Lynnette had moved on to talking about the official formation of the coven.

"Tonight each of you will pledge yourselves to the coven as the first step toward official membership," she said. Her gaze had been sweeping the group, but now it trained on me, and she gave me a pointed look.

I shifted my weight, suddenly wishing I could spring away, escape the circle, and disappear into the night. An invisible weight seemed to descend across my shoulders, and when I tried to lift one boot, it was as if gravity reached up through the earth to hold me tighter. For a second I thought it was Lynnette using her magic on me, but I recognized the same stir of energy that I'd felt when she had forced me to make good on our trade by agreeing to join her coven. She wasn't using any power on me, not directly. It was the bind of the promise I'd made that prevented me from fleeing.

A narrow, satisfied smile touched her lips.

Frustration flared hot in my chest, but I forced my fists to unclench.

She reached for something on the altar and then faced us with a long chain dangling from one hand. It had some sort of pendant on it.

"Now, to seal the pledge, we will each contribute magic to this charm." She raised the necklace. "Our energies will mingle, in a literal and symbolic manifestation of our collective magic."

An unpleasant shiver passed through me as I eyed the object she held. She turned to face the woman to her immediate left, a petite brunette with a sweet, round face, and presented the necklace.

"Repeat after me," Lynnette said. "I swear this oath of loyalty to my coven, trust in and transparency to my coven sisters, and protection of the coven's secrets. I freely open myself to the bond between us and hereby bind myself to this coven."

I felt none of the joy that radiated from the woman's eyes as she repeated the oath and then sent a tendril of magic into Lynnette's hands.

The exorcist witch moved on to the next woman, and the next, and then it was Deb's turn. I felt sick as I listened to my best friend swear herself to the coven.

When Lynnette stood before me, I saw that the object in her hands was indeed a locket, open and glowing with the magic that had been contributed so far.

My lips twisted with distaste, but I knew I couldn't get out of it.

Hating every second, I said the oath and added my tendril of green earth magic. I stared at the ground as Lynnette finished taking the locket around the circle. When she got back to where she'd started, she put the chain around her neck and lifted the locket so she could look down into it. She repeated the oath and then sent an arc of blue water magic into the locket. She snapped it closed and let it hang.

She said a few closing words, and then the women around me

burst into happy chatter. They hugged, a few even cried a little.

Deb touched my shoulder. "I know you didn't want this, but I can't say I'm sorry we're doing it together."

Not knowing what else to do or say, I gave her a hug. I silently swore to myself that I'd get us out of this, even if it meant I had to rip that chain from Lynnette's neck and battle her to the death. There was no way in hell I'd spend the rest of my life under her control.

Lynnette passed around a plate of crescent-moon shaped cookies and a large ornate tumbler of wine, from which all the women sipped.

I went up to the coven leader. "We need to talk about the new moon and the Baelman," I said, not bothering to conjure up a fake smile.

She nodded, her mouth pressing into a grim line. "Let's give them a moment to celebrate, and then I'll open the circle and we can go inside."

She spoke to me with an equality I didn't expect, which silenced me long enough for her to step away. She knew how to shift her mood and tone to disarm people, and I needed to stop letting her manipulate me so easily.

"So how's it feel, witch?" Jen appeared next to me.

I gave her a wry, narrow-eyed look, and she let out her throaty laugh.

"Not much of a fan of group activities, are you?" she asked, turning serious. She flipped a glance at Lynnette.

"Uh, that would be a resounding no," I said.

I suddenly wondered if Jen had guessed that I'd been compelled into the coven. She was eyeing me, and as I returned her gaze, I couldn't be completely sure, but I thought I saw a flicker of understanding there. Maybe she could be an ally.

When another woman got Jen's attention, I quickly pulled out my phone, turning partially away from the group to shield what I was doing, and sent a text to Damien.

I need to know everything about verbal binding magic. Help, please?

When I glanced around guiltily, one of the women was shooting me a disapproving look. She tilted her gaze pointedly at my phone. I jammed it back in my pocket, gave her an apologetic half-shrug, and felt my expression sour when she looked away.

For the love of my sanity, I needed to get the hell out of here.

I dropped my hold on the earth magic I'd drawn. Keeping a small tendril of it for the past half hour, or however long we'd been gathered was enough, to make me feel the beginnings of magical drain. I pressed my fingertips into my closed eyelids, trying to ward off the cranky fatigue that seemed to be seeping into my bones.

Lynnette got everyone's attention, and we assumed our positions around the circle as we had before.

She said some ceremonial words, thanking the directions and elements, and then walked counter-clockwise around the circle, releasing the sphere as she went. The third time around, she used a long, rustic broom to sweep at the salt, marking the circumference of the circle. It was more symbolic than a gesture of actual cleaning-up.

My relief was palpable as the group began to head back inside. I was chilled from holding onto my magic for so long and glad to be done with witchy ceremony.

We gathered in the kitchen again, and this time I was actually grateful for a warm mug of mulled wine in my hands.

Lynnette stood at the island, waiting for the room to settle a little. When she had the group's attention, she drew in a slow breath, her face sober.

"Though we are only at the very beginning of the process of binding to each other, we must draw together quickly. We must trust each other deeply. Unfortunately, the threat to our membership will reemerge soon. We don't have the luxury of time."

Ugh, we were only at the beginning of the witchy kumbayas? I wanted to groan at the thought of more magic circles, but I appreciated her gravity. We *didn't* have much time. You could have heard a pin drop in the silence of her pause.

"Our newest sister, Ella, killed the creature that took Amanda's life," she continued. Several gazes swung my way. "Another creature will come forth with the new moon. We assume that this one, too, will target us. Ella is working with Supernatural Crimes, but they have less to go on than we do, and she and I have realized that our best hope with this threat is our own collective magic. So, sisters, we will begin practicing tomorrow night, and we'll practice every night until the new moon. I, for one, will be asking the universe for strength."

She turned to me, and I realized she expected me to say something.

I cleared my throat. "Uh, thank you for welcoming me into your coven. I realize I'm taking the place of someone you cared about, and I wish the circumstances were . . . *different*." I shot a significant look at Lynnette. "I'll tell you everything I know about the creature, the Baelman. I know there's great power in this group. Come Samhain and the new moon, we're going to kick this Baelman's ass."

There were a few determined nods, and Jennifer even let out a little whoop.

Everyone turned back to Lynnette.

"We will be putting ourselves in danger, but I believe in facing an adversary head-on. We'll have Ella, who killed the Baelman that murdered Amanda, and we'll have each other."

I had to admit to myself that even I was getting a little bit pumped up by Lynnette's speeches. Maybe the collective magic thing wouldn't be so horrible.

"So," she said, businesslike. "We'll meet here at five every evening, work for a couple of hours, and then take a quick meal break, and then go until ten."

My face pulled into a grimace. *Five hours*? Every night?

"See you tomorrow night."

After the coven dispersed, I tried to get Deb to talk to me about Keith, but she begged off, saying she was too exhausted and needed to get a full night's rest if she had any hope of putting in the long hours Lynnette was demanding.

I didn't push it, knowing that her pregnancy, the stress of recent events, and her personal life were putting a very real strain on her. Besides, I knew her well enough to be patient—she'd talk when she was ready.

Back home, I called Damien to see if he could tell me anything about verbal binding magic. Also, I really needed to vent to someone.

"It went on *forever*," I said. "And I really don't like the fact that I put some of my magic into that locket. How the hell am I going to get out of this coven?"

"I'm sorry you got roped into this," he said, his voice genuinely sympathetic.

"No, I'm literally asking you. How do I get out of it?"

I'd been lying on my back across my bed with my legs dangling off, staring up at the ceiling. Now I sat up, cross-legged.

"The magic promise thing is killing me, Damien. When we were in the circle, I started thinking about running, and it was like gravity reached up and locked me down."

"Well, the most obvious answer is finding a loophole in the promise," he said. "You've already discovered that when you try to go against it head-on, it butts back. You've got to find a different way around it."

"Yeah, that makes sense." I plucked at a loose thread in the quilt folded at the foot of my bed. "I'll have to figure out where she might have made a mistake."

I wasn't feeling optimistic about outsmarting Lynnette. She seemed experienced with verbal binding magic and just very skilled at manipulation in general.

"I'll keep looking into it, maybe I'll find something." His words dissolved into a yawn.

"I'm sorry," I said. "I'm treating you like my own personal research department and keeping you up half the night. I owe you. Like ten times over."

"Don't worry about it. I came to Boise so I could independently continue my inquiries. I couldn't have met a better person to provide me with ample opportunities to study unusual supernatural phenomena."

A grin tugged at the corners of my lips. "Well, that's very generous of you. I'm lucky you're here. And I *will* make it up to you, somehow."

"You'd better rest up for your group magic rehearsals," he said with a snicker. "Oh, and Barnes wants us to come in to the SC precinct at ten in the morning."

I sighed, remembering that I'd gotten a text from Lagatuda

saying something along those lines. "Okay, I'll see you tomorrow. 'Night."

"Goodnight."

I got ready for bed and climbed in with Loki already curled on the quilt, forcing my legs off to one side.

"Bed hog," I said affectionately.

He exhaled a contented doggy sigh.

I was exhausted, but instead of sleeping I tossed from side to side. My brother Evan was on my mind. It'd been too long since I'd seen any visions of him, and I didn't even know if he was still in that vampire feeder den somewhere in the desert. Or if he was still alive at all. I had to believe he was, though, and since I'd become more skilled at driving minor demons I intended to use them to help me search for him.

My conversation with Jacob Gregori and his macabre confession about aiming to eliminate Lynnette's coven also resurfaced in my thoughts. I was part of the coven now. Did that mean he would try to kill me, too? I wasn't naïve enough to believe he held any true familial affection for me, not enough to outweigh his other goals, anyway, but . . . was he cold-hearted enough to try to murder his own niece? He almost had, when I'd posed as Deb. Atriul's intervention might have been the only thing that saved me.

After the coven took care of the next Baelman, we had to find a way to prove that the creatures were sent by Gregori Industries. A witch was dead, and Jacob should be held accountable.

My phone lit up on the bedside table, drawing my attention. I rolled over and pulled it onto the pillow. There was a text from

Johnny.

Hey sugar, been thinking about you. I hope you're behaving yourself and things are staying nice and boring. Looking forward to some uninterrupted time after I get into town.

The message ended with a winky face.

I typed a reply: *Not as boring as I'd like, but I'm still in one piece so that's something. Uninterrupted time sounds perfect. When are you coming back?*

I missed him but realized that any swoony feelings I might have had were getting buried under the distraction of everything I was facing. It was probably a good thing Johnny had a lot going on, too.

I stared at my phone for a few seconds, but when he didn't respond, I set it back on its charger. I turned over and burrowed deeper into the covers.

A normal date with no supernatural disruptions, no emergency calls from work? I didn't quite believe it was possible, but a girl could hope.

The next morning, my alarm was followed a couple of minutes later by a call. I was sitting on the edge of the bed, trying to muster up some enthusiasm for a morning run, and the name on the caller ID made me straighten in surprise.

"Atriul?" I answered.

"Hello, Ella."

"I've been meaning to get in touch with you. Is everything okay?"

There was a rustling noise, as if he was holding the phone

against his face. "I've heard some news, and it's not good. The new moon isn't going to bring just a Baelman. Apparently Gregori has something in the works that's potentially much worse."

I frowned. "What is it?" I found myself tensing, as if readying for a blow.

"For one, I think he's found a way to leverage the thinning of the veil at Samhain to allow more than one Baelman into our dimension."

"That's bad," I said. "If he's going to send a whole slew of those creatures, it could be very, *very* bad."

"I'm sorry I don't have more to tell you."

I squeezed my eyes closed and rolled my head to each side. I'd been up for ten minutes, and I was already wound tight. It didn't bode well for the day.

"No need to apologize, I appreciate the heads up. We've still got a few days, so if you could do your damnedest to discover more details about what Jacob has up his sleeve, well, you'll save lives." I gave a short, humorless laugh. "Not to put a dramatic spin on it or anything."

He chuckled, a surprisingly warm and human sound. "No pressure, got it."

I managed a tiny smile at his dry humor. "Thanks, Atriul."

There was a moment of silent hesitation on his end. "Would it be weird if I asked you to call me Rogan?"

My lips parted in surprise. "The name of the mage you . . . uh . . ." I couldn't think of a polite phrase for *the mage you extinguished when you ate his soul.*

"I know it might seem odd or even offensive to you, but I feel like it's a way to keep a piece of him in this world. It's the least I can do."

"Sure," I said. "Rogan it is."

"I will be in touch soon."

We disconnected, and I sat holding my phone for a few seconds. Would my reaper someday have a similar conversation with someone? Would it take my body as its own and then want to honor me by using my name? The image of the little nebula of collected souls welled up from my memory, and I shuddered. I didn't think my reaper was like Atriul. Somehow I doubted my reaper would be concerned with such things as memorializing the human it'd killed.

I raised my phone and flipped to my contacts, where I changed "Atriul" to "Rogan."

I dressed in sweats, a down vest, a knit hat, and gloves for my run. The temperature wasn't cold enough for the air to sear my lungs, but in a few weeks it would be. For the worst of the winter months I resorted to a treadmill in the gym at the station, but for now I relished the freedom of my shoes pounding over concrete and the chilly autumn air stinging my cheeks.

After my sit-ups and pushups, I ran through the magic drills Damien had instructed me to do daily and then spent about fifteen minutes practicing with my whip.

Pleasantly spent from the physical and magical activity, I carried a mug of coffee into the bathroom and jumped into the shower. After, I was once again faced with what to wear to the

Supernatural Crimes precinct. I put on the same form-fitting pants as last time, and found a blue chambray button-down shirt shoved to one end of my closet that wasn't too wrinkled.

Damien showed up at about nine, and we sat at my kitchen table with our chairs pulled together so we could both look at his laptop.

"There are ways to protect yourself from verbal magic," he said, scrolling through a document of notes he'd compiled. "You should take those steps for future protection, but obviously these won't do much good for your current situation with Lynnette."

"Could you send those to me?" I asked.

"Sure." With a few keystrokes he sent the info, and a second later my phone pinged with the received message. "Now, if possible I think what you should do is find a way to break her spell, but without her knowing it."

"Ah, I like that," I said with an approving nod.

"But it's the breaking that's the problem. You could try soaking in salt and herb baths and repeat some spell-breaking chants. A skilled spell caster might be able to stir something up for you. But I think the success of that approach is unlikely, considering that Lynnette is powerful and seems to be quite shrewd. She probably wouldn't cast a spell of verbal magic that would be so easily broken."

"Good point."

"Ideally, you need to find the spell cord that binds you to her and cut it," he said.

"Cord?"

"It's not literal, obviously. It's . . . astral, I guess you could say."

"It sounds a bit like the connection I feel with the demons I control," I said slowly. "It's like I mentally trace a line from my own mind to theirs. I've never felt that sort of thing between me and another person, though. I wouldn't even know how to locate it."

He leaned back with a thoughtful look, folding his arms across his chest. "Supposedly there are mages who can travel on the astral plane," he said. "I honestly don't know if that's just a legend or not, but I could try to find one for you."

I could hear the reluctance in his voice. He came from a family of renowned and powerful mages, and he was the only one with sub-mage abilities. He'd left his roots on the East Coast and come here, two thousand miles away, in part to escape the stigma of being a failure in the eyes of his family. I knew he had no desire to contact them or anyone in their network to beg for help.

I shook my head. "Thanks, but a mage's services are way beyond my price range. I need to learn how to handle Lynnette without throwing myself into a sinkhole of mage debt."

A tiny light bulb lit in my brain, and I picked up my phone to type a text to Rogan.

Any idea how to break a verbal spell on the astral plane?

My phone beeped, but it wasn't a reply. It was a scheduling reminder.

"Guess we need to head into the SC precinct," I said, standing with no small amount of reluctance.

"Hey, we got to spend the morning hanging out here drinking coffee in your kitchen instead of tromping around in the cold trapping demons," Damien said. His half-smile folded into concern. "You don't think we'll get in trouble, do you? After all, we're on the SC payroll right now."

"Nah. I was up til after ten last night with the coven. I'm counting that as work time, since the Baelman threat is my only personal reason for putting myself through that nonsense."

"The Baelman, and the spell that won't allow you to do otherwise."

I gave him an exaggerated pissy look. "Thanks for the reminder."

He pushed his fist against his mouth in a poor attempt to hide a wide grin. "Never fails. Every time I think of it, I get a kick out of the image of *you* in a magic circle with all those witches, chanting and holding hands and swearing oaths to each other."

He snickered.

I smacked his shoulder. "There was no fricking hand-holding."

Damien drove us to the SC precinct. I'd expected something like the briefing I'd attended before, but this time it was just us plus Lagatuda, Barnes, a couple of investigators, and an SC technology expert. They took us to a conference room that was more cushy and corporate-looking than the chief's office at my station.

"From now until the new moon, we're going to do daily briefings here at this time," Barnes said once we were all seated around a conference table. She sat at the head, of course. "That'll be seven days a week."

She paused to look at me and Damien, which I took as her way of asking us if we could accommodate that.

I nodded while Damien said something acquiescent. I didn't

love Barnes's tone, but I wasn't going to argue at a time when urgency was necessity.

"Lagatuda tells me your coven is prepared to perform collective magic to combat the threat," Barnes said to me, pinning me with her eyes. "He's also said you've learned something new about the Baelman that will emerge with the new moon."

For a second I thought maybe Lagatuda had somehow bugged my call with Rogan but then realized that no—I'd told him I knew who was behind the creature assassins.

Everyone seemed to shift forward, waiting for me to speak.

"My source has confirmed that Gregori Industries sent the Baelman that killed Amanda," I said. "I'm positive he's correct about that. He believes the next Baelman will come through at or near the Gregori campus. This morning he contacted me to tell me his sources think Gregori has found a way to get more than one Baelman into our dimension at once, using the thinning of the veil, and the dark power that will reach its peak at the new moon."

I expected Barnes to challenge me or demand proof of my claims. Instead, she gave me a grim nod and then rose from her chair. "Okay, we will fold all of this into our strategy, but it won't change the overall approach."

The screen on the wall lit up.

"SC has determined that it's too risky to involve a civilian coven," she said. "Please tell your coven that we appreciate the offer but must ask that they stay in their respective homes until we give them the all-clear. That includes you, Officer Grey. We'll have each of you under guard. Now, we're coordinating across several different supernatural departments—"

"Wait just a second," I interrupted. "You don't want the coven's help? You don't even want *mine*?"

"It would be irresponsible for us to involve the civilians that the creatures are going to target. Each witch needs to stay in her own home during the window of time we specify," Barnes said, her voice rising with a tone of authority.

I shook my head vigorously. "Sorry, but putting a couple of SC patrol cars on each witch isn't going to help them one damn bit. The coven will be much safer if they're—if *we're*—all together. That way I can protect them, and we can defend ourselves with collective magic if we have to. Forcing them apart makes them each sitting ducks, and it's just—well, it's idiotic. Surely you can see that, can't you?"

I could feel my face flushing, and it was all I could do to keep the volume of my voice under control. I stared at her with my hands raised in a near-plea. I could see what she was trying to force, and I couldn't let it fly. SC wanted to keep the women—the targets— spread out to mitigate the risk. I could easily guess SC's reasoning: if the women were all in one place, it would be too easy to attack them all at once; keeping them each in a different location was like taking a paper shooting target, tearing it into thirteen pieces, and letting the wind scatter it. There was a logic to it, except for one thing. Coven witches were stronger together.

I thought I saw a flash of agreement in her eyes, but then her face hardened.

"It would be irresponsible," she repeated, lowering her voice in a way that told me I was probably right—she didn't have a choice in this. Her orders came from above.

"You can't force us to stay in our homes. We're not criminals under house arrest," I said, matching her steady gaze and tone. I gripped the armrests so hard my hands began to cramp.

"Actually, we are prepared to use force if necessary." Her jaw muscles flexed. "We have to keep the potential victims under tight control. It's for their own good. For yours, too."

Hell, no. No one—especially not Barnes—was going to tell me I had to do something for my own good when it was so fricking clear that the opposite was true.

I seethed through the rest of Barnes's talk about how SC would bring in Strike Team as well as their own supernatural special forces. I wanted to holler at her that Strike's weapons were designed to combat arch demons. Their traps wouldn't work on Baelmen. Their people weren't trained for something like this. But I knew I couldn't try to engage in a convincing discussion. I'd ask Damien if he could plead the case that Strike Team was ill-equipped for such an assignment. Maybe Barnes would be more open to him. Anyway, at the moment I was too worked up to be any good.

A few times when she seemed to expect some sort of reaction from me, I just gave her vague nods. I could feel Damien's attention on me, the glances he was flicking my way when Barnes wasn't looking.

When she reached the end of her presentation, she leaned one hip against the table.

"Look, I know this isn't what you were expecting," she said to me, speaking as if we were the only two in the room. "But we'll be engaging resources that are way beyond your clearance level. We've dealt with unknown threats before. Have some trust that there's more to this than meets the eye."

I ground my teeth. "I see that I'll have to leave the execution of your plan to you," I said stiffly.

She nodded, apparently satisfied by my half-assed response.

"For now, we want the two of you to work on getting more specifics about what Gregori's going to throw at us." She flipped a glance between me and Damien. "You and Officer Stein are dismissed."

I managed to hold my shit together until we were in the parking lot.

"They're going to get Strike Team killed!" I burst out, my voice shrill with pent-up frustration. "And there is no way in hell they're going to force me to hide out in my house. Wait till I tell Lynnette. She'll shit a brick. I bet my entire SC paycheck that she has no intention of taking this sitting down, regardless of what anyone says. Can you even believe the nerve of this department? I honestly fear for the safety of the general public if this is how SC handles new supernatural threats. Piss poor approach, if you ask me. Fine example of bureaucratic idiocy."

He waited, his key fob in one hand and his weight shifted over to one hip, until I was finished with my tirade. I kicked at a small rock and sent it skittering across the parking lot, stalked in a tight circle, and then stopped near the rear bumper of his Lexus, facing him with my hands planted hard on my hips.

"Okay, I'm done," I said sullenly.

The car's locks disengaged with a smooth, soft *snick*.

We got in, and I took a slow breath.

"So what do you think about all of this?" I asked.

"I understand their desire to keep civilians out of the operation," he said. "But, I agree with you, it's wrong to try to keep the coven separated. They're making each one of you into sitting ducks."

"I know!" I burst out, throwing up my hands and smacking my elbow against the door. I cleared my throat. "Sorry. You were saying?"

He pulled out of the SC lot.

"And I've been doing some calculations," he continued, ignoring my interruption. "I don't think Gregori's creatures are going to emerge near the company grounds."

"You don't?"

"It doesn't make sense, from a magic standpoint. There's nothing special about the location of the Gregori Industries campus. Assuming that Jacob wants to maximize the dark power available at Samhain, he's going to want a spot that amplifies the magical energy."

I nodded, my eyebrows pulling low. "Yeah. Like a ley line?"

"Possibly. But ley line magic isn't specific to dark magic. I'd expect him to go with a location that caters to the type of power he's going to need in order to bring forth a horde of Baelmen."

"Hm. Do you have any candidates?"

"I have a short list of possible locations, but . . ." He shook his head and a look of frustration crossed his features. "I feel like I'm missing something."

"What about the Boise Rip?" I asked. "That seems like the most concentrated area of bad juju."

"Yes, it is. But it's so heavily guarded, it's a bad choice for him for that reason alone. Too much attention and too many eyes. Plus, the Rip isn't special to the timing of this year's dark harvest. As I've been able to discern, rips don't change with moon phases or other events on our earthly calendar."

"Okay, so you think it's a spot that might be dormant, or at least uninteresting, unless the conditions are right."

I realized we'd missed the turn that would have taken us back toward my place. Instead, Damien was driving us west on State Street.

"Something like that." He signaled left and then pulled into the parking lot of a popular local Mexican chain. "I'm starved. Let's grab something to eat, and then I'll get back to my calculations and you can talk to Lynnette."

After we were seated, I sent a text to Rogan and realized he'd never responded to my previous question about breaking verbal spells.

Got another one for you: what would you expect to be the most powerful dark magic location around here come Samhain?

Out of the corner of my eye, I saw a group filing through the restaurant toward a room that held tables that could accommodate larger-sized parties. When I twisted partway around, I expected to see a bunch of coworkers with matching corporate badges out to lunch together. But my gaze was met with the green sea-glass eyes of Rafael St. James, well-known activist and my one-time fling.

He raised a hand partway in greeting and veered over toward our table.

"Ella, I hear you've joined a coven." His generous mouth quirked with amusement. "Have to say I'm surprised."

I pursed my lips and gave him a look of chagrin, trying to play it down. I didn't want to let on just how badly I'd been snowed into joining the exorcist-witch's coven. "Yeah, well, you warned me before: Lynnette Leblanc should be handled with care."

"It'll be good for her to have someone to butt heads with." He let his half-controlled grin bloom into a full smile of appreciation, as if he were picturing me and Lynnette clashing and liked what he saw.

I shrugged a shoulder. "I'll do what I can. Hey, I have a random question for you. If you had to pick a place where dark magic would be the strongest at Samhain, where would you put your money?"

His amusement dissolved into trepidation. "You're not getting into the black arts, are you?"

"Good gravy, no," I said emphatically. I tipped my head toward Damien. "We're on temporary assignment with Supernatural Crimes, and well, I can't get into details but we're trying to combat something ugly. Just thought with your extensive travels you might have a guess."

He tilted his gaze up at a corner of the room. "I'm assuming you're looking for something beyond the obvious, so not any of the major rips. If you want to reach back in history, I'd say around Salem."

"Like witch trials Salem? Massachusetts?" I asked, surprised.

"Yeah. Site of some of the first European dark magical arts on this continent, right?"

"Good point," I said. I noticed one of his entourage trying to get his attention and nodded that way. "I won't keep you."

"Good to see you both," he said, and sauntered away.

I watched Damien watch Raf move through the tables to his group. Once Raf was out of sight, Damien took a long breath in through his nose and reached for his water glass.

"Yeah," I said. "He does tend to do that to a person."

Damien widened his eyes in a brief look of unabashed agreement.

"So is he your type?" I asked.

"I'm pretty sure Rafael St. James is *everyone's* type," Damien said drily.

I snorted a laugh. "Yeah . . . but is he?"

"Not important right now." He made a dismissive gesture. "I hadn't been thinking of distal locations, but now that changes things. Maybe Gregori's Baelman horde won't originate close by."

"You think Jacob is going to have them birthed—or whatever—in Salem, Mass, and then stick 'em on one of his private jets and fly 'em out here? First class, complete with blankies, champagne, and those little hot towels to wipe their faces when they land?" I said it to be funny, but Damien wasn't laughing.

"I don't know," he said thoughtfully. "But now I realize I need to widen my area of consideration."

We talked through a few possibilities, stretching lunch into the early afternoon. I'd been in a hurry to get to Lynnette and figure out what to do next but found that the extended break was actually welcome. By the time Damien dropped me at home, it was three in the afternoon.

I shut the door behind me and nearly jumped out of my skin when I looked up and found Deb scrunched in a corner of the sofa with her legs pulled up against her chest and her face tear-streaked.

"What happened? Is the baby okay?" I dropped my keys and went to sit next to her.

She looked at me with round, red-rimmed eyes. "Yeah, the baby is fine. I think—I think I just left Keith."

Her face crumpled as her tears started anew. I folded her into my arms until her sobs subsided to sniffles.

I went to the bathroom to grab a wad of toilet paper and brought it to her. "How did you get here? I didn't see your car out front."

"He sold it."

"*What?*"

Loki, who'd been lying on the floor near Deb, jumped at my raised voice and then stood and slunk into the bedroom.

"Jennifer and I were meeting up after I was finished with school anyway, so she came and got me and brought me here," she said. She pulled her lips in between her teeth and bit down and then shook her head. "It was just the last straw, I guess. It wasn't a fancy car or anything, but . . ."

"It was Deep Blue, the car you've had since high school. He had no right to do that." I blew out a breath through my clenched teeth, surprised at how angry it made me that Keith had gotten rid of Deb's old Honda. After all, this certainly wasn't the worst of his offenses.

I shifted to face her fully. "Is it for real this time? You're not going back?"

She set her chin, and her face hardened. "I'm not going back."

I hugged her again, my mind starting to spin. Deb was due in, what, six months? We'd have to get a bigger place. We'd need to buy infant things—a crib and bottles and stuff. And what would she do after the baby came? Daycare was crazy expensive, I'd heard. Oh shit, and then there were the divorce fees. Would Keith even have to pay any child support if he didn't have a steady job?

I reined in my thoughts before they could continue racing off in a hundred different directions. None of those details mattered.

I gently pulled her up by the wrist. "Come in the kitchen. I'm making you tea."

I sat her down at the little table and went about putting water on and finding a couple of mugs and my little-used canister of assorted tea bags.

"I don't know what I'd do without you, Ella," she said earnestly. "You and the coven are my world, my family."

I paused with my hand on the stove's knob. Luckily I was facing away from her so she couldn't see the perturbed look on my face.

Sh-i-i-i-t.

She'd never want to leave the coven, not now that she was on her own. And who would be a giant asshole for trying to talk her into it? *I know you desperately want to belong and feel a sense of family, but Deb, I need you to ditch all your new besties pronto.*

I masked a groan in a quiet exhalation.

"You know we're all here for you," I said and then joined her at the table when I was sure I could keep my expression neutral.

We talked for a bit over tea, and then Deb took a short nap.

By the time she woke up and we'd grabbed a quick bite for dinner, we had to head to Lynnette's for mandatory coven practice.

As the women were gathering, I pulled Lynnette aside and told her what Supernatural Crimes had decided.

Her eyes narrowed, and her nostrils flared.

"Screw that," she hissed. "We'll just have to make sure they can't force us apart. I'll come up with something."

"You think we should still be ready to use collective magic?"

"Absolutely. In fact, I *hope* the creatures come after us so we get to demonstrate what we can do. I'd love to show those SC bastards how wrong they were to try to shut us down."

With Lynnette's declaration, I was actually amped up to learn how to perform group magic. But it didn't take long for my enthusiasm to deflate like a month-old birthday balloon.

Apparently being a weak Level I on the Magical Aptitude Scale made me a poor fit for collective magic activities. I was like a baby elephant trying to hang with a herd of mature gazelles, in terms of skill level. And I tired much more quickly than everyone else.

But the real problem was that my aptitude was literally limiting how much magic the rest of the women could feed into the collective powers. We each sent a stream of magic to Lynnette, who was the focus for the circle. The thing was, each woman could only feed in the amount that the least powerful crafter—me, in this case—was able to contribute. It was a serious liability.

During a break, when everyone was milling around in the kitchen, I pulled Deb over by the sleek retro-modern coffee maker.

"I'm obviously holding everyone back," I said. "This isn't the only way I'm a crappy fit for this group, but I don't think we can deny that my lack of skill and ability is potentially putting everyone in danger."

I eyed the other women, trying to gauge whether any of them might be thinking the same thing. No one seemed openly concerned at this point, but I thought I caught a few less-than-thrilled glances coming my way. The fact was that we didn't have much time to get it right.

"I trust Lynnette on this," Deb said firmly. "If she thinks this group works, then we'll be fine. You'll get the hang of it."

"I appreciate your confidence, but does she have experience with collective magic? Does she even know enough to recognize that a replacement is needed?"

"She was in a coven before she decided to get her own charter. She's got more experience than anyone here."

"If you say so."

I eyed the locket around Lynnette's neck. It still gave me the creeps, knowing that a little blob of my magic was sealed up inside.

Lynnette called us all back into her great room in the basement—a space that was probably meant to have sofas, a big screen TV, and maybe a pool table, but that she'd left mostly empty so that it could accommodate a spacious magic circle. The circle was offset into one corner, and Deb had explained to me that it was positioned so that no pipes passed through the part of the magic sphere that formed below the floor. If certain drains interrupted the sphere—major tree roots, sewer pipes, and the like—they'd effectively break the circle. That meant the center part of the sphere that extended overhead and into the ceiling also had to be in a spot that was uninterrupted.

The space felt too cave-like, with heavy, dark curtains over the high half-windows and a painted concrete floor. Add to that the chill of magic fatigue and the throbbing in my temples from a couple of hours of focused crafting, and it was starting to feel like I'd never see the light of day again. Maybe if I were a practicing witch I would have felt more connected to the space, but I couldn't wait to escape.

We started to arrange ourselves inside the circle the way Lynnette had set us up—with us around the inside perimeter and her at the center—when she held up a hand.

"Let's try something different," she said. "I want to see what happens with Ella and myself acting as the focus."

One of the witches, a dark-complected curvy woman named Elena who was a hairdresser by day, pushed one hip out and planted her hand on it. "Wait a sec. How do we direct our magic into a double focus?"

"Use Ella as your target, and it'll pass through her to me," Lynnette said.

I half-raised my hand. "Whoa, I'm all for trying something new, but I have no idea how to be a focus."

The premise of collective magic was that the witches in a circle added their streams of magic one-by-one to a central witch—the focus—who then added her own power plus directed the magic of all the others. I'd assumed it required a large capacity for magic, which I didn't have, plus a lot of skill to handle that much power, also something I was lacking.

"Actually, I think you *do* know how to be a focus," Lynnette said.

She gave me a pointed look, and it dawned on me that she was talking about my reaper. I quickly covered the few steps between us, trying to ignore the confused and curious stares of the women surrounding us.

"That's not the same thing," I whispered as low as I could, trying to prevent the others from overhearing. "The—*you know*—is within me and works symbiotically with me. It's not channeling magic into me from outside. And how do you know they're not going to fry me with their magic, considering my low aptitude?"

"I think your low aptitude will make it easier for you—all you have to do is let it flow through you and into me. Don't try to hang on. If you do, that's where the harm could come in. Don't worry, I'll have them start small."

She patted my arm, and part of me wanted to slap her hand away. But everyone was watching.

I drew myself up, stepped back a few paces, and then squared off with Lynnette. "Okay, let's do this."

A tiny smile played across her lips as she shifted her attention to the group.

"Let's start with small threads of earth magic," she said. Then she locked eyes with me. "Take a deep breath and do what you normally do to most easily grasp your magic, but stop short of actually touching any elemental power."

I nodded, already focusing. A couple of slow breaths, and I sent my awareness down through my feet until I felt the anticipatory tingle of touching earth magic. But I held back, sensing it, but not reaching for it.

Around me, I felt the brush of magic like an electric breeze across my bare skin as the women drew their power.

When the first stream of earth magic hit me, pooling in my feet and then spreading through my body, I jolted as if a clap of thunder had startled me. It filled me with a sensation that was at once foreign and familiar. I recognized it as earth energy, but it carried the feel of the woman who drew it—something subtle but unmistakable, like the signature scent of a person's house.

Two more women added their streams of magic, and my head began to buzz. After a fourth thread of earth magic, I felt like my insides were swelling too big for my skin.

"Let it out," Lynnette said. "Exhale and direct it at me."

I did as she said, blowing out slowly and raising my dominant hand. I intended to send the magic outward at the triangular magic hologram she'd formed in the air as a target, but a fifth woman joined in and I couldn't hold it. A flash of green throbbed down my arm, off the tip of my index finger, and smacked against the concrete floor just in front of Lynnette's Doc Martens. The sound was like two large rocks smacking together, and a few bits of concrete flew up.

My hand flew up to cover my mouth. "Oh damn, your floor."

"No worries," she said. "You almost had it. Let's try again."

We repeated the exercise, but this time I accidentally let the magic leak down through my feet and back into the earth, grounding it instead of conducting it.

On the third try, I managed to direct a stream from myself to Lynnette, but only for a second before I lost my focus and sent it spraying wide. The women behind Lynnette ducked, but one of them wasn't fast enough and got clubbed in the forehead with a blob of green energy. She looked a little dazed when she stood but wasn't upset.

I, however, was completely freaked out. What if it had been a bigger blast of earth energy? What if it had been *fire* magic?

I drew a ragged breath. "Mind if we take ten?" I asked.

"Not at all," Lynnette said with a surprisingly patient look.

I waited until the women were milling around and talking in small groups before I started speaking.

"This is dangerous, Lynnette. I know you have your reasons for wanting me here and keeping me in your coven, but I could seriously hurt some of them. What in the world could be worth that? You need someone who's experienced. Someone who's *meant* to be here."

She regarded me for a moment, her kohl-lined eyes unblinking. "This is part of being in a coven, Ella. Sometimes we hurt each other, be it with careless words or misfired magic. That's what happens when you're close to people. It's okay. We all know this. We've all accepted the risk because we also know the rewards. All you have to do is accept them, too."

I pressed my lips into a hard line, looking straight back at her. But for a second I couldn't breathe through the tightness in my chest. The thing was, I still didn't *want* this coven. *I didn't want to be here.*

But I realized the others were depending on me. And yes, even knowing that I might weaken the group in some ways or even injure them, they accepted me. Lynnette wasn't going to let me out of the agreement. And even if she changed her mind at some point, I was in it until after the new moon.

They were giving me their trust. In return, I had to give them my best. And I had to be okay with the knowledge that I was going to fail over and over and possibly even hurt some of them in the process.

I didn't like it. I hated it, actually. I despised feeling so vulnerable, so intertwined with a dozen other people.

But I was going to do my damnedest to embrace it.

"Collective magic requires thirteen of us. I believe with the double focus configuration and some intense drilling together, nothing will be able to beat us," she said. "Remember, let it all *flow* through you. It's a river of energy, and you need do nothing more than let it flow from them, through you, to me. When you can do that easily, you'll add your own magic to the river."

The next couple of tries went a little better, but by then I was so drained I couldn't do much more. By the time Deb and I trudged out to my truck, I was shivering and dragging ass. I started the truck but didn't pull away.

"You need healing before you go to bed tonight," she said. She pulled out her phone and began to scroll through her contacts. "I'd do it or get one of the others to do it, but we're all a little tired right now. I'm sure I can find someone outside the coven who's still up."

I placed a hand on her phone, stopping her. "I have to tell you something."

I repeated what had happened after my last healing and didn't leave anything out. I told her how the reaper had looked upon the clinic healer's soul like it was a free steak and lobster dinner, how I'd scooted out of the clinic to keep from trying to reap a live woman's soul.

"I know I need healing, but last time it fueled the reaper's hunger so strongly I could barely contain it," I said. "If healing amps the reaper's strength, then I have to be ready for that. I might be able to hold it off for a while, but it's only through sheer willpower. It's gaining strength. Eventually, the reaper will demand to do its work."

She frowned with concern, but at least she didn't look horrified. The entire thing still turned my stomach.

"It might not be the same this time," she said. "Before, it was after you'd battled the Baelman, which nearly killed you. Plus, if you didn't tell the healer about your reaper soul, she may have read *it* as something that needed healing. Maybe she inadvertently stoked it with power. Yet another argument for letting me find you a referral instead of walking into any old Supernatural Urgent Care clinic."

She gave me a pointed, sidelong look.

I squirmed like I'd been caught stealing a ten from my mom's wallet. "Yeah, you might have a point there."

"In any case, you only need a small fraction of the healing you needed after the Baelman. That combined with the right healer who has a better understanding of your circumstances might make the whole thing go a lot smoother."

I dialed up the heater, shifted the truck into gear, and pulled away from the curb.

"I don't know, Deb. That's a whole lot of ifs, mights, and maybes."

"You only need a bit of restoration tonight," she said. "Let me do it."

I started to protest, but she held up her hand.

"I'll do the bare minimum you need, and we'll see how that goes," she said. "I can do another session in the morning."

"But what about you?" I asked.

"I'll be fine. Tonight's crafting didn't really tax me. I could do it all over again and still not require healing."

Deb performed about twenty minutes of healing on me, and the entire time I was braced for the soul-hunger to flood in. But when she finished, I only felt an echo of the voracious need I'd felt after my clinic healing. I lay awake for a while on the foldout bed in the living room, allowing Deb some peace in my bedroom, waiting for the feeling to grow. It never did, and exhaustion eventually claimed me.

The rude jangle of my phone awoke me sooner than I would have liked.

"Damien?" I answered, my voice scratchy.

"It's out in the desert." His voice was hoarse but excited.

I sat up, glancing at the closed bedroom door. "What's out in the desert?"

"The place where the Baelmen will emerge on Samhain," he said impatiently, as if I should have known what he was talking about. "Put your phone on speaker and look at the link I just sent to you."

I did as he instructed, tapping the link that popped up and expanding the picture.

"It's a satellite image," he said. "Gregori owns a chunk of that land. And it has some history. Natives used it for death-spirit ceremonies. It used to be tribe owned, but due to the bad magic associated with the area, they were more than happy to sell it off. There's some pretty fricking creepy lore about this area, too."

I scrolled around in the image. It was boring, visually speaking. Just a bunch of rocky, hilly high desert.

"Did you stay up all night working on this?" I asked.

"Yeah."

"How sure are you that this is the place?"

"Ninety percent," he said. "I need to do some more verification."

I moved past the bounds of the area Damien had marked with a blue dotted line, searching around the perimeter for any landmarks or distinguishing features. I scanned about fifty miles to the west, and something popped up.

I stared at it, and an ice cube seemed to drop down my spine.

I was looking at something *familiar*. It was only a small length of fence and a corner of what might be a house. The rest, where the remaining parts of the house should have been, showed only flat desert. It was as if the rest of the building had been cut off with the sharp edge of a blade. Or mostly masked using some image manipulation.

But certainty swelled like a tide inside my chest. I was looking at the edge of the compound where my brother Evan was being held.

"Did you manipulate the image at all?" I asked Damien.

"No, just added the blue line to show the demarcation of Gregori property," he said. "Why?"

"Go west sixty or seventy miles." I paused. "Do you see it? It looks like the corner of a structure."

"Yeah . . . huh . . . that's weird. This is from the government satellite shots that are available online. Someone's obviously messed with it. Maybe it's a bomb-testing site or some other military facility they don't want civilians gawking at?"

"I don't think so," I said. "Remember when I told you I believed Evan was in a vampire feeder den in some isolated place?"

"Yeaaah . . ." He drew the word out into a question.

"I'm pretty sure that's it."

"I'm not trying to stomp on your cupcake, but how could you possibly tell?" he asked. "There's barely anything there."

"I just knew as soon as I saw it that I'd seen it before. From one of the visions of Evan. Where is this, anyway?"

"It's out in the Nevada desert. That's why I thought it might be military. I'll send you the exact coordinates."

Damn. It was too far away for a day trip by car. I was hoping he'd say Idaho, or even Utah might have been manageable. I couldn't ditch the nightly coven activities to do an overnight trip.

My mind had shifted to thoughts of Evan, but I couldn't focus solely on my brother. Not with what we were facing at Samhain. I felt torn.

"This is amazing work, Damien. I have no doubt you're on the right track. You should catch some sleep, and I'll run interference for you at the SC precinct check-in. What do you want me to tell them about all this?"

"Nothing, just yet," he said around a yawn. "Let me look into a few more things that should increase my certainty about this hypothesis. I'll know better later today."

A few minutes after I hung up with Damien, Deb was up. She did another light healing session, and then we got dressed and I drove her out to her house to pick up some more things. I offered to come in, but she told me she preferred to go in alone. Keith and I had butted heads plenty in the past, so it was probably a wise call on her part. After about fifteen minutes she emerged pulling a large suitcase on wheels.

"How'd it go?" I asked as I helped her swing her luggage into the back of the truck.

"He begged me to stay and talk," she said. "But I told him there'd been plenty of time for that, and I wasn't interested in more empty promises."

My brows shot up as we got in. "Wow, that was gutsy."

She looked at me, her blue eyes suddenly doubtful. "Was it too mean?"

"No! I'm really proud of you."

She nodded and heaved a deep sigh. I could tell she didn't want to talk, so I kept sliding glances at her all the way home, trying to gauge how she was feeling. She appeared sober but also surprisingly peaceful.

I helped her get the suitcases inside and then left by myself to report to the Supernatural Crimes precinct.

Since I couldn't give them Damien's new information yet, I didn't really have anything to contribute to the briefing. I told Barnes that Damien was following up on a very strong lead and would let her know that afternoon what he'd found.

After the briefing, I got in my truck in the SC parking lot but didn't start the engine. I found Rogan in my contacts and called him.

"Hey, does this sound like a good candidate for the birthplace of a horde of Baelmen?" I described the spot that Damien had identified.

"Yes . . . yes, I think I know the location," he said. "I can't believe I didn't think of it. Your friend is quite a researcher."

"That he is. He'll be glad to have your confirmation." I paused, fiddling with the zipper on my jacket as an impulsive thought occurred to me. "After the business with the Baelmen is taken care of, would you be interested in helping me with a—well, a personal mission? There'd be some danger. Vampires."

He made a scoffing noise. "I'm impervious to vampires."

"So you're interested?"

"Sure, why the hell not. What is it?"

"I want to break my brother out of a feeder den. It's actually in the vicinity of the spot we're talking about."

"I'm in," he said without hesitation.

A slow grin tugged at my lips.

When I talked to Damien just before dinnertime, he told me he'd found information indicating that Gregori Industries was planning to move equipment or something to Nevada in the next week. He was all but certain that he had the location of Jacob's ugly Samhain surprise.

I relayed all of it to Lagatuda and told him that Damien would be happy to fill them in. And that night at the coven meeting, I told Lynnette we had the last piece of the puzzle.

A wicked smile came over her face.

"We'll just have to disappear before SC can get us on lockdown. Then we'll reappear in Nevada." She wiggled her gray-polished fingers in the air. "Like magic. And they won't be able to do a damn thing about it."

Things went slightly better in the circle that night, with me and Lynnette acting as a double focus. We moved our practice outside, and I managed to stream the circle's small bits of earth magic to her. Lynnette directed the power of the circle at targets she'd set up, a few ten-foot-high stacks of wood pallets, which were obliterated to sawdust each time she blasted them with the collective magic of the circle.

The third time, I threaded the circle's magic through the center of my chest, the spot where it felt like the reaper soul resided. With a jolt, I felt my newly discovered magic awaken. When my own blood-red power joined the stream, I gritted my teeth as lightning seemed to strike my organs. But I held on, and the collective magic flowed from me to Lynnette. She gasped and stiffened when it hit her but handled it without a glitch.

When the exercise was over, there was a burst of questions from the group.

Elena's voice rose above the rest. "What on god's green earth was *that*?" She tossed a wave of her elbow-length dark hair over her shoulder and stood with her chest out and her arms folded.

I saw Deb shifting out of the corner of my eye, but I didn't want her to feel as if she had to defend me.

I faced Elena with my hands on my hips. "You may have heard I temporarily died a while back. When I came to, there was something new. A different type of magic."

She squinted at me. "It's not like Jennifer's hot pink vamp magic."

"No, it's something different. Call it underworld magic, if you like," I said, using Rogan's term.

She nodded and gave a tiny shrug. "Cool. Anything we have in the coven that's rare gives us an edge."

The others seemed to agree. I wasn't going to reveal the part about the reaper soul unless forced to. And I planned to be out of the coven before we got to the point of spilling our every deep, dark secret to each other, anyway.

Even though my skill in the circle seemed to be improving, I began to have second thoughts about our plan. Since we knew where the Baelmen would appear on Samhain and it wasn't nearby, maybe the witches *should* step aside and let SC take care of it. They witches could still hide out together, but not go to Nevada to face the threat head-on.

It wasn't that I wanted to back away from a fight. It was more the sense that our options had opened up slightly, now that we knew the threat was more remote distance-wise. Out in the desert, SC would have the space to bring down the creatures without threatening civilian lives. They could turn on all their firepower full-throttle. And the witches could stay here in Lynnette's place. They could turn it into a fortress. I was sure I could talk Damien into staying, too. His magical prowess would be another weapon in our favor, in case they had to defend themselves.

I'd make it sound as if I planned to stay with them, but there was no way I'd miss out on the battle. I'd slip away and head to Nevada on my own. I was the only one who'd killed a Baelman, and SC needed me. If I could get Lagatuda on my side, I was sure I could convince Barnes that I should be on the front lines.

At the end of our practice session, I proposed it to Lynnette. She listened to my argument but with a gleam in her eye that put me on edge.

"I appreciate what you're saying." When she crossed her arms, I knew she was going to go against my suggestion. "But we as a coven have a huge opportunity. I know you're new to all of this, but let me put it this way. We're about to finalize our charter. At that point, we'll be trying to bring in as much work as possible, in the form of requests for our services. If we defeat the Baelmen on Samhain, it's going to be big news in the supernatural world *and* in the normal world. Enormous free publicity for the coven. Then, we'll be golden."

"But surely there are other ways to bring in business that don't put everyone at such a huge risk," I said.

"Ella, do you have any idea how many covens fail financially in their first year? There is a *lot* of competition out there. The fees I charge for exorcisms and my other services will go into the coven's revenue once the charter is official. But even with my rates, I can't single-handedly support thirteen witches plus the operating costs of the coven."

I pulled back, affronted. "I certainly don't expect you to support *me*. I'll still have my job with Demon Patrol."

"Your paycheck will go into the collective revenue of the coven. All coven income is distributed equally among the members on a monthly basis, after operating expenses."

"What!" My voice strained with outrage. "You never told me that was part of the deal!"

She arched a brow. "It wouldn't have mattered. You were joining us regardless. Remember?"

I turned on my heel and stalked away. It was either that or punch her in her smug, cherry red-lipsticked mouth. I forced myself to calm down, but I wasn't going to give up so easily. I just had to think of a way to circumvent Lynnette.

Anger actually seemed to help my crafting, and I was able to go longer without tiring. Back at home, Deb did a light healing session. We'd decided that smaller, more frequent healing would be safer. And since I'd had no trouble since she'd started helping me counteract the effects of crafting, we also thought it would be best if I didn't switch healers. A couple times a week, she would go to a practitioner outside the coven who specialized in healing during pregnancy.

After Deb was done with me, I told her about my exchanges with Lynnette.

"It's not right," I said. "She doesn't need to be risking everyone this way."

A faint mix of surprise and amusement crossed her face. "Look at you, the champion for the conservative route. I guess you've met your match." She trilled a little giggle.

I threw her a bitter look, which just made her laugh more.

"Seriously, don't you think it's stupid on her part?" I pressed.

Her mirth faded, and she looked down at her hands. "It's risky, yeah. But as head of the coven, it's her responsibility to do everything she can to ensure its success. She's ambitious, and it's one of the reasons I aligned myself with her."

"Lynnette isn't your only hope for independence. There are other—"

"Yes, actually, she *is*," Deb interrupted. Her face tightened, and her cheeks began to flush. "I'm probably going to have to declare bankruptcy to divorce Keith. My teaching salary is basically peanuts. I've got a baby coming, Ella, and I don't even have a damn *car* anymore. How in the world do you think I'm going to manage if I don't have the coven?"

I raised my palms in surrender. "Okay, let's just talk about it. I'm sure we can come up with something."

"No, you don't understand. I already have come up with

something—the coven," she said vehemently. She rose. "Just because you don't like it, or you have a problem with Lynnette, doesn't mean it isn't the right choice for me. I need this. I need *them*. So please, just stop trying to pull me away from something that's really, really important to me, okay?"

Her eyes welled as she turned, stormed into my bedroom, and then shut the door with a heavy thud.

I stood in the living room, staring at the door. Loki whimpered and came up and nudged my hand, and I absently scratched his head.

Why did it seem like things were suddenly unraveling? It was like I'd completely lost control of everything. I wasn't sure who I was more pissed with—Barnes, Lynnette, Deb, Jacob Gregori . . . or myself. But I was more and more sure that I needed to find a way to keep Lynnette from putting the coven in harm's way. The publicity wasn't worth the risk.

I only had three days to figure out how to foil her.

The next morning when I got back from my run, Deb was pale and withdrawn. I made eggs and toast while she was in the shower and insisted she sit down and eat them with a mug of the icky tea she loved.

I sat down across from her.

"I'm not going to try to force you to leave the coven," I said. "But I don't intend to stay. It just isn't me, and I know you see that. I hope none of this has to affect our friendship, though. We've been in each other's lives a long time, including since you became friends with the women in the coven. Things are changing, yes, but . . . we've been through lots of changes before."

I'd left a question hanging in the air between us—the question of whether we could continue to be friends the way we had up to now—and I realized that if things changed between me and Deb, it would crush me. There was a lot I could live without, many things other people seemed to desire and I'd never really felt I needed, but I needed Deb.

She looked down into her mug for a couple of seconds and then up at me. Her blue eyes were wide and sincere.

"You and I will be okay, Ella," she said. "The coven doesn't replace *us*."

The sudden loosening in my chest prevented me from speaking right away. I just nodded and sipped my coffee.

I set my cup down and looked around. "We're going to need a bigger place," I said. "Kind of a shame, the rent is really cheap in this building."

She lifted a shoulder. "It'll all work out."

The next couple of days were mostly an odd lull of routine, except for one glitch. Barnes denied my request to join the team in Nevada. It pissed me off but ultimately didn't change my plans. I didn't need an engraved invitation from Barnes to go to Nevada.

I showed up at the SC meetings with Damien, but after he gave them his info on the desert location, we didn't have much to contribute. I talked to Rogan a couple of times, hoping he had more news about what Jacob had in store for Samhain, but Rogan's network wasn't spilling any more details.

Our collective magic drills tightened up as I was able to handle larger amounts of magic with better control. The women were still only feeding me a trickle compared to what they could have done when directing it all at Lynnette, but when we reached the point where each woman fed in a greater amount of magic than I would have as a non-focus, I knew Lynnette had made the right choice in moving me to secondary focus. Our collective power was becoming more potent, and even I had to admit that it was pretty damn cool to watch Lynnette obliterate a large pyramid of rocks, all bigger than my head, with a flick of her fingers. I mean, those rocks practically ceased to exist—blasted so hard with earth magic and a few twists of fire that they exploded into a cloud of particles.

She'd set up sound-dampening wards around her property, and it was a good thing because the noise of the blasts was deafening.

Shame that I would have to fix it so that we wouldn't be using our collective magic against Jacob's Samhain surprises. In spite of the progress, I still had no intention of putting the coven in the middle of a battle out in the Nevada desert. Lynnette wanted to endanger the women for the sake of publicity, and I could no longer trust that she even believed the collective magic would be enough to protect them. I didn't believe she truly cared about the women as individuals. She'd quickly replaced Amanda with me, and there were plenty of other women who would leap at the chance to join the coven if a few of the current members happened to die in battle. The witches were just cogs in her grand plans for a dominant coven.

The morning before Samhain and the new moon was several degrees warmer than normal. I savored it on my morning run, knowing that soon I'd be forced indoors to the treadmill.

Things had gone back to normal between me and Deb, but what I had planned was going to piss her off big time. I could only hope that eventually she would see I did it because I wanted her to be safe.

I'd consulted with Damien and every online resource I could find to be sure I was correct about my understanding of my coven's collective magic. Though the charter wasn't yet official, we'd been sealed to each other via the little ceremony with the locket that Lynnette wore. The only way the coven's group magic would work was if every member was present and participating. So, if at least one member was unaccounted for at the time that Lynnette wanted to take off for Nevada, the coven couldn't make the trip.

Well, they *could* make the trip, but they wouldn't be able to use collective magic. My plan was based on the assumption that Lynnette wouldn't be so stupid as to take the coven into the middle of the Samhain shit-storm without the power and protection of the group's collective magic.

I hated the thought of ditching them, and part of me felt like a traitor. I could hardly believe I'd come around to agreeing with Barnes and SC about not involving the coven. I wasn't succumbing to the house arrest they wanted to impose, but it still irked me that I was basically going along with their desire to keep the women all swept out of the way.

The hardest part was going to be slipping away from Deb. The coven was supposed to convene at Lynnette's. From there, we'd pile into the three rented SUVs that she had hidden in her huge garage and then caravan away.

The new moon wasn't exact until around dawn the following day, and SC was planning to put us under guard just after sundown tonight. Lynnette had given SC the impression that the coven would be complying with the house arrest, and I almost felt a little guilty that they'd be suckered into her ploy. Someone was sure to get in trouble when SC discovered that none of the witches were at home where they were supposed to be.

When Deb and I had our overnight bags packed and were about to leave my place for Lynnette's, my phone went off with a loud jangle.

"Damn, Barnes and Lagatuda want me and Damien to come by," I said, keeping my head down as I pretended to send back a reply to the fake message I'd set up to ping my phone. I carefully averted my eyes. I was a terrible liar, and I knew it.

"Oh no, why?" she said. "They don't suspect that we're up to something, do they?"

"I don't think so, but I'd better go just to make it look good," I said. "Take my truck to Lynnette's, and I'll get Damien to give me a ride and then drop me when we're done at SC."

"Okay, good idea," she said. "I'll see you at Lynnette's."

I slumped with relief when I heard the truck rumble away. Deb almost always knew when I was up to something, but she must have been preoccupied with the coven's covert mission.

I ditched the overnight bag and got my backpacking pack from the pantry where I'd hidden it. I held Loki's face in my hands.

"Damien's going to check on you while I'm gone," I said. I kissed the top of his head. "Be a good boy."

Then I went to the back yard where my mountain bike was chained to the gas line that went into the side of the house. I unlocked it, kicked away the leaves that had collected around the tires, and swung my pack onto my back.

I let myself out of the gate and then hopped onto my bike and headed toward Foothills East. When I was a few blocks away from my place, I stopped and pulled out my phone. I scrolled to the app that allowed SC to track me and communicate with me through their system and deleted it. Then I restarted my phone, just to make sure the change stuck, and shoved it back into the pocket on the side of my thigh. Lagatuda would be furious with me, and Barnes would probably blow a gasket when they figured out I'd deleted their app, but tomorrow was the last day I was on the SC payroll anyway.

I also sent a text to Rogan: *I got away and am heading to the cave.*

I'd managed to recruit Rogan to go with me to Nevada. I had no qualms about involving him because he couldn't be hurt. And if by some strange fluke he did get killed in the battle, it was what he wanted anyway.

I pedaled hard, keeping to alleys and side streets, in case SC noticed I'd dropped off their sensors and decided to come looking for me right away.

By the time I turned off the paved road onto the dirt lane leading to Tablerock, my shirt was glued to my back with sweat under my pack. I stopped and walked my bike away from the road, down a slope so that no one driving by would see me.

I stopped to catch my breath and tap out a text to Damien. First, I turned off all GPS and locator functions on my phone.

Deb is going to be looking for me, and she'll be pissed, but I can't let her or the rest of the coven know where I am. I'm fine, just not playing into Lynnette's plan to force the coven into the middle of a battle. I swear I'm okay, so please don't worry. Check on Loki tonight?

I was a little earlier than the time I'd arranged to meet with Rogan. My eyes kept flicking to the sky, searching for the black-winged shapes of his demon pets.

Reluctantly, I pulled out my phone. There was a text from

Damien that said he thought it was dangerous for me to be in a location no one knew about. And there was a missed call from him.

And then there were the texts from Deb. I read through a few of them but then tucked my phone away. It would only make me feel guilty and anxious to keep reading the messages that I had to ignore.

I stood on a rock so I could see the sun lowering toward the horizon. The sky turned peachy over the city, and I watched as night fell. I knew there would be a lot of people furious with me later, but for the moment I almost felt peaceful.

My phone stopped vibrating for a while, but then it started up again. This time, it was Deb trying to call. Three calls, and then nothing.

Alarm pinged in the back of my mind. She'd left a voice message. I played it.

There was rustling and a scream in the background. My heart lurched.

"Ella, the Baelmen have found us!" Her voice was raw with panic. "I don't know how they got here early, but we're—"

The call had cut off, ending the message.

My hands shaking, I dialed Rogan and he picked up on the first ring.

"The Baelmen are attacking the coven. I'm at our meeting point. I'm going to start running back down the road. Please, leave now and look for me!"

"I'm on my way."

I let my bike tip to the ground, tore off my pack and dropped it, and began sprinting. I ran, my shoes pounding the pavement in the weakening light of dusk. Headlights glared in my eyes, and a car scraped to a fast stop next to me. It was an old Jeep, and Rogan was at the wheel. I threw myself into the passenger seat.

"The Baelmen," I panted.

"I know," he said grimly. "They're early."

"How?"

"Not sure. Gregori may have stashed a few away, somehow. I can't imagine they're the Samhain Baelmen. Even Jacob Gregori doesn't have the ability to speed up time."

I called Damien and told him what was happening and where I was headed. He took off for Lynnette's.

Then I dialed Lagatuda.

"We've been trying to locate you for hours. What the hell happened?" he demanded.

"The Baelmen are here," I said, ignoring his question. "Lynnette Leblanc's house. I'm headed there now."

There was a second of shocked silence. "But that's not possible."

"I know, and yet it's happening," I said flatly, finally starting to catch my breath.

He let out a string of curse words. "We've already deployed the team to Nevada."

"How far out are they?"

"Too far to help us in the next few minutes," he said, talking fast. "I've gotta call the higher-ups and get them to turn around. I'll call you back."

He disconnected.

I turned to Rogan, who was swerving around cars and gunning the engine whenever the road was clear ahead.

"All of the resources were deployed to Nevada," I said. My stomach plummeted as the reality of it really sank in. "Lagatuda is getting his bosses to call them back, but I don't think they'll arrive in time to be much help. I think we're on our own."

I grabbed the ceiling handle near the top of the door and braced my other hand against the dash as he began disregarding stop signs and red lights, laying on the horn and weaving through the traffic.

When he slammed to a stop in front of Lynnette's place, we jumped out. Damien's Lexus screeched up to the curb right behind us, and he slammed the door and ran to where we stood. I squinted up at the looming house. It was completely dark and eerily silent.

"No," I choked out, and began running. "Please, please let us not be too late."

As soon as I crossed the magical threshold of Lynnette's home, sound exploded against my eardrums, and I realized the apparent silence had been due to her noise-dampening ward.

I reached for my whip and held it coiled in my hand as I burst through the front door.

Currents of magic buffeted me. I kept running, following the sounds of unearthly screeching, through the house and out the French doors to the back yard.

I pulled up short when I took in the scene. The women had formed a magic circle, but the glow of the sphere flickered every time it was hit by a neon-blue-laced blast of smoke-black magic from one of the hellish creatures swarming the yard.

The women were shooting magic out through the sphere, lighting up the yard like a fireworks show. But I could see they weren't going to be able to hold out for long. I quickly counted the Baelmen—six, I was fairly certain. Two dead on the ground and four still in flight.

"Ella! Get in the circle!" Deb was screaming at me.

"Go, I'll cover you," Damien said behind me.

Magic rushed over me and surrounded me in a multi-colored orb. Like a gerbil in an exercise ball, I began running across the yard toward the women. Two of the Baelmen dived at me, screaming and bouncing away when they impacted Damien's protective sphere.

When I was halfway to Deb and the others, the magic surrounding me faltered, and then it winked out. I looked over my shoulder to see Damien down on one knee. Rogan was defending himself and Damien against a Baelman trying to dive-bomb them like a demonic bird of prey. Damien looked dazed, but I couldn't turn back to see if he was hurt.

I pushed faster toward the women. Then a Baelman dropped to the ground in front of me, landing in a crouch.

I skidded to a stop, unfurled my whip, and grasped for earth and fire magic.

The creature looked up, its hellfire gaze trained on me, and its lips stretching to show its razor teeth. It raised an arm, flashing the curved sword-like bladed claws that grew off the end of each index finger. It almost seemed to savor the moment of our face-off.

It sprang at me with unearthly, blurring swiftness. My right arm came up, a reflex born of hours of practice, and sent the whip curling toward the Baelman as my magic flowed into it and amplified in the charmed weapon.

The creature leapt up, using its wings to propel the jump higher, just out of the way of the whip.

Then it changed direction and dove at me, baring its claws. Without time to lash out again, I took the defensive. I lunged and rolled out of the way at the last second and scrambled to my feet to see the Baelman gearing up for another dive.

The creature's wings froze, and it dropped straight down at me. My whip lashed out again. The Baelman dodged, but I could tell my weak elemental magic wasn't doing much to intimidate it.

It was out of reach of my whip. Screams from the circle drew my attention. I needed to end this. Eyeing one of the boulders left from Lynnette's magic target practice, I got a running start. I jumped up to the rock and pushed off to launch myself higher. Twisting in the air, I snapped my wrist again. The end of the whip caught the Baelman's ankle, curling around it. As I crashed back down to the ground, I yanked as hard as I could before the creature could react to stay aloft. It flailed its wings but couldn't catch air. With a screech, it landed on its back.

In the next blink I realized I was bathed in a pulsing halo of maroon magic. A current of it shot down the whip and surrounded the Baelman, too. It went rigid as I quickly penetrated its mind.

There was someone it called "father" or "maker"—actually, some combination of the two words in a language I only understood through the creature's understanding. The Baelman's maker had given it one purpose in life, to kill Lynnette and her coven. The faces of the women flashed like a slideshow, whirling through the creature's mind. I had a split-second to see that I was not included among them, but Amanda was.

Rogan was right. This Baelman must have been created earlier and had been given its mission some time ago, before Amanda had been killed. And Jacob had not kept his word about Deb—her face was on the hit list.

With a spike of adrenaline, I realized my whip had nearly

sliced clean through the creature's ankle. I gave it one more yank, and then the Baelman was free, leaving its severed foot behind and frantically taking flight as white liquid frothed and dripped off the end of its leg.

I took the opening to race the rest of the way to the magic circle. A vertical white line appeared in the sphere, and I squinted against its brightness. It was an opening, a slice barely wide enough for me to slip through.

"Hurry!" Deb screamed.

I turned sideways and threw myself inside the protective sphere shoulder-first, stumbling and crashing into a couple of the women. They righted me and then pushed me forward into the center, near Lynnette.

"I won't be able to hold the circle when the collective magic hits me," she called out to us. "I'll have to drop it."

I nodded, already opening myself to receive and channel the streams of magic from the other women. I let it swell, building up until it was almost painful, and then raised my right hand and opened the floodgate. Fire magic, earth magic, and my own blood-red energy streamed from my fingertips to the triangular hologram that Lynnette appeared to hold floating between her hands as a target.

The protective half-sphere around us winked out, and the Baelmen were ready. There were three left in flight—Rogan and Damien must have killed one—and they descended on us.

Lynnette turned and whipped a giant boulder of magic at the nearest one, and it exploded in a fiery burst of magic sparks, leathery skin, and white goo. I reeled as her blast seemed to create a vacuum in our collective magic, sucking more of it through me.

One down, two to go.

The remaining creatures pulled back when their comrade was obliterated. They circled higher, apparently regrouping. Lynnette was taking aim, but they were high enough that they were difficult to spot in the dark of the night.

When they dove, it was clear they were aiming for Lynnette. Twin streaks of pale flesh and wing, accompanied by glass-shattering screams. They separated, obviously trying to evade one big hit, but Lynnette was ready. Her hands moved apart, and two more holograms formed. I kept streaming magic into the central one, and the power amplified from the central hologram into the other two.

She pushed her palms outward, and there were two ground-shaking booms. The Baelmen vaporized. There was literally nothing left of them except an oily mist and the smell of death in the air.

Victory flashed hot in my chest, even as the chill of magical exhaustion descended over me like a cloak of snow.

Shivering, I rushed to Deb. We fell into each other's arms, but there was no time to celebrate.

Around us, women were collapsing. Some stayed on their feet, and bent to try to help the others. Deb and I hurried over.

"We didn't close the circle right away," Deb said, her voice hoarse and shaking. Her face grim, she lifted Elena's limp wrist to check her pulse. "Some of the women expended themselves early.

Their bodies and minds have shut down as a defense mechanism."

"Are they going to be okay?" I asked.

"If they get emergency healing, they should be. Let's get them inside."

We focused on working together to lift Elena.

"They protected me," Deb said softly as we carried the unconscious woman. Elena's long hair trailed along the ground. We walked around a still-bubbling puddle of pale Baelman blood. "Because I'm pregnant. They didn't want me to endanger the baby."

The look on her face—a teary mix of guilt and gratitude—nearly broke my heart.

Dazed, those of us still conscious carried the collapsed witches inside, and Rogan and Damien helped. There were two more Baelman corpses near the house. I hadn't even realized that more creatures had arrived. That made eight dead Baelmen in total.

"You guys killed these ones?" I asked Damien.

He nodded, and I swallowed hard, looking up at the sky. I knew we'd killed them all—I'd sense any live ones if they were nearby—but I couldn't help wondering if there were more out there.

Damien was pale and winced when he moved but seemed mostly okay. Rogan appeared completely unharmed and untouched by magical exhaustion.

"I've got three Level III healers on the way," Lynnette said as we all scrambled for blankets to cover the unconscious witches.

She knelt next to Jennifer, whose freckles stood out on her slack, pale face and took her limp hand. Lynnette pressed it between her palms for a moment. She went around to each fallen witch, worrying over them with unexpected softness.

The healers arrived and began working on the unconscious women first. Lagatuda and Barnes came not long after with an SC crime scene crew that took care of the Baelman bodies in the yard.

I huddled under a quilt next to Deb on one of Lynnette's velvet sofas, watching all of it as if it was something happening far away. Deb seemed equally dazed. The healers spent hours on the unconscious women and eventually moved their still forms into bedrooms to allow them to keep recuperating away from all the commotion.

"Are they really going to be okay?" I asked Deb.

"If the healers know what they're doing, the women will wake up with the equivalent of bad concussions. Dangerous if they don't take it easy for a while, but with the proper rest and care, they should all recover. I'm sure they'll be fine. Lynnette called in the best."

When the healers were ready to turn to the rest of us, I prompted Deb to go before me. Objectively speaking, I probably had a worse case of magical exhaustion due to my low aptitude and resulting low threshold, but I was wary of letting anyone but Deb heal me.

The healers worked through the night, and at some point I drifted off for a few minutes. I awoke to Deb's hand on my arm. She had me lie down and performed some light healing, which lulled me into the floaty space between sleep and wakefulness.

"How are the others?" I asked after she finished.

I sat up, feeling some of the fog of magical exhaustion lifting.

We weren't doing deep healing, to avoid waking the soul-hunger, so I was still chilled and a little slow thinking.

"They're sleeping now. Real sleep, not a burnout coma," she said.

"Oh. That's good." I scrubbed my hands up and down my face. "How did you guys end up in the yard? When the Baelmen attacked?"

"Lynnette wanted to do a little ritual while we waited for you," Deb said. "For strength. We were out there when they came."

"I'm sorry, Deb."

She closed her eyes and shook her head. "No, don't be. If we'd been on the road when the Baelmen attacked us, it would have been so much worse. We would've been separated in different cars, maybe even miles apart. Because we were waiting for you, we were delayed. But it meant we were together. We were able to fight them together as a coven. And Rogan and Damien . . ."

She gave a little sigh.

"I don't understand where all the Baelmen came from," I said. "We're still, what, hours away from the official new moon?"

She looked at her phone and frowned. "Actually, we're right on top of the new moon."

I stood abruptly, swiveling around and searching for Lagatuda. Not finding him among the people sitting and milling in the main living spaces, I went out to the back yard.

I found him holding a little notepad and pencil, making notes. The crime scene people were still working, snapping pictures, recording video, and taking samples of the Baelman gore left behind in the grass.

"Hey." I hurried over to him. "We just hit the new moon. What's the word from Nevada? Is Jacob Gregori cooking anything out there in the desert or what?"

He looked up, his eyes distracted for a moment. Then his gaze sharpened, and he shook his left sleeve back to check his wristwatch.

Before he could respond, his jacket pocket began blaring a harsh emergency signal. He pulled out his phone and began running toward the house. I wheeled and ran after him, trying to catch any snippet of what was going on.

Deb stood up, alarmed.

"What's going on?" she said.

"I don't think this is over. He's on the phone with Nevada!" I said to her over my shoulder as I followed Lagatuda out through the front door.

There was a fancy, high-tech SCSI van like the one that had been parked outside Jennifer's house on the curb, and Lagatuda was beelining toward it with his wool trench coat flapping around his long legs.

I skidded to a stop next to him as Barnes came out of the van.

Both of them were shouting into their phones, and my attention ping-ponged between them.

"You're estimating *how* many of them?" Lagatuda demanded.

Barnes was shaking her head. ". . . containment percentage can't be correct . . ."

"How long do we have?" Lagatuda asked and listened for a

second.

Then he lowered his phone, even though whoever was on the line was still speaking. His eyes were full of dread.

"We need to secure the women," he said to me. "A horde of Baelmen is headed here."

"How long?" I echoed his question.

He blinked a few times. "I don't know how it's possible, but they're moving at a rate—"

"*When will they get here?*" I interrupted.

"We've got twenty minutes. Twenty-five tops. They're estimating hundreds of creatures."

$\mathcal{P}$art of the Nevada team had been recalled here, but some had already been stationed near the Gregori Industries property in the desert.

The SC people were scurrying around red-faced and shouting into their phones. I left the bureaucratic chaos behind and sprinted back into Lynnette's house. I found her and then frantically waved Damien over. Rogan trailed behind him.

"We're not done," I said, my heart pounding like a jackhammer. "Gregori hatched a horde of Baelmen in Nevada, and they're headed here now."

Lynnette's mouth dropped open, and her makeup-smudged eyes widened.

"But the women." She gestured toward the hallway that led to the bedrooms where the witches were recuperating.

"Yeah, we're not going to be able to rely on collective magic. New plan." I glanced at Rogan. "You up for this?"

His brows twitched up in anticipation, and his eyes gleamed. "Oh, yes."

He and I were the only ones who stood a real chance against the horde. He couldn't be killed, and I was pretty sure my reaper wasn't going to let me die, either. The reaper couldn't keep me from frying my brain if I pushed myself into the danger zone of magical burnout, but we'd be sure to put up a hell of a fight up until that point.

I turned back to Lynnette and Damien. "You two are the strongest crafters here, and you're in decent enough shape to keep slinging magic if you have to. Work out a plan with whoever else is still standing to defend this place from the inside. Rogan and I are going to be out there. I assume SC will gather all the forces they can, but we've only got twenty minutes, and I don't know how fast they can slash through the red tape."

Lynnette clapped her hands sharply and began hurriedly waving over the other witches, including Deb. My best friend listened to Lynnette for a moment and then Deb's eyes found mine. She looked terrified.

I blinked hard and turned to Rogan. "Okay. We need a strategy that doesn't rely on huge amounts of magical power because I'm a little lacking in that area."

"We have other tools at our disposal," he said. If I didn't know better, I'd guess he was relishing the thought of this fight. Or maybe he was hoping it would finally be his end, and he could escape his earthly form and get back to the *in-between*.

"Demons," I said. "Would arch-demons be any kind of match for Baelmen?"

"Depends on who's driving them," he said. "How many can you control at once?"

"Uhh . . . I've actually never driven an arch-demon before," I admitted. "You?"

There were the sounds of sirens in the distance, and I heard voices on megaphones out front. It sounded like they were trying to initiate a lock-down protocol in the neighborhood. At least it was early on Halloween morning. I couldn't bear to think about what might happen if the timing were different, if the streets were full of little kids out trick-or-treating.

"A few dozen," he said. "Maybe more if I'm really on."

I gaped at him. "A few *dozen*? Do you realize that makes you one of the most highly skilled necromancers in the world? You might even give Phillip Zarella a run for his money."

He modestly shrugged a shoulder.

"Okay, we've gotta tell SC so they can inform everyone that we're going to have demons working on our side." I beckoned him to follow me outside. "Last thing we need is to have a Strike Team race in here and try to shoot down our weapons."

We informed Barnes that Rogan would be driving some arch-demons and told the detective to make sure everyone understood that unless an arch-demon went for a human the Rip spawn were to be left alone. Her mouth pinched in an unhappy grimace, but she nodded.

"There's only one problem," Rogan said. "I doubt there are that many arch-demons just roaming around here. In fact, there may not be any."

"*Shit*." I ground my teeth in frustration. "Wait, I think Lynnette might be able to help."

I could practically feel the clock ticking down as we ran back inside and looked for the exorcist witch. I explained our plan and our problem.

She nodded, looking grim. "I'm going to have to be out there with you to open a rip and summon arch-demons through it. I can't do it from within the house."

I didn't like the implications at all—either that she'd be outside and exposed, or that she could so readily produce a bunch of arch-demons for Rogan to drive. But it was what we needed, and I'd worry about the implications later. If we all survived.

Lagatuda burst through the front door. "We've got about eight minutes before the horde reaches the city limits. We're going to be on lockdown in our armored vehicles out front. Three mages are going to be projecting to this location, and they'll do what they can to help."

Mages projecting . . .? I didn't have time to ask for an explanation.

Lynnette started her own lockdown that erected magical shields over the doors and windows. Rogan and I followed her out into the backyard, and she shielded the door behind us.

"I'm going to open the rip directly overhead," she said, her eyes already unfocusing as she started to go into trance. "It might provide some cover from the horde, but it also puts us at risk because the arch-demons will be coming through very close. I hope you know what you're doing." She flicked a glance at Rogan.

He gave a single nod, already turning his attention within. Lynnette raised her hands, and above us a streak of black appeared, slashing a few feet across the pale light of early morning that illuminated the sky. I could see her lips moving but couldn't hear the words. The black line appeared to smoke, and it writhed like a snake. Then the center of it split open and began to widen. The smell of brimstone and death filled my nose, and my stomach tightened into a hard ball.

The rip widened, and the black smoke around the edges was shot through with bolts of neon blue. I felt the brush of magic. It stung my bare skin like lemon juice in a cut, and my eyes watered.

My reaper was responding, and the shadows framing my vision danced furiously. The cold, sickening feeling of the blood-red magic began to fill me, too. In the next blink I stood in the gray swirl of the *in-between*, where Rogan was a spectre bathed in blood-red power. I looked down to find that I appeared the same.

A low whir in the air pulled my attention to the world of the living. The noise swelled. I tipped my head back to look around the edges of Lynnette's rip.

High above, a moving dark blot smeared across the innocent pale blue of the pre-dawn sky. The blob was descending. The roar of the Baelmen horde's wings began to beat against my eardrums. It was starting to circle downward, forming a spiral of winged bodies that were indistinguishable from each other.

A black shape sprang through the rip, and I sensed Rogan reaching out for the arch-demon's mind. When the creature streaked upward to meet the leading edge of the horde, I knew he'd assumed control. Three more arch-demons came through, as if birthing from their dimension into ours, and Rogan caught their minds and sent them upward.

I held my whip in my hand, but if the horde got close enough for me to use it, we'd be doomed.

When the horde ripped the four arch-demons to nothing, my heart plummeted. There were too many Baelmen.

A white point of light streaked upward and then burst like a firework. A second later a booming report shook the ground and sent us staggering. Expanding like a giant web, the white light scooped at the horde like the yawning maw of a giant, hungry whale. When it closed around them, it began to shrink, tightening smaller and smaller until it winked out.

Mage magic. It had to be. No ordinary crafter had the power to enclose a hundred Baelmen and then squeeze them out of existence, not even Damien.

Another white spark lit in the sky, scooping more of the creatures. But this time, they knew what was coming and they scattered, rendering the spiral formation into a chaos of winged bodies.

The mages were focused on making broad grabs of the creatures, but dozens of strays were escaping their dragnets.

"The stragglers!" I shouted. "We need to focus on those!"

Panic swelled in my chest as I watched Baelmen begin to descend overhead. I had to do something. Rogan's demons weren't making a dent. Ground forces were starting to shoot at the individual creatures, but it was like throwing darts at a swarm of flies. I started to move my focus inward to reach for the maroon underworld magic when light caught my eye, and I glanced down to see that the sigils on my arms were glowing so intensely they shone through my clothes.

My arms throbbed, and again I flashed over to the *in-between*.

Somewhere in the back of my mind I remembered Roxanne telling me that the strange sigils on my arms had the feel of ley lines—rivers of magical energy that ran through the earth. In the *in-between*, I pulled at the pool of blood-red magic in the center of my chest and on instinct sent it into the glowing tattoos. The markings hovered in the air above my skeletal arms. Their light became blinding, and power surged through me. But there was something new, a sort of rhythmic ebb and flow that vibrated beneath my feet.

I sent my awareness downward, searching for the source of the pulse.

Deep below, there was a channel of power. I took in the vastness of it and lost my breath. Or maybe in the *in-between* I needed no air.

Understanding filled me: the *in-between* had its own ley lines. The sigils on my arms were the passwords to access the power.

My hands joined in front of me, and I read the sigils from left to right in a voice that sounded like nails scratching concrete. I didn't know what the words meant, but when I reached the last sigil, I reached my awareness out to the river of power. It rushed at me, into me, filling me.

It was like an electric tornado had burst to life in my blood vessels. My entire being pressurized with the onslaught. It was too much. If I couldn't squeeze the flow down, I'd explode.

I struggled, pushing against the rush of power. The pressure was building, and my every cell seemed strained to the edge of bursting.

I couldn't contain it, and I couldn't stop the tidal wave of power crashing into me. The screeches of Baelmen brought me back to the battle waging overhead in the dimension of the living. I was blinded by the rush of power, the pressure obliterating my earthly senses, but I could feel them. Remembering how I'd let magic flow through me in the circle of the coven, I stopped struggling. I let go, hollowing myself and letting the magic burst from my hands.

I didn't remember raising my arms, but I looked upward into the sky above Lynnette's yard. Silver glinting magic streamed from each of my palms as if a dam had burst inside me. It was way too much power for someone with my aptitude, and yet somehow I wielded it.

It consumed every Baelman who dared to plunge from the sky, reducing them to ash that floated down like snow. The mages were still at work, casting their magic high above. And below, I obliterated the creatures that slipped through.

It seemed to go on for an eternity, the power rushing through me from the *in-between* to the world of the living. I was the bridge, the connection between the dead and the living, funneling magic that didn't belong to this realm.

Silver power surged through me until the last stray Baelman was gone.

I lowered my arms, but the magic still pounded into me. I pushed back, but my efforts were fruitless. I tried to release my grasp as I would have with earth or fire magic. But it just kept coming.

It was going to scrape me raw like a hundred razors, burn me up like a white-hot flame. I'd be nothing but ash, like the Baelmen I'd just destroyed.

Buzzing filled my ears. The sound surged, seeming to vibrate my brain. I fell to the ground and curled up, trying to shut it out. I knew I was screaming, but the sound in my head drowned out my own voice.

Shadows began to crowd in. I stared at the morning sky, unable to move, watching as darkness pushed in from the edges, shrinking the sky to a tiny point.

I lost my grasp on the world.

W(hen awareness returned, it felt foreign.

I stared up at a ceiling I recognized, my eyes tracing a crack that made gentle bends like a stream on a map.

I knew where I was, yet nothing felt the same as before.

Before . . .

Now I remembered. The Baelmen. The power of the *in-between* surging from there, through me, to here.

The bed beneath me shifted. A furry face came into view. Loki. I reached up to pat his flank. Hellfire pulsed deep in his irises, like windows into another dimension.

He whimpered and then licked my cheek.

I pushed up to my elbows, still trying to pinpoint what felt different. There was a very distinct *before* and *after* demarcated in my mind, yet I couldn't say what it was.

There were candles on my dresser. Small spell candles, four of them lit. The ashy, musty smell of spent incense hung in the room.

Loki's attention shifted to the doorway, and I turned to look, too.

"Ella." My name fell from Deb's throat as a half-sob as she came to my side.

I started to sit up. Something tugged at my arm, and there was a sharp pinch in my inner elbow. For the first time, I noticed there was an I.V. pole next to my bed, its line leading to my arm. Deb pressed my shoulder, gently forcing me to lie back.

"Don't try to get up," she said. She wiped a tear from under her eye and gave a little laugh. "Thank god you're awake. Another hour, and they were going to insist on a catheter."

I frowned, still trying to discern why I felt a strange emptiness in my head.

"I don't feel right." My words were a barely intelligible series of croaks. And then a bolt of realization and alarm burst through me. "My magic. I can't reach it. I can't even *feel* it."

My hand shot out and clutched at the hem of her shirt as my entire world reeled. For one crazy moment I thought maybe I'd destroyed the world's magic by pulling the power of the *in-between*.

"It's a charm," Deb said, gently trying to loosen my fist from her t-shirt. "We didn't know what else to do."

Johnny came through the doorway and quickly moved around the bed to my other side. He was saying something in a soothing voice and tried to take my hand, but I wouldn't let him.

My breaths were coming too fast. I was on the verge of hyperventilating. I kept trying to send my awareness down to draw earth energy as I'd done hundreds of times. But there was nothing there.

"Ella, don't panic," Deb said. She held my face firmly in her hands, and after a second or two my terror dulled.

I knew she'd used her magic on me, but I'd felt no whisper of it over my skin. No stirring of elemental energy. I suddenly realized

I couldn't feel the reaper, either.

I knocked her hands away. "What did you do?" I demanded.

Someone else came in.

"It's a charm that prevents you from drawing magic, but it's not permanent," Damien said.

"I can't feel the reaper anymore, either." My eyed flicked back and forth between them.

He and Deb exchanged a glance.

"The reaper soul is still there," Deb said. "After the battle, you were hanging on by a thread. You were channeling enormous amounts of magic. We had to shut it off. We barely did it in time."

She reached for my left hand and lifted it. For the first time, I noticed a heavy metal ring around my index finger. There was another one on my right hand. I wiggled my fingers free of her hold.

I grasped the left-hand ring to pull it off. "I'm okay now, I don't need a charm."

"No!" Damien lunged and snatched at my hand. "You can't do that, Ella. The reaper nearly consumed you. You're teetering right on the edge of losing the battle, of *dying*."

His voice had gone ragged.

"Numbing you from supernatural power seems to have halted the reaper's consumption of your soul. Those rings are keeping you alive," Deb said.

The emptiness inside me, the feeling of being in the world but cut off from magic, seemed to pressurize my insides. The loss was overwhelming, and it was growing worse by the minute.

"How do you know?" I demanded. "How do you know the reaper almost has me?"

"Johnny scanned you," Deb said.

I glanced over at Johnny, and then closed my eyes. "How much of my soul is left?"

"Less than two percent," he said.

I felt like a numb, hollow version of myself. And I wasn't even sure if it was because I was cut off from magic or because I was hanging onto myself by a tiny slice. Maybe both.

I slowly raised my eyelids. "Can you take this thing off my arm?" I tipped my head at the I.V.

Deb nodded and slipped out, returning a second later with a woman I recognized as one of the healers who'd come to Lynnette's.

"We haven't formally met," she said. "I'm Gina. Supernatural healer and conventional nurse."

I winced as she removed the I.V. needle.

"Thank you," I said to her.

She nodded without looking up and quickly bandaged my arm and left us alone.

Deb carefully got onto the bed and sat cross-legged next to Loki. Damien sat on the edge with one knee pulled up. Johnny slipped his arm around me and pulled me into his side.

I sighed heavily. "Thank you for saving my life. Really, I owe you more than I could ever repay. I *am* grateful." I looked at both of them in turn, my eyes drilling into theirs. "But I can't live like this. There's just no way."

I spoke quietly, but my words seemed to echo in the silence

that followed.

"I'll be fired from Demon Patrol. Lynnette will kick me out of the coven. I can't save Evan from the vampire feeder den if I'm completely defenseless. And I can't live with this horrible, gnawing ache of emptiness." I pressed my hand into my stomach as if the pain were centered there in my body and then snorted a soft, humorless imitation of a laugh. "How ironic that I never had much appreciation for my weak-ass ability, but now that it's gone, it's the only thing in the world I want."

Damien scrubbed his hands down his face. "Can you live with it for a few days?" he asked. "Give us some time to try to come up with an alternative?"

I nodded reluctantly and finally allowed myself to relax against Johnny.

"Hey, is Jacob going to get nailed for murder and attempted murder or what?" I asked, ready for a change of subject. Anything to distract me from the ache.

Damien huffed, and his expression turned angry. "SC is working on it, but it's going to take time."

I felt my face screw up into bafflement. "Even though the horde originated from Gregori property? How much more blatant could it be?"

Deb shook her head. "They're actually having trouble making a formal connection. Yes, it was Gregori Industries property, but apparently nothing else that was used there can be definitively tied to the company."

"Unbelievable." I looked up at the ceiling, seething. The anger felt good. It dampened the emptiness just a hair.

"SC has a good working theory about how he was able to produce so many Baelmen," Damien said.

"Do tell," I said wryly but found I really was interested.

"They think he somehow saved up some from past new moons. Specifically, the handful of Baelmen that attacked in the first wave. He might have stored them interdimensionally somehow, to avoid breaking the law of having more than one at a time in our world."

"And the horde that came later?" I asked.

"Theory is that he borrowed against future new moons."

My eyes widened. "But there were *hundreds*. If there are around twelve new moons each year . . ." I blinked several times, trying to do the math.

"Yeah, if it's true, he's basically used up future Baelmen for something like a century," Damien said. "SC still has no idea how he managed to get so many to exist simultaneously, though. They suspect some very volatile and rare magic was at play, strengthened by the conditions of this particular new moon."

Something pinged in my mind, and I had a strong suspicion about why Jacob had been so desperate to keep Lynnette from harvesting magic from the edges of interdimensional rips. If that was the power he'd employed to break the physical supernatural law that prevented more than one Baelman at any one time—and had allowed hundreds to exist at once—it was an exceedingly powerful force.

Suddenly aware of how full my bladder was, I threw back the covers and Damien and Johnny each held an elbow while I hobbled to the bathroom. They waited for me at the door despite my protests. Deb wouldn't let me shower—they were all afraid I wasn't steady enough yet—and they forced me back into my room and brought me oatmeal and eggs in bed.

It seemed to reassure them that I was able to clean my plate and drain two glasses of orange juice. Deb and Damien both looked absolutely exhausted. I moved to the sofa with a promise that I would get up only to eat or use the bathroom. Gina took my vitals, and satisfied with what she saw, she left me her card and departed. Damien went home, and Deb sent a quick update to the coven and then crashed in my room.

Johnny shifted me so he could sit down and then leaned me back until my head rested on his lap. He stroked my hair back from my forehead in soothing movements. I turned the TV on with the sound muted but stared out the front window instead of the flickering screen. It was late afternoon, the first of November. I'd missed most of Halloween. I rotated the rings around my index fingers using my thumbs, feeling the thickness of the metal bands.

After a few minutes, Johnny's hand stilled on my hair. I glanced up to see his head tipped back as he dozed. Noticing my phone on the coffee table, I reached for it.

Then I typed a message to Rogan: *Did you hear that I've been de-magicized?*

He responded within a few seconds.

But the good news: you're alive.

I snorted at his dry humor, but the emptiness quickly sucked away my mild amusement. That seemed to be my new normal—

anything I felt was greedily snatched away by the void within me.

I can't do this. It feels like a living death.

My words looked a little dramatic, and I admitted I was looking for some sympathy. But it was no exaggeration—I felt like a wisp of a person living the barest shell of existence.

You'd be surprised what a person can learn to live with, he texted back.

So much for sympathy.

A long sigh escaped my lips. I couldn't summon up the will to reply. The screen on my phone went dark after a minute.

Another minute or two passed, and then a new message lit up the screen.

What are you willing to do to find an alternate fix?

I typed without hesitation: *Anything.*

I'll see what I can do.

I blinked at his message, realizing that I actually felt a tiny spark of hope. I closed my eyes and focused on it, urging it to swell and light up some of the void. I lay perfectly still, unaware of time passing, clinging to that pinpoint of possibility.

I tried to think of the good: if SC was right, the Baelmen were gone for good, never to return in our lifetime. Deb was safe. The rest of the coven was no longer threatened. I wasn't dead. I didn't feel particularly *alive*, but I supposed this was better than the alternative.

But other thoughts forced their way in.

I finally knew where Evan was, but I couldn't storm a vampire den with no magic and no reaper to keep me alive, even with

Rogan's help. Evan was my brother, and I couldn't go into a rescue mission as dead weight.

Johnny woke up and shifted so he could lie down with me wrapped in his arms. He told me about work, and after a while I gave him my account of the battle against the Baelman horde. He held me like that on the sofa for hours despite the fact that I desperately needed a shower. I pressed the side of my face into his chest, and lulled by the vibration of his voice and his warm, masculine scent, I dozed.

There were no visions through demon eyes, no glimpses of my brother's strung-out face. But I did dream of the giant demon, the creature that had towered above Lynnette and called me by name.

Its skin, made of iridescent blue-black scales, seemed to burn with coal-black flames. At first I thought it was smoke, but it danced the way only fire moves. I gasped as I recognized what it was: rip magic, the same energy that had licked around the edges of the rip Lynnette had opened, and the magic that had spewed from the Baelmen's mouths. The dark energy surrounded the hulking demon and poured off it the way blood-red magic sometimes emanated from me and Rogan. The creature appeared to be deep in slumber, its body curved in rest like a dog napping, the huge tail curled around the muscular body.

Instead of fear, I felt an odd kinship with the creature.

Its eyelid lifted suddenly, revealing an iris that burned with hellfire, and I jolted awake.

For a moment I teetered, still on the edge of the dream. But when it dissipated, the void crashed down on me once again. Johnny's even, slow breaths brushed my cheek.

I carefully disentangled myself from his arms and began looking through the house, searching for my service belt. I puffed my cheeks with a long, relieved exhale when I found the belt on the kitchen counter. But when I unsnapped my whip and held it coiled in my hands, deep loss scooped out my insides again. I'd thought I was already hollowed out, but the whip was like a dead thing, a coiled corpse.

I dropped it and leaned both hands against the edge of the counter as cold sweat sprang up on my face, neck, and chest. With slow, shaking breaths, I squeezed my eyelids closed and fought back the nausea that threatened to swell up my throat.

When I could finally open my eyes, my gaze landed on one of the rings. I held my hands up close together so I could see both bands. If I pulled the rings off for a second, just the merest flash of a moment, to remind myself how it felt. . .

There was a flurry of moment in my periphery and a heavy bump against my thigh, forcing me to catch myself against the edge of the sink.

Loki. He whined and cocked his head, looking up at me.

"Okay, boy. I'll leave them where they are," I whispered.

I straightened and went to the back door, opening it so he could bound out into the yard. I followed him, standing on the cold concrete of the patio in my bare feet.

Tipping my head back, I gazed at the dark sky. Before I

could save my brother, I would have to save myself. And I would. Somewhere out there, either in this world or some other, was something that would give me my life back.

Look for the next book in the series:
Demon Born Magic (Ella Grey Book Three)

For updates on new releases, fun giveaways, and free books go here to join Jayne Faith's Insiders List: http://bit.ly/JoinJayne

For new release and sale alerts only,
text CCJFBOOKS to 24587.

Made in the USA
Middletown, DE
13 September 2017